Far

T.A. Williams lives in Devon with his Italian wife. He was born in England of a Scottish mother and Welsh father. After a degree in modern languages at Nottingham University, he lived and worked in Switzerland, France and Italy, before returning to run one of the best-known language schools in the UK. He's taught Arab princes, Brazilian beauty queens and Italian billionaires. He speaks a number of languages and has travelled extensively. He has eaten snake, still-alive fish, and alligator. A Spanish dog, a Russian bug and a Korean parasite have done their best to eat him in return. His hobby is long-distance cycling, but his passion is writing.

Also by T.A. Williams

Chasing Shadows
Dreaming of Venice
Dreaming of Florence
Dreaming of St-Tropez
Dreaming of Christmas
Dreaming of Tuscany
Dreaming of Rome
Dreaming of Verona
Dreaming of Italy

Escape to Tuscany

Under a Siena Sun
Second Chances in Chianti
Secrets on the Italian Island

Love from Italy

A Little Piece of Paradise
An Escape to Remember
A Chance in a Million

Beneath Italian Skies

Never Too Late
Change of Heart
Far from Home

T.A. WILLIAMS

Far from home

CANELO

First published in the United Kingdom in 2024 by

Canelo
Unit 9, 5th Floor
Cargo Works, 1-2 Hatfields
London SE1 9PG
United Kingdom

A CIP catalogue record for this book is available from the British Library.

Print ISBN 978 1 80436 623 3
Ebook ISBN 978 1 80436 624 0

Cover design by Rose Cooper

Cover images © Arcangel, Shutterstock

Look for more great books at www.canelo.co

Printed and bound in Great Britain by Clays Ltd, Elcograf S.p.A.

1

To Mariangela, without whose help my books would be all the poorer.

Chapter 1

'Tough day?'

'Tougher than yours by the look of it.'

Amy dropped her briefcase onto a chair and slumped down alongside Gavin on the sofa, feeling completely washed out. He must have stopped off at his place on his way here from work and she saw that he had had time to change out of his suit into jeans and a T-shirt. From the way he was sprawled out on the sofa, he looked as if he'd been here for hours. His eyes were glued to the vast TV screen that occupied most of the opposite wall. He had persuaded her to buy it last Christmas and nowadays he was round here almost every night, and he seemed to spend an inordinate amount of time just sitting staring at movie after movie – when he wasn't out schmoozing clients. Tonight she immediately recognised *The Wolf of Wall Street* with Leonardo DiCaprio and she snorted. Talk about coals to Newcastle.

He waved vaguely in the direction of the bottle of Sancerre Premier Cru that she had been saving for a very special occasion. It was on the table in front of him and already half empty. 'Drink?' There was only one glass and that was in his other hand, and she debated whether to get up and go and look for one for herself, before deciding she was too weary. Needless to say, he didn't offer to get one for her.

She glanced back at him. 'Have you eaten?' No reply, so she nudged him with her elbow and tried again – louder. 'Gavin, have you eaten?'

He nodded absently. 'I had a burger at the squash club.'

She glanced at her watch. It was nine fifteen. He must have left work really early – unlike her. Theoretically her working day was supposed to finish at five, but it had been getting longer and longer as she climbed the ladder towards the glass ceiling. There were some – like her immediate boss, Scott – who reckoned she'd already smashed her way through it, but she knew better. Before she got that corner office on the seventeenth floor she knew she'd have to be prepared to fight tooth and nail in what was still very much a boys' club.

She was mildly surprised to see Gavin pause the movie and turn towards her. 'You look shattered, Amy. What's happened?'

She stretched her arms above her head in a vain attempt to relax her neck muscles and chase away the nagging headache. 'Nothing bad... but it could have been a disaster.' Seeing his enquiring look, she explained, 'We had a thirty-seven-million-pound deal going through involving yuan, rupees and ZAR. For a while this afternoon it was all looking very wobbly and we stood to lose a small fortune.' She corrected herself. 'Make that a large fortune. You could have cut the tension in the office with a knife. It finally all went through just a matter of seconds before close of play in Cape Town.' Even just the memory brought a cold chill to her stomach and she reached out, grabbed his glass of wine from him and drained it without tasting it. Yes, she thought to herself, it had been a tough day.

'Still, think of it this way: your bonus this year is going to beat all records.' He returned to his movie and she knew she'd be lucky to get any more out of him for another hour or more.

'Yes, I suppose you're right, but I could do without days like this.'

Something in her voice must have got through to him, although he didn't take his eyes off the screen. 'Why don't you have something to eat? You'll feel better afterwards.'

Pleasantly surprised, she mustered a little smile, despite his attention still being trained on the movie. 'What's in the fridge?'

'Not a lot, unless you like carrots and onions. Don't ask me why you have so many.'

'I thought for once you were going to do the shopping.' It had sounded too good to be true when he'd offered last night.

'I was running late for squash. Don't worry, I'll do it tomorrow – or you can.' He somehow managed to reach for the phone without taking his eyes off the TV and handed it to her. 'Get yourself a pizza. It should be here in twenty minutes or so.'

They had already had pizza twice this week and she shook her head. 'I'm not that hungry. I'll go and make myself a bowl of porridge and then I'm crashing out.'

'Cheer up. Tomorrow's Friday and then you'll have the whole weekend to rest and recuperate.'

'The way I feel right now, I'll probably sleep straight through to Monday morning. God, I'm tired.'

She heaved herself to her feet and went through to the kitchen, feeling unusually dopey. The porridge packet was in the cupboard alongside the slick Neff oven and she bent down to retrieve it. As she did so, her head started spinning, everything around her blurred and she toppled forward into unconsciousness.

–

'You had me worried back there for a while.'

The touch of his hand on her arm roused her and she opened her eyes to see Gavin sitting alongside the bed with an expression on his face that somehow managed to combine concern and relief at the same time. She gave him a little smile.

'I had me worried, too, Gav.' Her voice sounded as weak as she felt.

'At least it wasn't a heart attack.' His expression darkened. 'But it was the next best thing. The paramedics were really worried and the doctors in A&E were all over you like locusts. They told me what they think it was but I've forgotten the word. Basically a collapse due to overwork and excessive stress.'

'What time is it?'

'Eight thirty.'

'AM or PM?'

'It's eight thirty in the morning and, before you ask, it's Friday.'

'Have you been here all night?'

He shook his head. 'No, after they sent you to this ward last night, they told me to go home and get some rest. I'm okay.' As usual he looked impeccable, without a hair out of place, and his crisp white shirt – which she had ironed – didn't have a single crease in it.

'Have you any idea how long they're going to keep me in?'

'The nurse outside told me they won't know until the specialist does his rounds later on this morning.' He glanced at his watch and stood up. 'To be honest, she said I wasn't supposed to come in here, but I turned on the charm.' *I bet you did*, Amy thought to herself. 'She said just two minutes, so I'd better disappear before she gets into trouble.'

Amy caught hold of his hand and gave it a squeeze, impressed that he had made the effort. 'Thanks, Gav. I'm sorry you've had all this bother. Will you call Scott and tell him what's happened? Tell him I'm sorry and I hope to be in on Monday morning.'

He bent down towards her and wagged his finger at her. 'You'll go back to work when the medics say it's okay for you to go back to work and not before. Got that?'

'Yes, sir.' She gave him another smile. 'And thanks again.'

He kissed her on the cheek and left. She lay back against the pillows, reflecting that this was the most attentive he'd been for months.

The day passed unexpectedly quickly – mainly because she spent a lot of it sleeping. The highlight was the appearance of the specialist accompanied by a cohort of junior doctors. Amy had been expecting this to be an august older gentleman in a pinstripe suit, collar and tie – probably as a result of watching too many movies with Gavin – but this turned out to be a tall, good-looking woman only a few years older than Amy, and she was wearing red scrubs. She announced to Amy and to her coterie of junior doctors that she believed the collapse had been due to nervous exhaustion, but that there was still the possibility that it might have been what she called a 'heart event', and she wanted to keep her in for another night while they did a series of tests. Amy thanked her and all of the staff around her for their care.

In the course of the day she had her blood pressure checked over and over again, more blood taken for analysis through a cannula taped to the back of her hand, another ECG, an X-ray and a CT scan. From what she could glean from the junior doctor who popped in to see her on a number of occasions, the results were looking 'promising' and he predicted the specialist would discharge her next morning. This news heartened Amy and she even managed to eat some of the chicken pie and mash at lunchtime followed by orange jelly – something she hadn't had since she was a little girl, and after eating it she felt pretty sure it would be another thirty years before she would feel like trying another. She was just finishing her meal when she received a visitor. It was Lucy, her best friend from work, and she came in looking far more worried than Gavin had been. In her hands was a packet of grapes from the Waitrose shop near the office.

'Amy, look at you!' She sounded genuinely concerned. 'What have I been telling you for the last God knows how many years? You need to start looking after yourself.'

Amy looked up and smiled. 'Hi, Luce, thanks for coming. There was no need.'

Lucy set down the grapes on the bedside table and pulled up a chair. 'There was every need.'

'How're things at work?'

'Forget work. It's like I've been telling you: you'll work yourself into an early grave if you go on like this.'

'You sound like my mum.' Thought of her mother wiped the smile off Amy's face. Of course her mum was never going to be able to tell her anything ever again.

'And she was right. Is it true you had a heart attack?'

Amy shook her head and related what the specialist had said, but Lucy wasn't convinced. 'You've got to take it easy. Your health's far more important than work.'

Gradually Amy managed to wean her off the subject of health, but Lucy steadfastly refused to talk about work. In fairness, she worked two floors below in Insurance and probably didn't know much about the foreign exchange side of things anyway. Instead, she recounted how things had gone with her latest conquest – the most recent in a seemingly never-ending stream of paramours. Amy never ceased to be amazed at her friend's voracious appetite for men. By the time Lucy mercifully changed the subject, Amy was feeling slightly dazed at the degree of anatomical detail Lucy had shared with her. Certainly the two of them, although best friends, were very different in that respect.

Needless to say, Lucy then queried yet again when Amy and Gavin might be going to formally move in together and Amy's answer to that one remained the same as ever – not yet. Their conversation then changed to the weather and politics, and Lucy's latest attempt to lose weight – which she didn't need to lose – by joining a gym. Her parting words were a further exhortation to take it easy. Easier said than done.

Amy spent much of the afternoon dozing and by the time Gavin reappeared at half past five she was feeling much more like her normal self. This didn't go unnoticed by him.

'You look a whole lot better than you did earlier. My nurse friend tells me she reckons you'll be out of here in the morning.'

She held out her hands to him and he bent down to give her a kiss, somewhat hampered by the apparatus alongside the bed. 'I can't stay long. I have to take a couple of Taiwanese gentlemen out for dinner a bit later on and I'm just on my way home to change.' To reinforce the message that this was only a flying visit, he shot an ostentatious look at his watch and didn't take a seat. She wasn't surprised and her first question probably didn't come as a surprise to him either. They both knew each other so well after more than a year of going out together.

'Did you speak to Scott? What did he say?'

'Yes, I called in this morning on my way to the office.' Gavin's firm was in the next high-rise block to hers. 'He was very sympathetic and he told me to tell you to take all the time you need.'

'And the South African deal? No complications?'

'He thought you'd ask that, and he says to tell you it's all fine.' He reached down to his Louis Vuitton briefcase – her present to him last Christmas – and brought out a long envelope. 'By the way, I popped round to your place on the way here and I found this.'

She took it from him and recognised it immediately as being from the firm of solicitors who had been handling her mother's affairs. Even though her mum's death had been almost three months ago now, Amy felt tears springing to the corners of her eyes as it awoke so many memories. She slit the envelope open and pulled out a letter along with another, slightly smaller, envelope. The letter was from Diana Carstairs, the solicitor dealing with her mother's estate, and it was brief and to the point.

Dear Amy

I hope this finds you well. This envelope has been forwarded to us by the agents handling the sale of your mother's house. They found it on the mat and thought it looked important.

Yours sincerely

Diana

Amy set down the letter and picked up the enclosed envelope, noting that it bore an Italian stamp and it had been addressed to her, care of her mother's old address. Considering that she hadn't lived there for almost thirteen years, she was intrigued. She opened it and pulled out a formal-looking letter from a *notaio*, a notary, in a place whose name she didn't recognise. Correspondence from Italy in itself wasn't too unexpected, as Amy's mum had originally been from there. Since her death, Amy had been receiving sporadic letters, cards and messages of condolence from old friends of the family in and around her mum's birthplace near Turin. Her mum had always spoken Italian to her as she grew up, even though Amy had been born and brought up here in the UK, and so she had no trouble reading it. As she digested the contents of the letter, she did a doubletake and glanced up in amazement.

'Gav, you're not going to believe this. It's from a notary, a lawyer in Italy...'

'What does it say? Is it bad news?' Amy didn't react. She just went on staring blankly at the letter in her hands. He pulled out the chair and sat down, leaning towards her. 'What is it, Amy? What's the matter?'

It was a while before she managed to tear herself away from the letter, struggling to take in what she had just read.

'It appears that I've just been left a house.' She could hear the disbelief in her own voice. 'In a little town in Tuscany.'

'A house? Who by?' He looked at her with increased interest.

Amy shook her head blankly, her mind still trying to digest this totally unexpected news. 'That's the thing. It makes no sense. The man's name is... was... Martin Thomas Slater.'

'Doesn't sound very Italian. Are you sure you don't know who he is? One of your mum's friends maybe.' He was looking happier now and he grinned at her. 'Not some secret lover you've never told me about?'

She was still shaking her head in bemusement. 'Nope, I've never heard of him.' For a moment an image appeared in her head of her Italian grandparents' old house in the foothills of the Alps and the happy holidays she and her mum had spent together over there, and another little wave of melancholy swept over her. 'And, of course, there's no way Mum will ever be able to tell me now.'

'And this guy's left you a house? Are you sure?'

Amy looked up and nodded. 'Yes, that's what it says, but why...?' Her voice tailed off helplessly.

'Let's see where it is. What's the name of the town?'

'Sant'Antonio.'

He pulled out his phone and tapped in the name but immediately raised his head again. 'We might have a problem. Do you know how many places in Italy are called Sant'Antonio? As saints go, he must have been a popular chap.'

'This place is in the province of Pisa, if that helps.'

'Hang on.' A few seconds later it popped up and he read the results out loud. 'Sant'Antonio is in Tuscany, thirty-eight kilometres southeast of Pisa. Main industry: agriculture, principally olive oil and wine production. According to this, there are 2497 inhabitants. Not the biggest of towns, but it does have the remains of a medieval castle. There's a photo. It looks quite pretty actually.' He held his phone out so she could see. 'And some random man has left you a house there? What does this mean? Are you going to have to take a trip to Tuscany to see for yourself?'

'I suppose I should.' Amy was still trying to get her head around what had just happened. 'It's just so weird... Mum was from the very north, up in the foothills of the Alps. As far as I know she had no connections with Tuscany... or with anybody called Martin Thomas Slater.'

'Does the letter say anything about the man, or the house for that matter? Seeing as the guy's got an English name, could he be some distant relative or friend of your dad's? He was British after all, wasn't he?'

Amy nodded. 'Yes, but I've no idea if he had friends in Italy. He and Mum met when she was already living and working in the UK and she said the first time he ever went to Italy was to meet her parents just before they got married...' Her voice tailed off. 'And then he was killed only a year later.'

'Is there anybody you could ask?'

'He only had a handful of relatives in the UK and, to be honest, Mum had pretty well lost touch with any of them.'

'What about your grandparents? Your British ones, I mean?'

'Dead, just like my *nonna* and *nonno* in Turin.' She shrugged helplessly. 'I can't think of anybody I can ask now that Mum's dead too.' She glanced back down at the letter in her hand. 'Maybe this Alfredo Lucchese, the notary, will be able to fill me in. It's just plain weird.'

Chapter 2

Amy was discharged from hospital on Saturday morning with a clean bill of health as far as her heart was concerned but with strict instructions from the specialist to 'Take life a bit easier'. She did her best to heed this advice and rested on Sunday and stayed at home on Monday, but by Tuesday morning she couldn't resist returning to Canary Wharf where she was greeted by a surprise. Just minutes after she got there, Scott called her into his office and laid it on the line.

'I've been talking to Karl, and we both feel you need to take some time off. You've been burning the candle at both ends for years now and you need to start thinking about your health.' He held up a hand to stave off her protests. 'This is non-negotiable, Amy. You do a wonderful job but nobody's indispensable, and we'll get by without you while you take a good long holiday. I want you to just relax and recharge your batteries. You're due a whole heap of time off anyway. Christian will be only too happy to step into your shoes for a month or so.'

Amy had to struggle hard to avoid grinding her teeth. Christian, with his Oxford degree and his plummy accent, had been cosying up to Scott for years now and openly eyeing Amy's job. Amy knew the man would be overjoyed to step into the breach and she felt sure there would be trouble when she returned from her compulsory break and tried to evict him from her office. Still, she heard the resolve in her boss's voice and couldn't miss the fact that it sounded very much like what the tall specialist had told her, so she nodded meekly and agreed.

She left Scott's office and went back to her own and, sure enough, barely a minute later she spotted slimy Christian leering at her through the glass, obviously relishing the prospect of taking over her desk. She shot him a disarming smile while growling to herself and set about collecting her things. As she did so, she realised that this did at least resolve one problem. She could now head off to see the Italian lawyer and, hopefully, find out what this bequest was all about.

She called Gavin to see whether he might be able to take a few days off and accompany her. He was a bit reticent at first but he finally agreed to see if he could get Friday off. That way he could make it a long weekend and only miss one day of work, if you could call it that. He worked for an international property company and his job seemed mainly to consist of trips to exotic locations – most of which had been without her because of the pressure of her own job – and games of golf and squash with clients, plus slap-up dinners at the top of the Shard. Nice work if you can get it.

She dropped into Lucy's office on her way home where the news that she was taking a holiday was greeted with satisfaction by her friend. When Lucy heard about the mystery bequest and the forthcoming trip to Italy she sounded enthusiastic.

'How amazing, Amy! And you have no idea who the guy is? Wow! How long are you going over for? Did you say Tuscany? I've never been there but everybody says it's gorgeous. If you need company just say the word – I still have a few days' holiday left over from last year. I was going to go off to the Caribbean for a dirty week with a guy from the gym, but he can keep.'

'I've no idea how long I'll be staying. Maybe just a day or two. I guess it'll depend on the state of the property. Gav's coming with me on Friday but if you can keep your gym guy on the back burner for a day or two, I'll give you a call at the weekend and let you know.'

–

Amy and Gavin flew to Pisa three days later and rented a car at the airport. Gavin drove while she checked the map and they headed inland to Sant'Antonio. The drive took them less than an hour and the little town was visible from some way off, set on the flank of a gently sloping hill in the middle of a sea of other gently sloping hills that stretched off into the distance. The approach was up a good, if winding, road through olive groves and vineyards, which occupied most of the hillside apart from the ubiquitous umbrella pines and cypress trees that dotted the landscape.

After passing the sign announcing their arrival in Sant'Antonio the road narrowed as they entered the *centro storico*. On both sides of the increasingly tortuous Via Roma were typical Tuscan town houses, some bare sandstone and others in varying hues of ochre from the palest cream to faded pink and even rich orange, all with the trademark Tuscan matt green louvred shutters. They drove past a small selection of shops ranging from what looked like a traditional butcher to an ironmonger with galvanised buckets and rolls of hosepipe stacked outside its doors. Beyond them was a *pasticceria* emanating a wonderful aroma of freshly baked pastries that wafted enticingly into the car and reminded both of them that they had skipped lunch.

Beyond these the road widened and levelled out into a slightly lopsided piazza that was unmistakably the town centre. Old stone houses ringed the square, with the remains of the medieval castle on the right-hand side dominating the surroundings and overlooking the valley below. Behind the row of houses on the opposite side of the square they could see the hillside continue to rise, cloaked in a series of vineyards, fields and olive groves. A hotel/restaurant with tables and chairs added a burst of colour to the scene with its red and blue parasols, and the overall impression was quaint, historic and quintessentially Italian.

Along the top end of the piazza were a series of imposing, probably Renaissance era, buildings on either side of the town hall which was recognisable by the green, white and red flag hanging limply outside, while a branch of the Credito degli Agricoltori bank occupied the far corner. Plane trees at regular intervals provided welcome shade, casting deep shadows beneath their branches and there was a dusty *bocce* court over to one side although it was currently empty apart from a couple of elderly men sitting on a bench under the nearby tree. All in all, it was a charming place and the views down over the wooded hills as far as the hazy blue sweep of the Mediterranean, only twenty or thirty kilometres away with its golden beaches, were equally delightful.

On Amy's instruction, Gavin drew up in the shade of a particularly leafy tree and turned off the engine. 'That looks like the lawyer's house right there.' She pointed towards a grand-looking building directly ahead of them that bore the number 5. A fine brass plaque below it announced the offices of Alfredo Lucchese, Notary.

The whole journey had been surprisingly smooth; the flight had been on time, Pisa airport not too crowded, and Amy found she was relishing being in Italy again. In fact, she hadn't been back for about five years now but, growing up, she had spent most of her summer holidays in the north. Tuscany was completely new to her and from what she'd seen so far today, it looked gorgeous. Warm sunshine was a real bonus after one of the coldest, wettest Aprils on record back in the UK and she felt remarkably relaxed. She reflected that the tall specialist would no doubt have approved. She opened the door and climbed out, breathing deeply, glad to be out in the open air.

'What time do you make it, Gav?' He got out as well and stretched. He was looking happier now, no longer sulking about having to miss a tennis match scheduled for tomorrow.

'Three fifteen. The solicitor said any time after three, didn't he? Go on. I'll wait for you here. On second thoughts, I'll wait for you in the café over there. I really fancy a real Italian ice cream.'

Amy rather fancied the idea of an ice cream herself but that would have to wait. She left him and walked across to the lawyer's chambers. When she reached the front door, she rang the bell. It was an old bell pull and the noise reverberated around the interior of the building. A few moments later the door was opened by a mature lady wearing a dark skirt and a sober white blouse. She produced a welcoming smile.

'Signora Sherwood?'

Amy nodded and shook the extended hand. Although she wasn't married, she knew that women her age were generally addressed as Signora, rather than Signorina, and she answered in Italian. 'Good afternoon. Yes, I'm Amy Sherwood.'

'Please come in and take a seat. Signor Lucchese will be with you shortly.'

The woman showed her into a grand waiting room, furnished with a fine sofa and matching armchairs, with portraits of austere men on the walls. A crucifix took pride of place over the door. A low table was set out with a selection of leaflets dealing with everything from buying and selling houses to burying the dead. She picked up a copy of that day's *Il Tirreno*, the local newspaper, and flicked idly through the pages, wondering once more just who this Martin Thomas Slater was and what his connection with her could possibly be.

Less than five minutes later the door at the end of the waiting room opened and an elderly couple emerged. Behind them was the lawyer. He was immaculately turned out in a dark suit, white shirt and sober tie and with his perfectly trimmed military-style moustache he wouldn't have looked out of place in the Royal Courts of Justice in London. He shook hands with the old couple and saw them out through the main door before turning to Amy and giving her a formal bow of the head.

'*Signora Sherwood? Benvenuta a Sant'Antonio*.'

Amy shook hands, after which he ushered her into his study. This was a magnificent room, dominated by an enormous bookcase filled with worthy legal tomes. Behind him, French windows opened onto a charming garden surrounded by high stone walls swathed with bougainvillea. Amy sat down opposite him with the elegant desk between them, and the notary wasted no time in getting down to business. He began speaking slowly and clearly but speeded up as he saw that she appeared to have no difficulty understanding. After taking a copy of her passport to confirm her identity he outlined the situation.

'Signor Martin Thomas Slater passed away on the sixteenth of June last year. I have copies of the death certificate for you here. He died at home of a heart attack, brought on by his existing serious heart condition. It was very sad. He was only sixty-five years old.' He glanced up. 'I know the local doctor well and he told me Martin must have died almost instantly.'

Amy noted his use of the first name. Presumably the notary had known Mr Slater personally, too, so that boded well for an explanation of just who he was and, more to the point, what the connection might be between him and her.

'Thank you. Can I ask you something, please? How is it that I've only been notified of his death now, almost a year later?'

The lawyer shook his head and reached into the file on the desk before him. 'In total, four letters were sent to you at the only address we had for you. Alas, we never received any response at all until your email last Monday.'

Amy shook her head in disbelief. 'That's my mother's address. I don't know why she didn't tell me. Four letters, you say?'

The notary nodded. 'Here, we keep copies of all correspondence – you can see for yourself.' He passed a handful of sheets across the desk to her.

Amy checked the address to which they had been sent. There was no mistake. Her mother must have received them and, yet, she had said nothing. How very strange.

'I'm at a loss to explain why she never mentioned them to me or passed them on to me. And now I'm afraid she's died as well, so we may never know. I'm very sorry you've had all this extra work.'

The notary waved away her apologies. 'It's nothing, Signora. My condolences for the loss of your mother. The important thing is that we've finally been able to locate you as the beneficiary of Martin's will. Would you like me to read it to you?'

Amy sat back and listened as the lawyer read the words written by this unknown man. There were a number of bequests to local charities, including ten thousand euros each to the local fishing and tennis clubs, but when he reached the part where he left everything else to his *beloved Amy*, she felt genuinely moved, if greatly puzzled, and she found herself wiping moisture from the corners of her eyes.

'The will is undisputed and so you are now the owner of his house, l'Ospedaletto, here in Sant'Antonio, the contents of the house, garden, garage and cellar, all lands surrounding it, and the sum of just over eight hundred thousand euros remaining in his bank account after payment of death duties, taxes and notary's fees. My secretary has prepared documents, duly notarised, to that effect. If you present a copy to the bank, they'll be able to transfer the money to you. It's the Credito degli Agricoltori bank just along the square from here.' He sat back and waited for Amy to reply. It took a few moments as she was still digesting the fact that she had been left not only a house but also a hell of a lot of money.

'Thank you very much, that all sounds amazing. The trouble is...' Amy took a deep breath. 'I have no idea who Signor Slater was. I've never heard his name before and I can't begin to imagine why he should have left me his possessions.' She looked across at the notary. 'Can you enlighten me, please?'

The notary's face was a picture. He now looked as puzzled as she felt. 'You don't know who he was?' He leant towards her, elbows on the desk. 'But, surely, you must know. After all, why should he name you in his will if you and he weren't connected?'

Amy shook her head before replying. 'It's a total mystery to me. Did you know him well?' The notary nodded. 'And he never told you anything about me or my mum?'

'Absolutely not, Signora. I must confess this is the first time in my professional life that I've come across a case like this.' There was an awkward silence for a few moments before he shrugged helplessly and returned to the matter in hand. 'Anyway, the property is undeniably yours, whether you knew Signor Slater or not. You'll find l'Ospedaletto only a short walk from here. If you turn left on the far side of the piazza and then immediately right you'll come to it in a matter of minutes. It's one of the oldest and finest buildings in Sant'Antonio. As you'll see from the deeds, the property comprises not only the house, but also six hectares of land – some of it currently rented to a local farmer, Signor Emanuele Montalcino – mostly planted with vines.' He allowed himself a smile. 'As I understand it, the annual rent is paid in wine, and I can confirm from personal experience that it's excellent.'

Amy grinned as the notary continued.

'Here are copies of the deeds, some other documents and a bunch of keys. There's also an envelope in there addressed to you. Maybe that will explain his connection with you.'

He handed over a small ring of keys, followed by a hefty brown envelope of documents. 'If you need anything else, please don't hesitate to contact me.'

'I wonder if you could tell me more about Mr Slater? What sort of man was he?'

'He was a fine man – generous and kind. He was well liked in the town.'

'And what did he do?'

'Do? You mean his job? I don't think he worked. He never talked about what he did before he arrived here. Maybe he took early retirement from a well-paid job. I often wondered if it had been something in finance, seeing as he was well-off but, like I say, he never spoke of it.' He smiled. 'Who knows? Maybe he was fortunate enough to come from a wealthy family.' He glanced at his watch. 'I'm afraid I have another appointment now. I wish you a good afternoon but don't hesitate to contact me if you have any queries.'

Chapter 3

Amy left the lawyer's studio and spotted Gavin sitting under a parasol outside the bar across the square so she went over to report back. She found him sipping a glass of what looked like Prosecco, an empty dish in front of him.

'Meringue and black cherry ice cream. It's amazing. You have to try it.' He must have noticed the shell-shocked expression on Amy's face. 'What did the man say, Amy? You look as if you've seen a ghost.'

'I've just been left a whole heap of money.'

'As well as the house?'

'Yup.'

Amy went on to outline the details of Mr Slater's will and he looked delighted. 'That's fantastic! Looks like we've got ourselves a holiday home.' She noted his use of the plural but didn't comment as he continued, 'We need to celebrate. Is it too early for champagne?'

A waitress appeared through the gaudy plastic fly curtains and Amy resisted the temptation to order a bottle of booze and just asked for ice cream and sparkling mineral water for herself and another glass of fizz for Gavin. After the woman had gone off, Amy recounted in more detail everything the lawyer had said and she saw a puzzled expression on Gavin's face. This was the same expression she had been seeing in the mirror herself every time she tried to get her head around the identity of her mysterious benefactor.

'So even the notary hasn't been able to help you find out who Mr Slater was?' He swigged down the last of the wine in his glass, ready for the next one. 'Surely he must have been able to tell you something?'

'He was as mystified as we are. It's just plain weird.' She had been using that word a lot recently.

'What about the stuff he gave you? Did you say there was a letter?'

Amy nodded and reached for the bulky envelope. 'That's what he said. You never know – maybe that'll give us the explanation.'

There was a brief delay while the waitress brought out a heaped dish of ice cream, a little bottle of cold mineral water, and another glass of Prosecco for Gavin. As she set it down in front of him he shot her a sparkling smile that actually made the woman's cheeks flush. Amy sighed. He had always had a way with women – herself included. Relegating that can of worms to another time, she took a mouthful of the excellent ice cream and followed it with a big swig of water before locating a slim white envelope amid the package of documents the notary had given her.

Unusually, this envelope was securely sealed with a large blob of dark red sealing wax. On the outside was a single handwritten word: *Amy*. She broke the seal, slit open the flap at the top of the envelope with her finger and reached inside.

The letter, written in a shaky hand, was short and quite bewildering. If she had been baffled before, she felt even more confused by the end of it. She read it through twice before handing it across to Gavin without comment.

My dearest Amy

Initially this may puzzle you, but you will find that these are key questions. Keep them safe.

1) On what day was your mother born?

2) On what day were you born?

3) Your mother has a brooch in the shape of an animal. How many diamonds are there on the brooch?

4) The pub opposite the church where you were christened – how many bells on the sign?

All my love

The letter was signed with an illegible scrawl.

Gavin read it carefully and then looked across at Amy and raised his eyebrows. 'Well, he certainly wasn't wrong about puzzling you! What the hell is this all about?'

She shook her head. 'I haven't the foggiest idea. Maybe he was trying to check that the stuff got given to the right person. But, if that's what he's trying to do, surely the questions should have been answerable in front of the notary? Could it be some sort of code or maybe he was just going a bit bonkers in his final years?' She snorted. 'Whoever he was.'

She took the letter back from Gavin and checked the date. 'April last year, barely a month or two before he died. That's when he wrote that, and it's not as if he was even that old. From what the solicitor said, he would have only been sixty-five or so – hardly senile.'

'So, what about your mum's brooch? Did she have one in the shape of an animal?'

Amy looked up and met his eye, ever more struck by the surreal feel of all this. 'In fact, she did. She had a rather fine brooch in the shape of a silver stag, complete with antlers, and she wore it to church every Sunday. She kept it in her jewellery box back home. There were quite a few little stones set in it, but I must admit I didn't realise they were real diamonds. It's in one of the cardboard boxes that came from her place that are stacked up in the cupboard at my flat back in London now.'

'So, assuming that's the brooch he's alluding to, how on earth did he know about it?'

Amy was also thinking about this. There was only one logical explanation. 'He must have known my mother, and she must have known him. Maybe he even gave her the brooch. But the funny thing is that she never mentioned him to me.' She looked across at him and shook her head. 'I can only guess that she didn't want me to know.'

'An old boyfriend, maybe?'

'I don't think she had boyfriends. After Dad's death, to my knowledge, she never went out with another man.'

'And before your dad?'

Amy hesitated. She, too, had been wondering about this. Might this mystery man have been a former boyfriend who, somehow, had never forgotten her mother? But how had he got to know her daughter in that case? She sighed with frustration. 'I honestly don't know. It would all have been so long ago.'

'But your father was killed just before you were born, wasn't he? Even allowing for some years of mourning, surely she must have got to know other men after his death?'

Amy sighed again. 'I really don't know. Nobody special, I'm sure, and certainly nobody while I was growing up.'

Thoughts of her parents, and now this other man, all of them dead and gone, made Amy begin to feel unexpectedly emotional and tears sprang to her eyes. She sat there for some minutes, trying to collect herself. After a minute or two, she heard Gavin's voice again, sounding pensive.

'Amy, I was thinking... Now look, the last thing I'd ever want to do is to malign the memory of your mum, but have you considered that this Mr Slater might have known her very well indeed?'

She caught his eye. 'You mean he and she might have had an affair?'

'It's just a thought...'

'And what you're saying is that you're wondering whether he might have been my father?' The same thought had been occurring to her on and off for days now but hearing it out loud for the first time was bizarre. She did her best to sound expressionless. 'You're not the only one, Gav. I've been thinking along the same lines ever since I heard about him.'

'And the way he addresses you in this letter as "dearest" and signs it "all my love"; that's pretty intimate, considering the two of you never met.'

'I know. That's been bothering me, too.'

'How did your dad die? It's not something you've ever really talked about.'

Amy took another mouthful of water before answering. 'He was killed on active service in the First Gulf War in 1990, the year I was born. He died in what they described as a friendly fire incident – a missile strike by an Allied warplane that went badly wrong. The really sad thing is that he never even saw me, nor me him. I was born five months after his death.'

'And he would have been, what? Thirty or so?'

'Thirty-one or thirty-two, I believe. I think Mum said he was a couple of years older than her, but I can check. Somewhere in all the boxes of Mum's stuff there's a load of old documents, including both of their birth certificates.'

'The notary said Mr Slater died at the age of sixty-five. How old did you say your mum was when she died?'

'Sixty-four.'

'So when you were born, your mum and dad were both roughly the same age as you and me now, as was Mr Slater. So, how about this as a scenario? Your mum has an affair with Mr Slater – presumably while your dad was away on duty somewhere – and then she finds she's pregnant. She decides to have the baby – that's you – and either hopes to convince your dad that you are his or confess to him and get a divorce. In the meantime, he gets killed. I wonder how it would have gone down if he'd survived the fighting.'

By this time Amy's head was spinning – even though she had already done these same calculations in her head over and over again all week. She reached for her glass of water and rather wished she had gone for wine after all. 'In that scenario my mum doesn't come out of this looking too good, does she?'

'These things happen. We all make mistakes – besides, it's just as much Slater's fault, maybe more.'

Amy nodded reflectively. 'But if that's really what happened, what I don't understand is why she and Mr Slater didn't get together once my dad – the man I think of as my dad – died. Surely that would have been the obvious thing to do.'

'There may have been a reason why he and she didn't get together. Like him maybe being married to somebody else for instance...'

'Or they had a major falling-out and that explains why she never spoke about him and never replied to the notary's letters...'

'Who knows?'

At that moment his phone started ringing and while he answered it, Amy folded the letter back into the envelope, wiped her eyes and set about consuming her rapidly melting ice cream. This was as delicious as Gavin had said but she barely tasted it. By the sound of it, his phone call was from one of his many friends and he was soon laughing uproariously at some funny story or other while she finished her ice cream and looked around. In the distance, behind the row of historic houses lining the far side of the piazza, she could see vineyards covering part of the hillside. The notary had talked of vines and she wondered whether some of these fields now belonged to her. In spite of her bewilderment, it was an exciting thought. She waited until Gavin's call ended and then pointed up the hill.

'What do six hectares of land look like?'

He followed the direction of her eyes. 'A lot. A hectare's roughly two and a half acres, two point four to be precise.' This was his job, after all. 'Two point four times six is around fourteen and a half acres, which sounds to me like what we can see up there, plus a bit more. Maybe you should give up the day job, move over here and take up farming.'

'And what would you do if you came with me?'

'Quality control for the wine, of course.' He laughed and she laughed with him but, deep down, she found herself wondering not for the first time if they really were destined to spend the rest of their lives together. Determined not to let this rare weekend away together disintegrate into vain conjecture, she skirted around that subject and pointed across the piazza once more.

'He said the house is a five-minute walk in that direction. I've finished my ice cream so shall we go and take a look?'

They settled up and, leaving the car in the shade of the trees, walked over to the far side of the square. Tree roots had done an effective job of breaking up the surface in places and they both had to keep their eyes trained on the ground to prevent themselves from tripping. Leaving the piazza, they turned left and then right as instructed. The roads here were even narrower and completely deserted. Barely three or four minutes later, as predicted, they found themselves on the edge of the town and came to a huge pair of ornate iron gates. They crossed the road towards l'Ospedaletto and peered through the bars. The fine stone building was surrounded by trees and an overgrown garden, and it was simply enormous. The name of the property translated as the Little Hospital but the building was far from little. It was hard to believe that all this was now hers.

'Wow, what a place, Amy. It looks seriously old, and very, very lovely.' Gavin sounded impressed – and it took a lot to impress him.

Before she could comment, Amy heard a voice behind them and they both wheeled around.

'Good afternoon, can I help in any way?'

The voice came from the shadowy garage belonging to an old stone house directly opposite. Inside they could just make out an ancient Fiat and an even more ancient lady in the gloom. The elderly lady rose to her feet remarkably nimbly and set down her knitting. An equally elderly-looking black and white cat immediately jumped onto the chair and settled down on top of the knitting. The lady came across the road towards them, her hand outstretched, and Amy and Gavin met her halfway. The fact that they were now standing in the middle of the road didn't seem to matter to the lady in the slightest and Amy reflected that she hadn't seen a single car since leaving the piazza. Clearly this was not a major thoroughfare.

'*Buongiorno, mi chiamo Grande*.' Her accent when she introduced herself was strong Tuscan but Amy understood her well enough. She had already worked out in conversation with the lawyer that in Tuscany the locals often pronounce a 'c' as an 'h', but she was getting used to it.

'Good afternoon, Signora Grande. I'm Amy Sherwood and this is my friend Gavin.' It occurred to her, after she had spoken, that back home she normally introduced him to people as her 'boyfriend'. The fact that she had just chosen to just call him 'a friend' wasn't because she didn't know the right vocabulary. Maybe, subconsciously, it marked a change in the way she was starting to think about him, but Signora Grande didn't give her time to dwell on the subject for now.

'Welcome, welcome. Signor Lucchese, the notary, told me to expect you today. I've been keeping an eye on Martin's house.'

'You knew him well?'

Signora Grande paused for thought, idly scratching the back of her head. 'Giovanni, my husband, knew him better, but I lost him to a coronary in January this year.' Her voice broke momentarily but she rallied. 'Mind you, I knew Martin well, too, maybe as well as anybody around here. He was very sociable and he had a lot of friends. At least, until the illness struck him.'

'I'm so sorry to hear about your husband. The notary said Mr Slater had a serious heart condition and that was what killed him.'

'That's correct. But he also contracted an illness of the mind. In his final months, he changed completely. He started to fear he was being watched. He thought everybody was against him. He didn't trust anybody, even me.' She caught Amy's eye and shrugged. 'I knew it was an illness, but it was hard, after so many years of friendship.'

Amy turned and gave Gavin a brief translation. Presumably this explained the cryptic nature of the letter.

A strangled yelp followed by furious scratching came from the old lady's house and she excused herself. Amy watched as she hurried back to her house and opened the door. No sooner had she done so than a large black dog came rushing out, its tail wagging furiously. As it did so, the cat leapt surprisingly athletically from the knitting to the top of a tall cupboard at the back of the garage. Ignoring the cat, the dog came charging across towards them and almost knocked Amy over with its enthusiastic greeting. Signora Grande hurried after it, doing her best to sound authoritative. 'Max, Max, come here. Bad dog. Leave the nice people alone.'

Amy bent down to make a fuss of the dog and looked up to reassure the old lady. 'It's perfectly all right. I love dogs. He's quite young, isn't he?'

Signora Grande sighed. 'Yes and he's got so much energy. I just can't cope. Taking him for a walk is getting impossible. He almost drags my arm out of its socket.' She explained. 'He's barely two years old and he's a lovely friendly dog, but I just can't manage. My husband, God rest his soul, got him as a puppy but then, of course, he passed away four months ago.' She produced a handkerchief from her sleeve and wiped her eyes. 'I've been struggling to look after Max ever since. It hasn't been easy. Anyway...' She reached into the pocket of her apron. 'Did the notary give you the keys? I have one here if you'd like it back.'

Amy shook her head. 'No, please hang onto yours.' She pulled out the envelope the lawyer had given her. 'I've got a load of keys here.'

'Knowing you were coming, I went into the house this morning and turned the electricity and water back on. Take a look around and if there's anything you need, you know where I am.' She glanced up at the cloudless sky and fanned herself with one hand. 'Never seen anything like it. It's still only the beginning of June and it's almost as hot as August. I think I'll go back to the shade.' She called the dog, who had been occupying himself marking all the trees along the pavement, and Amy was pleased to see him return obediently, although his tail had stopped wagging as he realised he was going back into the house. 'Goodbye for now.'

Amy thanked her warmly and watched as Signora Grande shooed the reluctant dog back inside and then made her way slowly back into the relative cool of her garage, presumably to engage in a struggle for territory with her cat. Evidently, this was the most comfortable place for her to sit and do her knitting. No doubt, the garage also had the advantage of giving her a good view of any passers-by and the opportunity for a chat. Amy was turning away when she had a thought and glanced back.

'I'll be here for a few days. If you like, I can come and collect Max and take him for walks.'

'That would be wonderful, thank you, my dear.'

Amy smiled back at her. It would appear that she had made a friend – two, if she included the Labrador.

Chapter 4

They headed across the road and Amy gave Gavin a brief translation of what Signora Grande had said before selecting the biggest key from the bunch and using it to unlock the massive gates. Although the lock looked a bit rusty, it opened without protest and they walked through onto a broad gravelled parking area in front of the building. Around this were fine tall oleander bushes, even taller clumps of bamboo and a series of vicious-looking spiny cactus plants, some almost as big as she was.

L'Ospedaletto was built of dusty sandstone, the mortar weathered by the passage of the seasons and many of the joints dug out over the centuries by generations of birds and animals. Massive wooden doors right in front of them in the lower part of the building protected the entrance to a cellar or garage under the property, and the house itself was accessed up a flight of old stone steps that led to a terrace. An ancient rambling rose sprawled across the whole façade with buds already well formed. It wouldn't be long before they flowered and when they did this whole area would no doubt smell divine. As Amy climbed to the front door, families of lizards scuttled into crevices in the walls. She caught Gavin's eye and grimaced. Hopefully they weren't going to find the house full of reptiles.

At the old wooden front door, one of the more modern keys turned the lock and they stepped inside, glad to get out of the direct sunlight. It was cool and dark in the house and the drop in temperature compared to outside was welcome. Amy stood on the doormat and breathed deeply. The last hour had been unexpectedly emotional. It was good to have a moment to herself. She stood there, vaguely conscious of Gavin moving about, before light suddenly flooded into the house and along with it she felt a wave of warm air from outside as he went around the room, opening the windows one by one and pushing the heavy wooden shutters outwards. The sound of birds twittering in the trees outside suddenly became much louder and Amy shook her head, emerged from her daze and stared about in wonder before glancing at Gavin.

'Wow! What a place.'

He looked equally impressed. 'You aren't joking.'

The front door led straight into a single, remarkable room. The walls were bare stone and the arched window surrounds were made of carved stone. The ceiling was very high – two or three times the height of her flat back in London, but it was the shape of the ceiling that was most impressive. It was ribbed all along its length with stone arches that supported the massive dark timbers that in turn carried the floor above, giving the room an almost ecclesiastical feel. The ceiling timbers were very old beams, likely oak, and the plaster between the beams had clearly not been painted for a long, long time. It could almost have been a chapel, or the great hall of a castle, although it was completely without ornamentation. The room was enormous and a hundred people would have been able to fit in here without trouble.

'Mr Slater certainly had no shortage of space if he felt like entertaining. You could shoot *Strictly* in here.' Gavin sounded as awe-struck as Amy felt.

Amy stared around the room. The floor was paved with ancient terracotta tiles that looked as though they had been there since the dawn of time. In the middle there was a huge old table, surrounded by a dozen chairs. Against the side wall were numerous bookcases and at this end of the room, a leather sofa was positioned in front of the monumental fireplace, with a number of old rugs strewn across the terracotta-tiled floor. At the far end, a stone archway led to a kitchen area. The overall impression was of immense space and a terrific sense of history.

'Come and take a look out here, Amy.'

Amy glanced across and saw that one of the huge archways along the right-hand wall had been transformed into a pair of French windows leading into the garden. She followed him out onto the patch of gravel that served as a patio. This was flat, although the hillside sloped steeply upwards to their left and down towards the road to the right. All around them were bushes and cypress trees, many of them considerably overgrown, and a strong scent of rosemary was in the air. A fine palm tree towered above them, almost as tall as the house. The result was a dappled area of blessed shade where the air temperature was not only bearable, but delightful.

'What a place!' She couldn't help repeating herself. 'The house is amazing and the garden could be a real gem with a bit of effort.'

She saw Gavin shudder. Manual work had never been his thing. 'A bit? You'd need a gang of labourers with chain saws.'

'But it's gorgeous, even if it is a bit overgrown. Mr Slater certainly had an eye for property.'

Gavin was fiddling with his phone. After a few seconds, he waved it at her and pointed up the hill. 'The signal here's rubbish. I need to make a call. I'll be back in five minutes.' And, without giving her a chance to say that she might like to come with him, he disappeared through the trees.

She sat down on an old bench and admired the view, soaking up the warmth and the clean country air. For a few moments she allowed herself to dream of giving up her life in London and coming over here to live. In fact, she had been considering it from the moment they had pulled up outside the notary's office. Of course, that wasn't going to be possible for two reasons: her job and Gavin. He didn't speak a word of Italian and she couldn't imagine him ever being willing to give up his job, his friends or the big city. But, for a few minutes, she let herself enjoy the thought. There was something about Italy that felt so familiar and yet so exciting.

She was still sitting there ten minutes later when he reappeared. 'I had to walk halfway up the hill before I got a proper signal.' His tone made clear what he thought of such a primitive place. 'Maybe the peasants here make do with jungle drums.' He sat down on the bench beside her. 'What are we going to do about accommodation for tonight? You're not planning on staying here in this house, are you? A hotel will be far more comfortable.' And Amy knew how important Gavin's personal comfort was to him.

'I suppose we might stay here, but first we'd better check out the rest of the house before I commit myself to anything I might regret. I'm still a bit worried where all those lizards disappeared to.'

They went back inside and walked slowly through the house. Apart from the huge living room on the ground floor, there was a kitchen, a bathroom and another room piled high with junk. The kitchen itself wasn't a pretty sight. The units were all in good repair, but very old-fashioned and covered in a thick coating of dust. The mould growing around the sides of the sink would probably have got Alexander Fleming very excited and Amy could see there was a major cleaning and disinfecting job to be done here. She opened the fridge and rapidly closed it again. The contents had doubtless been there since well before Mr Slater's death the previous year. No amount of cleaning would remove the amorphous brown mass that had slid through the bars of the shelves before congealing in the vegetable compartment at the bottom into the sort of droopy, melting shape that would have made Salvador Dalí proud.

She started to compose a mental list of things she would need before the place could be rendered even remotely habitable. *Fridge* occupied the top line. She felt Gavin's eyes on her and gestured towards the fridge.

'That'll have to go, and I'm afraid the cooker's had its day.'

He grimaced. 'It looks positively lethal.'

The rusty cooker was attached to a gas cylinder by a length of seriously corroded rubber pipe. This had probably started life red or orange, but it now reminded her of a rather wrinkly poisonous snake.

Gavin ran his finger across the worktop and it came back not only black, but sticky. He removed a tissue from his pocket and fastidiously wiped his hand clean. 'New kitchen: stick it on your list.'

'How do you know I'm making a list?'

'Because that's what you do. Well, go on, deny it. Tell me you aren't preparing a list of things you'll need to do.'

She just shrugged sheepishly and carried on with her survey.

Halfway along the wall of the living room was an ancient wooden staircase that led up to the first floor. It creaked ominously as they climbed – and it was a long way up. On the upper floor they found no fewer than six large bedrooms and a study. There was a big, solid wooden bed, stripped of all bedding, and some hefty matching furniture in the first room, with two beds and a dressing table in the next. Otherwise, the other rooms were quite empty, except for the study at the far end of the corridor. When they got there, Amy paused at the door and looked around.

It felt strange, almost improper, to be invading this very personal space. The floor was covered in odd bits and pieces, ranging from a couple of tennis racquets and a fishing rod to what looked like a rusty cannonball, while the desk was piled high with books and papers. Light filtered in through the louvred shutters as far as the other wall, which was filled by a floor-to-ceiling bookcase, packed with books. A battered old Remington typewriter took pride of place on the desk, and alongside it, a pen was lying on top of a pad as if the owner had just popped out to make himself a coffee. But, of course, Amy found herself thinking with a twinge of regret, he wouldn't be coming back ever again – whoever he had been.

'He certainly liked reading, didn't he?' Gavin was clearly amazed at the number of books squeezed onto the shelves that lined the walls.

He went over to the window, twisted the handle to open it and unfastened the shutters. As he pushed them outwards, sunlight came flooding into the room.

'Wow! There's quite a view from up here.'

Amy joined him at the window. They were now at the back of the house, looking out over a sea of vines that stretched up the hill above them. The leaves of the vines were a wonderful bright green, not yet burnt brown by the onslaught of the summer sun. Nevertheless, even now in early June, the stone surround to the window frame was hot. High summer here was likely to be boiling. Amy wondered how cold it would get in winter. She glanced sideways at Gavin.

'Did you see any radiators?' He shook his head. 'That's what I thought. Although it seems almost unbelievable on a day like this, I imagine it can get pretty chilly here in the winter. Take a look at that heater.'

In a corner of the room was an antiquated electric fire. It looked as if it had been manufactured around the year of Mr Slater's birth, or even earlier. The twisted brown flex that snaked out of the back of it looked even more potentially deadly than the gas hose downstairs. *Central Heating System* went onto Amy's mental list. This was rapidly getting longer and longer and it was time to write it down. She picked her way through the piles of clutter across to the desk and sat down on the fine old wooden swivel chair. The floor and the chair both creaked as she did so.

She located a pencil and picked up a piece of paper to write on while Gavin poked about on the bookshelves.

'I wonder if he was a historian. There are loads of history books here – in English and in Italian.'

'Who knows? Maybe the lady across the road can fill us in.' Another thought occurred to Amy. 'You said there wasn't a mobile signal; what about an Internet connection? I haven't seen a computer, so does this mean the Internet hasn't reached Sant'Antonio yet?'

'By the look of it, he only used that old typewriter. How antiquated can you get!'

While he checked his phone again and shook his head, she found a clean sheet of paper and started to write. After *New Electrics*, *Internet Connection* and *Plumbing*, she looked up. 'I haven't seen a bathroom up here, have you?' He shook his head so Amy added *New Bathroom upstairs* and they headed back downstairs.

Chapter 5

One peek into the bathroom on the ground floor was enough for Amy to see that it was going to need a complete makeover so that, too, was added to her list. Gavin was quick to point out the ramifications of this for them tonight.

'Well, it's pretty clear we aren't staying here, are we? Where's the nearest hotel?' He shook his head in frustration. 'And I can't get any kind of Internet connection anywhere in here. Have we somehow travelled back in time to the eighties?' His tone made clear his disapproval.

'That restaurant in the square, didn't it have *Hotel* on the sign? I'll go and ask Signora Grande in a minute. She'll know. If not, the coast's only half an hour away or there's Pisa itself. There must be loads of hotels in this area. It's all right, Gav, you won't have to sleep in a ditch.'

Directly opposite the bathroom was a door. It was locked, but the key was in the lock. Amy turned it and pulled the door open, revealing a steep, narrow staircase, no doubt leading down to the garage beneath the house. The light on the stair wasn't working, so she waited at the top, holding the door open so as to give enough light for Gavin to make his way tentatively down to the bottom.

'It's all right.' His voice floated back up as lights flickered on. 'The lights down here are still working.'

Amy wedged the top door open with an old stool and went down. The fairly modern strip lights in the garage looked a little less dangerous than the ones upstairs and allowed them to take a good look around. The floor was bare earth and it occupied the same surface area as the floors above. It was more like a warehouse or a cellar than a garage. Along one wall were three absolutely huge wooden barrels mounted horizontally on concrete supports, each almost the size of a small van. Beyond them were various barely recognisable objects, some made of wood and some rusty metal. Presumably these had all been used for winemaking or farming. At the front of the building were the two solid wooden doors that gave access to the parking area by the main gates. The rest of the space to their right was a mass of clutter, with everything from antique agricultural machinery, including half a tractor with no wheels, to bales of equally ancient straw. The whole untidy mass appeared to be welded together under a dense canopy of dusty cobwebs.

A vast woodpile started beside the entrance doors and ran halfway along the side wall of the building, piled up to shoulder height all the way, and she wandered over to it.

'Well, at least there's no shortage of firewood.' But if the fireplace upstairs was going to be the only source of heat, she knew it would be woefully inadequate when winter came. How had the mysterious Mr Slater managed?

Gavin threw in a caveat. 'Just mind what you're doing if you start lifting those logs, though. God knows what nasty bugs and spiders live in among them, let alone rats and mice.'

Amy's mind had been working very much along the same lines. Strange, curved tracks in the earth floor made her wonder if there might even be snakes down there. She shuddered, suddenly quite keen to get back up to the house again.

'I think I've seen enough for now.' She turned back towards the stairs. 'Shall we head back up?'

She noticed that he didn't hang about either.

Back up on the ground floor, Gavin made a welcome discovery. In one of the kitchen cupboards there were a dozen unmarked bottles of red wine. In the cupboard directly above, he located a corkscrew. He picked up a bottle, pulled the cork and held it up hopefully.

'Seen any glasses?'

The only glasses she could see on the worktop were covered in a thick layer of dust and cobwebs so she checked in a few cupboards and rapidly closed the doors again. She had limited experience of mice and rats but the host of droppings in there looked sinister.

She shook her head. 'Nothing I feel like using. We'd probably catch bubonic plague.'

Undeterred, he wiped the neck of the bottle on his tissue and took a tentative sip. He had a bigger swig, grunted approvingly and then passed it across to her. She took a little taste and smiled at him.

'Mmh, that's really good. Did I tell you the notary said the guy who looks after the vines paid Mr Slater rent in kind – wine.'

'Now you're talking.' Gavin grinned at her. 'I wonder what the going rate in litres for all this land is. There are rows and rows of vines up there on the hillside. Quite a few bottles, I would imagine. And if it's all as good as this, we can spend our holidays drunk as skunks all the time if we feel like it.' From the expression on his face she could see that the place was beginning to redeem itself in his eyes.

Together they walked back out onto the gravel patio and sat down again on the old iron bench. Here they were shaded by the criss-crossed branches above. Down the hill to their right was a fine view over faded, red-tiled roofs, the ramparts of the castle, and onwards across the low hills that ultimately separated them from the Mediterranean in the far distance. To their left, the rows of vines on the hillside rose up with mathematical precision towards uncultivated land and rocky outcrops near the top. It was a stunning view and it was so quiet all she could hear was the buzzing of bees in the rosemary bushes.

They sat down side by side and drank some more wine. A few moments later, they heard movement in the branches of an ancient fig tree and to Amy's delight she spotted not one, but two, gorgeous little red squirrels chasing each other about and, by the look of it, having great fun in the process. She sat and gazed at them in wonder while Gavin drank in the view – and the red wine. He took another couple of mouthfuls and offered her the bottle. She took it distractedly and sipped, lost in her thoughts, until he brought her back to the present.

'It's almost five. We need to sort out somewhere to stay for the night.' There was a brief pause before he added, almost casually, 'You know I said I'd stay till Sunday? Well, it turns out I need to get back tomorrow after all. That call I made earlier: the Taiwanese are keen to proceed with the purchase of a hefty chunk of Knightsbridge and I need to be there to seal the deal.'

Amy felt a wave of disappointment and immediately found herself analysing it. It didn't take her long to recognise that her disappointment wasn't so much the prospect of being separated from him, as the thought that if she were to accompany him to London tomorrow, it would separate her from this lovely place. She made a quick decision.

'Of course, your job has to come first, I understand. But I think I'll stay on for a few days more. After all, everybody's been telling me I'm supposed to be taking a break. Are you sure you won't be lonely by yourself?' That, she knew, was a rhetorical question. If she knew Gavin – and she did – he wouldn't be on his own for long.

He nodded. 'I'll be fine. What about you? Are you sure you want to stay here all on your own?'

'A bit of peace and quiet will do me good. Besides, I need to concentrate on finding a plumber to sort out the kitchen, bathroom and central heating – the stuff on my list, remember? That'll give me something to do.'

'So what's the plan? Are you thinking of keeping it as a holiday home? That would be a very expensive luxury, particularly considering that you normally only manage to get away for a week or two every year.'

'That's the old me, Gav. I'll tell you this: that fainting thing last week frightened the life out of me, and I know I need to start taking things easy – or at least *easier*.'

He looked sceptical. 'I'll believe it when I see it. That's just the way you're built and it's the way the job is. I wouldn't mind betting you'll be back to your old frenetic self within a matter of weeks.'

She shook her head. 'The specialist at the hospital didn't mince her words. What's the point of working myself into an early grave?' Lucy had said the exact same thing as well. 'No job's worth a heart attack.'

He still wasn't convinced. 'So you're telling me that you'd be quite happy to let slimy Christian take over your job while you do something more menial?' He caught her eye. 'Pull the other one.'

She wasn't convinced either, but she put on a brave face. 'I'll sort myself out, don't you worry. And as for it being too expensive to keep this place, I've just been left three quarters of a million pounds, remember. Add that to the money I've saved over the last five or six years of healthy bonuses and I could probably survive quite happily for the next ten years, or even twenty, without doing any work at all.'

'But you'd be bored stiff and you know it. If I were you, I'd put this place on the market and use all that money to buy us a decent flat in London.'

She didn't answer immediately. This was just about the first time she had ever heard him refer directly to them moving in together. Her continuing doubts about the longevity of their relationship threatened to surface but she didn't want to get into that now. The time for the two of them to talk seriously about the future was rapidly approaching but, for now, she intended to follow the doctor's advice and avoid any extra stress. In consequence, she opted for prevarication.

'Well, either way, I need to get the plumbing sorted out. I'll get onto that over the next few days and, when it's all been done, I'll make a decision.'

She took a final mouthful of wine and stood up. It was a delightful afternoon, and the temperature here in the shade of the trees just perfect. Somewhere in the distance a dog was barking and she wondered if it might be Max, the black Labrador. She glanced around the garden, which she felt sure could become spectacular with a bit of time, care and effort, and the house itself was to die for. She had never owned her own home before and this was so far beyond her wildest expectations, it was hard to believe it was truly hers. It was a dream of a place: stylish, ancient, and redolent with character, even if it was clear it was going to need a good bit of work. The fact that it had been owned by the mysterious Mr Slater added to its fascination. Hopefully, if she asked around over the next few days and searched through all the papers upstairs in his study, she might be able to find out more about this man and just why he'd seen fit to leave her his house. She looked across at Gavin, who was ensuring that none of the remaining wine went to waste.

'Come on, let's go and check out the hotel.'

Chapter 6

The Corona Grossa turned out to be very pleasant. The woman at the reception desk gave them a charming room with a little balcony overlooking the ruins of the old castle. Amy told her she intended to stay for a number of days, but she wasn't quite sure for how long. The receptionist was very laid-back about the exact length of stay, telling her to let her know in due course. The first half of June until the schools broke up for the summer holidays, she informed them, wasn't yet high season and the place had plenty of availability.

That evening they went downstairs to the restaurant to eat and Amy was glad she had booked. Almost all the tables outside on the square were taken and theirs was the last one free. Whether this was just because it was an exceptionally warm Friday night or the restaurant's normal state was unclear, although Amy thought it was probably the former. With a population of only a couple of thousand and with it not yet being high season for tourists, she couldn't imagine the restaurant being busy every night of the week.

The menu was remarkably comprehensive and she lost no time in deciding to have mixed antipasti, followed by a seafood *fritto misto*. Gavin also opted for the antipasti but predictably decided to follow it with a steak. The waiter who took their order returned a minute later with a bottle of red wine, a bottle of water and a basket of bread. As he set these down on the table he gave Amy a friendly smile.

'Here on holiday?'

'Sort of. I'm just staying a few days to check out a house here.'

The man's smile broadened. 'Really? You're thinking of buying a place here? Well, welcome to Sant'Antonio if you do. It's a great place to live. My name's Giuliano and my wife and I run the Corona Grossa.'

Amy held out her hand. 'I'm Amy Sherwood. The house is just around the corner.' Taking advantage of being with a local, she decided to do a bit of digging. 'It used to belong to a man called Martin Slater. I don't suppose you knew him by any chance?'

She was delighted to see the restaurateur nod his head.

'Yes, of course. He used to be a regular client of ours here and everybody knew Martino. We were all sorry the learn of his death last year. Did you know him well?'

Amy decided to dodge the question for now. 'A bit.'

'I didn't see you at the funeral.'

'I'm afraid I only recently found out about his death.'

'What a pity. Well, it was a good funeral. A lot of people from the town came along. He was very popular here.' Before she could ask for more information, he flashed her another smile. 'Enjoy your meal and enjoy your time in Sant'Antonio.'

After he had gone off, she translated what Giuliano had said and Gavin gave her an encouraging smile. 'That's good to hear, isn't it? A lot of people went to the funeral. Somehow I've had this image of him living and dying all alone. This makes it better, doesn't it – particularly if it turns out he really was your biological father.'

She nodded. It really did.

Gavin filled their glasses and raised his towards her. 'Well, cheers, and here's hoping you find out who the guy was. One thing's for sure: he was certainly generous to leave all that to somebody he barely knew.'

'I just wish I knew why.'

She gave a frustrated shrug of the shoulders and they clinked their glasses together. The wine was excellent and she checked the label. It came from a producer in the next village. Clearly, the winemakers in this region knew what they were doing.

She cast her eyes, and her ears, around the other tables. As far as she could tell, everybody else was Italian and it felt good to get back into an Italian environment again. Down here in the Tuscan countryside life promised to be very different from the cosmopolitan atmosphere of London, but that wasn't necessarily a bad thing. She felt a smile forming on her face. So far, Sant'Antonio had proved to be welcoming and friendly, although the big unknown question of just who Martin Slater had been still loomed over her head.

The meal was very good and by unspoken agreement, they didn't discuss Amy's mother or Mr Slater while they ate. The antipasti they had chosen was called *affettati misti* and consisted of no fewer than six different types of salami and ham, mushrooms in olive oil, sundried tomatoes and fat green olives from the local trees, accompanied by warm focaccia bread. Her *fritto misto* that followed was a mix of lightly fried prawns, squid, octopus and little fish and it was exquisite; and with a fresh green salad it was perfect. Gavin's steak was enormous with a pile of fries and even he struggled to clear the plate – but he did. By the time they had finished up with panna cotta and blueberries in syrup, they were both pleasantly full and much more relaxed.

Over the course of the evening, Amy checked out the other diners and was impressed at the general demographic. There was a good mix of young and old, even a couple of families with small kids who spent most of the evening running around noisily. She knew restaurants in the UK that would have taken a dim view of such uncivilised behaviour but here nobody batted an eyelid and it just added to the homely feel of the place. Somehow, she had been expecting to find this area full of people on holiday or older folk who had chosen to retire here, and it came as a pleasant surprise to see as many young people as the elderly. She glanced across at Gavin.

'I'm glad the place isn't just full of OAPs. From what you hear, so many young people have gone to the big cities and some of these Italian villages and towns have turned into retirement communities by another name or, even worse, ghost towns of empty second homes, apart from a few weeks in summer. But here there are people of all ages.'

'That's good.' Gavin nodded vaguely, his attention trained on his glass, and she wondered rather ungenerously whether he had even been listening.

Amy continued her scan of their fellow diners and found her eyes drawn towards the last table at the end of the terrace where two men were sitting. The one with his back to her had broad shoulders and short-cropped fair hair, and the one facing her was searching for something on his phone as he ate a plate of pasta. He looked as if he was around her age, with a long mane of dark hair and wearing a faded red T-shirt. His cheeks were covered in stubble and a diamond ear stud glinted in the twinkling lights that festooned the trees around them. What was funny was that, in spite of the fact that this rather unkempt character looked a million miles away from most of the men who had been in her life – like the one who was here with her now – she rather liked the look of him.

Back in London she would never have dreamt of checking out some random, long-haired man in a restaurant, but here in Sant'Antonio it felt right. This was instantly followed by a feeling of guilt. Whatever her reservations about their relationship in the long run, she was with Gavin and there was no place in her life for another man – at least for now. She glanced across at Gavin, who was still appreciatively studying the ruby red colour of the wine, and she was glad he appeared oblivious to what had just run through her head.

Her thoughts were interrupted by an Italian woman's voice from the next table.

'I hope you don't mind, but I wonder if you could do me a favour?'

The owner of the voice was a well-dressed lady, maybe in her sixties. She was sitting opposite a man with a neatly trimmed white beard.

Amy gave her a little smile. 'Of course.'

'Coco's got herself tangled up in the legs of your chair. You couldn't just lean forward so I can get the lead back, could you? We have to go.'

Amy looked down and, to her surprise, saw a pair of big brown eyes in a black face looking up at her from under the neighbours' table. It looked like a carbon copy of Max, the Labrador. She leant forward so that the lady could retrieve the tangled lead and felt she had to comment.

'What a well-behaved dog! I had no idea she was even here.'

'Coco's not always so well-behaved, but she's tired today. We had a good long walk this afternoon so she's been sleeping most of the time – until she decided to get up and start exploring.'

Amy bent down and made a fuss of the Labrador, who ended up stretched out on her back, grunting happily as Amy rubbed her tummy. 'I love dogs, but I work in London and it's impossible for me to keep one.'

'What super Italian you speak. I so envy people who can do languages. Did I hear you telling Giuliano you're looking at a house here?' She held up her hand in apology. 'I promise I wasn't eavesdropping. I just happened to catch a snippet of the conversation.'

Amy gave her a reassuring smile. 'That's all right. And yes, we arrived in Sant'Antonio this afternoon.'

'Well, welcome.' The lady held out her hand. 'My name's Rosa Grosseto and this is my husband, Vincenzo. Are you planning on staying long?'

'I'm very pleased to meet you both. I'm Amy Sherwood and this is my friend Gavin.' She gave them both a smile and the husband smiled back at her as his wife resumed the conversation.

'And did you say you're interested in Martin's old house? Is it for sale? I didn't know.'

'No, it's not for sale, it's a bit complicated...' Amy's voice petered out as she searched for the right words, but Signora Grosseto was quick to fill the silence.

'Martin was a lovely man. It was so sad that he died. Are you a relative of his?'

So these people had also known him. Giuliano, the restaurateur, hadn't been joking when he had said that Martin Slater had been well-known here. Amy shook her head. 'Like I say, it's complicated. Did *you* know him well?'

'Indeed we did.' Signor Grosseto spoke for the first time. 'He lived here for many years and we knew and liked him. We used to see a lot of him.'

'Until his illness.' His wife's voice was suddenly sombre.

'Yes, until his illness.' Signor Grosseto's face fell, too. 'Such a pity. More or less overnight, poor Martin became a hermit. Didn't want to talk to anybody, didn't go out. Such a shame. Still, it didn't last long. His heart gave out only a matter of a few months later. It was probably for the best, really.'

'What was his background? You see, I really know next to nothing about him.'

What Signor Grosseto said next made Amy sit up in surprise.

'I reckon he used to be a gangster, or a spy.'

'Don't listen to him. He's just kidding.' His wife frowned at him. 'Of course Martin wasn't anything of the sort.'

Amy was relieved. 'So if he wasn't a gangster, what was he then?'

'Nobody knows.' Signor Grosseto gave her a little smile. 'He hardly ever spoke about himself. For all we knew, he could have been an English milord or a paid assassin... or maybe he was hiding out here under an assumed identity, living under a witness protection scheme.'

'Vincenzo, stop it.' Signora Grosseto stepped in to silence him. 'My husband has a strange sense of humour. Martin was a lovely man. There's no way he could have been a criminal.'

'Well, that's good to hear.'

'What's happening with his house, if you don't mind me asking?'

Amy decided the time had come to come clean. 'It's all a bit strange. I'd never even heard of him before last weekend, but I've just discovered that he left it to me in his will.'

'You knew nothing about him and yet he left you his house?' Signora Grosseto sounded as bemused as Amy herself had been feeling, but fortunately she just nodded a few times and was polite enough not to probe further. 'Well, it's a wonderful old house – even though it'll probably need a bit of work.'

'A *bit*?' Signor Grosseto shook his head. 'Martin never did anything to it. He said he liked it as it was. You'll probably need to start from scratch.'

'And are you thinking of moving in? It would be lovely to have some new blood in the town.' Signora Grosseto gave Amy a reassuring smile as she repeated what the restaurateur had said. 'Sant'Antonio's a lovely place to live.'

'I honestly don't know. I have a job and…' Amy cast a quick glance at Gavin, whose nose was buried in his phone. 'It would be difficult for us both to uproot and move, but I want to make sure the house is habitable before I make any decisions. Maybe we'll keep it as a holiday home.'

'Make sure you come back as often as you can. We're very pleased to have met you.' Signora Grosseto stood up and gave Amy a warm smile. 'I do hope we meet again before too long.'

Chapter 7

When Amy dropped Gavin at Pisa airport early next morning, she felt little or no sense of abandonment. Very much the opposite, in fact. As she waved goodbye to him and put the car into gear, the main feeling running through her was one of relief: relief that they had been able to spend a pleasant twenty-four hours together without arguing, but also relief that she was now free to do whatever she wanted. Since her health scare last week she had been doing a lot of reassessing of her personal life, on top of her working life. What had been emerging ever more clearly had been the fact that she and Gavin didn't really have very much in common, apart from both thoroughly enjoying their respective jobs. Now that she found herself – for just about the first time in years – with time and leisure to think about something other than work, all the doubts that had been floating around inside her head for over a year had begun to coalesce.

She still liked him and, when he was being attentive and unselfish, she still probably loved him. He was very handsome – and he knew it – and he was the life and soul of any party, but she had started to see him for the thoughtless character he really was. She knew, for example, that when she got home from Italy in a few days' time, she would find that he had spent more time at her apartment than at his – no doubt lured by the attraction of the big-screen TV – and her sink would be full of dirty dishes. It wouldn't surprise her either if she found a pile of dirty laundry discarded by him that he would expect her to wash and iron. The idea of doing housework never even entered his head, and the closest he got to preparing food was ordering takeaways.

Yes, he'd made the effort to come and see her in hospital twice, but the day after she'd been discharged with orders to take it easy, he'd dropped in to see her at the end of an afternoon at a corporate golf event, clearly expecting her to make him dinner. When she'd told him she was still feeling washed-out and had just made herself a salad, he'd looked far from happy. The simple truth was that the most important character in Gavin's life was Gavin, and unless she could make him change, she felt in her bones that the relationship was doomed.

When she got back to Sant'Antonio, she parked the car at l'Ospedaletto and looked across the road towards Signora Grande's house. The shutters on the first-floor windows were open and, on impulse, she went across and knocked on the door. A volley of barking then ensued and she heard footsteps approaching and the old lady's voice admonishing the dog in a stage whisper.

'Max, do be quiet. Stop it, Max!'

The door opened to reveal Signora Grande clutching the excited dog by the collar. Amy was relieved to see that she was fully dressed, so she hadn't been woken up.

'Good morning, Signora Grande. Sorry to disturb you, but I wondered if you'd like me to take Max for a walk.'

At the sound of the word 'walk', the dog suddenly became even more excited and almost knocked his mistress over. She steadied herself and gave Amy a warm smile. 'That's very kind of you. He'd love that. Where are you thinking of going for your walk?'

'I haven't had a proper look at the land that belongs to the house yet, so I thought I'd go up the hill and through the fields with him.'

'That's an excellent idea. In that case you won't need his lead, which will make life much easier for you. He does pull so, when he's on the lead.' She stepped back and released her hold on the dog, who came leaping out of the door and stood up on his hind legs, pawing at Amy's waist as he produced excited little whining noises. She patted his head.

'He won't run away, will he?'

Signora Grande shook her head. 'No, he's very good. If you call him, he always comes back.'

Amy and the Labrador crossed the road and set out on a walking tour of the vineyards and fields above and around it. As she had told Signora Grande, she was interested to see the extent of the property that now belonged to her. The rows of vines occupying the land immediately above the house were clearly well looked after and underneath the new leaves she could already see the bunches of hard green grapes, little bigger than peas for now, but by the time of the autumn *vendemmia* – the grape harvest – she knew they would have quadrupled in size. There was no sign of Signor Montalcino, who tended the vines, so she and the dog had the vineyard to themselves.

There was almost complete silence, apart from the sound of the happy Labrador as he charged madly about between the rows of vines, emerging every now and then with a stick that he deposited at her feet. She obediently picked this up and threw it for him to retrieve and the game carried on as they climbed. Even though the town was no longer within shouting distance, she didn't feel vulnerable or alone. If anything, it felt wonderfully relaxing after the hustle and bustle of life back in London, and the company of the big, friendly dog was reassuring. The sky was a deep cloudless blue and the air temperature at this time of the morning absolutely perfect. The higher up the hill she walked, the better the view became and she could feel a smile on her face.

In spite of having had to get up early to see Gavin off, she wasn't feeling so tired today, and she walked all the way to the top of the vineyard and then into a series of open fields of rough grass and scrub. Clearly, although this was an agricultural area, Mr Slater hadn't been interested in farming. She thought back to what Gavin had said yesterday about taking up farming, and on a beautiful day like today the idea was tempting, although she felt sure that on a cold wet winter's day it would be a very different proposition entirely. Besides, as a Londoner born and bred, she didn't know the first thing about animal husbandry, and precious little about crops or even gardening. Agriculture was probably best left to the experts. Mind you, she thought, if she ever did decide to move over here, the first thing she would do would be to get herself a pet. This was the most wonderful space for a dog and if she needed any proof, the broad smile on Max's hairy face provided it.

Towards the far side of the second large field, she spotted a depression in the ground and saw what looked like the remains of an old earthwork or maybe a quarry. Interestingly, somebody had been digging here fairly recently as there was a little pile of rich orangey-red soil drying in the sun. A sturdy fence marked the end of her land and beyond it she could see that the neighbouring farmer had been busy planting what might have been maize, but she wasn't sure. Whatever they were, the young plants were already coming up strongly.

She stopped and took a couple of photos showing the extent of the land and the wonderful old house down the hill in the far distance with the roofs of the town and the ruined castle beyond. She also called the dog and made him sit while she took a photo of him as well. She saw that she had both a phone signal and an Internet connection up here so she sent some photos of the house and grounds to Lucy in London and then settled down to call her as promised. Needless to say, Lucy was immensely impressed by the photos and insisted that Amy tell her all about what she'd learnt the previous day about her mystery benefactor, which wasn't that much. Amy ended up sounding pretty clueless.

'So I now know that the guy left me not only a phenomenal old house and a load of land but also a pile of money, but I'm no closer to knowing who he was. Everybody I've spoken to so far in the town says that he was well known, well liked and popular, but what the connection between him and me really was still remains to be seen.'

Lucy then went on to voice the same conjecture that Gavin had come up with about Mr Slater maybe even being Amy's father, and once again all Amy could do was to give a frustrated sigh. 'I honestly don't know and there's nobody left in the family that I can ask. Maybe he and Mum were close once upon a time, maybe even very close, but how do I find out?'

When the call ended, she made her way back through the vineyard to the top corner and out of a little gate in the fence onto the open hillside. Presumably this marked the boundary of her land. The Labrador, having exhausted his first burst of energy, trotted along beside her most obediently. Evidently Signor Grande had trained him well. There was a rough track leading upwards so she followed it up to an old hut high up on the hill that had presumably once contained somebody's agricultural equipment. Now it looked as though the next gust of wind would blow the rotten timbers over. The shed faced down the hill, and a bench – fortunately still structurally sound – to one side looked welcoming, well positioned so as to catch the morning sun and provide valuable shade later in the day. Church bells were ringing in the town below and Amy remembered it was Saturday and wondered if there was a wedding taking place. She sat down, leant back cautiously against the sun-bleached planks of the rough wooden wall and, while Max set off on a mission to sniff and mark the surrounding area, she let her mind roam.

The bells reminded her that not that long ago she had been convinced that her relationship with Gavin would lead to a wedding, but that now felt less and less likely. They had never discussed the subject and he had shown no sign of wanting even to start the conversation. Of course, her mother's sudden illness and death earlier in the year had served to relegate such things to the back of her mind, but now that she had time to think, she realised that she no longer felt the same way about marriage or about him. Maybe if he were prepared to make a few changes, but not the way he was.

She thought fondly of Lucy. She was a really good friend and she had been so helpful and supportive during the aftermath of the death of her mother. Although relations between Amy and her mum had never been that close, at the time it had felt to Amy as if her whole world had crumbled to dust, but Lucy had been a tower of strength, always there for her. And particularly over the last few months, helping her with all the paperwork and practical arrangements relating to winding up her mum's affairs and selling her house, Lucy had been a rock. Amy remembered what Lucy had said about maybe coming over to join her for a few days and she decided that in view of the huge sum of money she had just been left, she would get in touch with her again and ask her if she'd like to come and stay with her at the hotel as her treat. Besides, a few days' R&R away from all her men friends might not be a bad idea.

She was shaken out of her thoughts by the sight of not one, but two, black Labradors charging up the hill towards her. As she dissuaded them from trying to climb onto her lap, she looked around to see where the other dog's owner might be and saw the familiar face coming up the hill towards her. As she had suspected, it was Signora Grosseto from the restaurant. She waved and Amy waved back. A minute later she reached the hut and took a seat alongside Amy, while the dogs flopped down at their feet, tongues hanging out.

'Hello, good to see you again, Amy. And this is Max, isn't it? I'd recognise him anywhere. I haven't seen him out and about since Signor Grande died.' She sounded a bit out of breath after the climb.

'That's right, I told Signora Grande I'd take him for walks while I'm here. She finds it hard going. And you're Signora Grosseto and that's Coco.'

The other woman nodded. 'Call me Rosa, please.'

'Do you bring your dog up here often, Rosa?'

'Coco and I come up the track to here most days. I live just over there, so we're close by.' She pointed down the hill towards a small cluster of fairly modern-looking villas, probably little more than three or four hundred metres from Amy's new house. 'I often used to meet Signor Grande and Max out here. Such a shame he died.'

'We're almost neighbours, then. My house is just down there... but of course you already know that.'

'I know Martin's house well. It's the most amazing historic old place, isn't it?'

'It's gorgeous. I just wish I knew more about Mr Slater, even just his job. What do you do, Rosa, if you don't mind me asking?'

'I used to teach history, but now I'm retired.'

'I imagine Sant'Antonio's a pretty good place to retire to. I love it already.'

'Both Vincenzo and I were born here. We've known each other since nursery school. I've lived here all my life and I taught history at the *liceo* in Pontedera. Vincenzo had a spell in Rome for a few years but he soon came back. He's an accountant. And what about you, Amy? What do you do?'

'I work in finance. I'm based in London.'

'How come you speak Italian like a native? Congratulations, by the way.'

'Thanks. My mum and my grandparents were Italian and we always spoke Italian at home.'

'Over here or over there?'

'London, I've always lived in London.'

'Sant'Antonio must seem very quiet in comparison.'

Amy answered honestly. 'Yes, but quiet in a good way.' She decided not to mention her health scare and just limited herself to adding, 'Maybe my life's been getting a bit too frenetic. It's wonderful to relax, and Sant'Antonio's a perfect spot for that.'

'Martin used to say the exact same thing. How strange that you didn't know him.'

Amy shook her head. 'I know. I haven't a clue who he was. Before I got the notary's letter a week ago, I'd never even heard of him.'

'And yet he left you his house? That's incredible.'

'You can say that again.'

Rosa turned her head and gave Amy a shrewd look. 'But the fact remains that he knew you. Maybe Vincenzo's idea of him living under an assumed name is closer to the mark than I thought.'

Amy snorted. 'But even if he originally had another name, I just don't know anybody well enough for them to leave me a house. I just can't fathom it out.'

Rosa nodded. 'In that case all you can do is try to enjoy it. Do you think you'll move over here for good?'

'I honestly don't know. Like I said last night, whatever I decide, first of all I'm going to have to do an awful lot of work to get the house up to scratch.'

'Martin didn't do much to it. He lived quite a Spartan life, really, considering how wealthy he was. Of course it's a very ancient building – the oldest in Sant'Antonio, even older than the castle.'

'Do you have any idea how old?' Amy was very pleased to have bumped into Rosa, who seemed to be a fount of local knowledge.

'The house is early medieval; it used to be a hospice for pilgrims on their way to Rome.'

A lightbulb switched on in Amy's brain. 'Hence the name, l'Ospedaletto. Wow, so that means the place is, what, seven or eight hundred years old?'

'1215, if I remember right, so that's over eight hundred years. It's a sobering thought that this place was standing before the Duomo in Florence.' Rosa smiled. 'That's why I love history. And the stonework inside is a delight, isn't it. Those arches are amazing.'

Clearly Rosa was no stranger to the house and its owner. 'So you knew Mr Slater really well. Can you tell me any more about him?'

Rosa reached down to pat the head of her Labrador, and Max immediately crawled over to be petted as well. 'Yes, Max, you're a lovely dog as well.' She glanced up. 'Max and Coco are brother and sister. Martin got him the same time we got her. He was such a nice man. Vincenzo played tennis with him most weeks and we both saw a lot of him and liked him. We often met for a coffee or a drink. He used to come to our house for dinner at least once a month and every Christmas Day.'

'On his own?'

'Yes, that's why we always invited him for Christmas dinner, to stop him being all alone.'

'How sad.'

Rosa shrugged her shoulders helplessly. 'We could never work out why he chose to be alone.'

'Didn't he have a wife or partner?'

Rosa hesitated for a few moments before replying. 'I honestly don't know. I'm sure he must have had a few lady friends – he was a good-looking man after all – but I don't think there was ever anything serious. He was just a very solitary person. Vincenzo and I felt awfully sorry for him really, but I suppose that was his choice.'

Amy was fascinated and would have asked for more information, but at that moment Rosa glanced at her watch and stood up.

'Anyway, I'd better get back. Are you going on with your walk?'

Swallowing her disappointment, Amy shook her head. 'No, I don't think so. I reckon Max has had enough for now and I need to start looking for a good plumber.'

'The best plumber by a long way is Angelo Rossi. The trouble is that he's always so terribly busy. I'll give you his number anyway, but don't be surprised if he can't fit you in for months.'

They set off back down the hill together and Mr Slater was no longer discussed. Instead, they talked about tradesmen. Rosa had had a lot of work done on her house and she was able to rattle off quite a few names of people to use and those to avoid. Unfortunately, she also added a codicil to her endorsement of Signor Rossi the plumber. Apparently he had a reputation for not turning up when he said he would.

'If you can get Angelo Rossi into your house, lock the doors and take his mobile phone away. It's the only way.'

Amy gave her a smile. 'I look forward to meeting him. Can you recommend a builder as well? I have a feeling I'm going to need one.'

'The best in the area by far is Lorenzo Pozzovivo. He's an absolute sweetheart. If you can get him, he'll do everything to perfection.' Rosa produced a remarkably cheeky grin. 'He's absolutely gorgeous: intelligent, but muscular with it.' She rolled her eyes. 'Oh, to be thirty, or even forty again. As for Angelo, the plumber, he's very good at his job, but let's just say he's not quite in the same league when it comes to physique and looks.'

'I look forward to meeting them all – especially the handsome builder.'

Chapter 8

Amy called the plumber – once she had found a spot just up the hill from the house where there was a phone signal – and, to her surprise, when she told him the address of the property, he promised to be there first thing on Monday morning to take a look at what needed doing. Remembering what Rosa had told her, she decided to suspend her disbelief for now. If he didn't show up, it wouldn't be the end of the world. Her new friend had given her another two names to try.

She spent the rest of the morning poking about in the house before deciding to make a start on cleaning up the worst of the dust and dirt. The first thing she discovered was that there appeared to be no hoover, no mop, no disinfectant, and the only bucket looked as though somebody had used it for mixing concrete. She went across the road to speak to Signora Grande again, who endorsed Rosa's choice of plumber – with the same caveats about how busy he was – and offered Amy a coffee. They sat in the old lady's spotless front room and Amy wondered how long it would be before the floors of l'Ospedaletto would shine like these. Max came over and stationed himself at her side, his nose on her thigh, staring up at her adoringly, and Signora Grande smiled.

'I think you've got a friend for life there. Thank you so much for taking him out.'

'I should thank you. He's super company and very well trained.'

They chatted and Amy learned a lot about the town and its customs, but little or nothing more about Martin Slater. All she got from Signora Grande was confirmation of what Rosa had told her about the man having led a very solitary life: few friends and no women in his life. The only other piece of information was that he had spent a lot of his time writing, but the old lady had no idea what he might have been writing. Amy remembered all the history books in his study and it occurred to her that he had maybe been an academic.

She left them and went back to the piazza and turned down the main street to the ironmongers she had spotted the previous day on the way into town. When she got there she found herself inside an Aladdin's cave packed with everything from nappies to chainsaws and she emerged laden down with cleaning products, a mop, bucket and an electric kettle, although the storekeeper told her she would have to look further afield for a vacuum cleaner. She went into a little supermarket and bought tea bags and milk, as well as a couple of packets of biscuits, and managed to cart everything back to l'Ospedaletto, although it was a struggle.

Back at the house, she made herself a cup of tea after locating and scrupulously disinfecting an old mug celebrating the marriage of Charles and Diana in July 1981. When she switched on the kettle, the light over the sink dipped in sinister fashion and she hoped she wouldn't fuse the whole place. She stood and looked on anxiously but the water heated rapidly and when it came to the boil and clicked off, the light immediately returned to normal brightness. The resulting tea was okay, although the long conservation milk gave it a funny taste. Still, it allowed her to feel more at home.

She spent most of the rest of the day cleaning the house and turfing out all manner of junk. This ranged from a worm-eaten bench that almost crumbled in her hands, to a tin basin that looked as though it had been part of the house's original fittings way back in the Middle Ages. One positive thing to emerge as a result of her efforts was the fact that the bathroom, while far from attractive, was still functioning and hot water soon began to emerge from the hot tap and the shower, albeit an unappealing brown colour for the first few minutes until the pipes cleared.

She managed to scrape away most of the dust and dirt from the kitchen worktop and in so doing discovered that underneath all the dust and grime was actually a rather nice piece of marble. The sink cleaned up reasonably and both taps worked, but she avoided drinking the water without boiling it until she had checked with Signora Grande. She had already mentally condemned the fridge so she unplugged it but found it too heavy to cart outside. The same applied to the cooker, which she had no intention of touching for fear of blowing herself to smithereens. Still, she told herself, as she stopped for more tea and a couple of biscuits at lunchtime, if she was careful with what she bought and if she could make do with cold food, and an occasional meal at the restaurant, she could actually squat here relatively comfortably if she wanted. The unused holiday entitlement Scott had told her to take amounted to twenty-five working days, and although she now had ample money if she chose to stay in the hotel for five weeks, the natural frugality instilled in her by her mum made her seriously consider moving in here. First, though, she needed to see when the plumber might be able to start work. There would be no point moving into the middle of a building site.

At four o'clock she decided that enough was enough and headed back to the hotel for a glass of lemonade followed by a snooze. It had been a long, but satisfying, day and she realised that she hadn't thought about foreign exchange transactions even once. She had dinner in the restaurant again and saw that the table where the man with the long hair had been sitting was now occupied by an elderly couple. There was no sign of him, but she gave herself a strict talking-to. Apart from anything else, there was the not-so-small matter of her boyfriend. She had never been the sort of girl to cheat and she had no time for people who did. Certainly, she wasn't going to start now, but she couldn't help questioning, once again, how long the relationship with Gavin would last. She had asked him to text her when he arrived home safely, but she had heard nothing. She didn't even bother checking the news for possible plane crashes because she knew this was just typical Gavin. He was probably concentrating on his Taiwanese property deal and had relegated her to the back of his mind.

After a seafood risotto followed by a glorious mixture of peach, lemon and raspberry ice cream, she was in bed by ten o'clock and sleeping like a log.

–

Amy woke up on Sunday morning to the sound of church bells pealing out, summoning the faithful to early morning mass. She went to Signora Grande's house at nine and took the bouncy Labrador for another long walk. After delivering him back to the old lady, she spent most of the day in the house, continuing her herculean cleaning efforts, before returning to the hotel in the late afternoon for more cold lemonade and to use their Wi-Fi to catch up on her messages and emails. She was touched to see that she had received half a dozen messages from friends at work wishing her well but, needless to say, there was nothing from Gavin. She was just sighing to herself when a shadow fell across her and she glanced up and found herself looking straight into the eyes of none other than the man with the long dark hair and the diamond ear stud. Today he was wearing what looked like a fisherman's smock, splattered all over with paint or mud. There were even a few brown specks on his cheeks and she had to restrain the urge to reach up and wipe them off. He gave her a little smile.

'Hi… um, my name's Danny.' He sounded unexpectedly hesitant. 'Am I right in thinking that you now own Martin's place? Signora Grande told me I'd find you here. I remember you from the other night, but I didn't know who you were then or I would have said something.' The last sentence came tumbling out in a jumbled rush that Amy only just understood.

She blinked a couple of times as she digested the fact that he was speaking to her not in Italian but in English. From his soft accent she thought he might be from the West Coast but she wasn't too good at identifying American accents. She smiled up at him. 'That's right, my name's Amy, Amy Sherwood.'

He nodded his head a few times and as he did so, she felt a mix of feelings sweep through her. On the one hand, she was happy to see him again, but at the same time there was relief that, close up, he didn't inspire a sense of physical attraction in her, after all. Attraction, in the sense that he looked like a nice guy, but not a physical one, which removed the nagging feeling of guilt that she might somehow risk being unfaithful to Gavin by associating with him. This instantly made it all the easier for her to respond in a relaxed way. 'Can I help you?'

He nodded again, a curious, almost birdlike bobbing up-and-down movement, and she could see that he was struggling to find the right words. It was strange to see such a good-looking man appear so reticent and, yes, shy. 'Yes, um, right, you see, Amy... um, Ms Sherwood, I'm the potter.'

'Call me Amy.' She answered automatically while trying to make sense of what he had just told her. She pointed to the empty chair on the opposite side of the table. 'Would you like to sit down?'

'Um, yes, thanks.' With another birdlike nod, he pulled out the chair and sat down. 'You see, it's like I said, I'm the potter...'

His voice tailed off helplessly and she stepped in to help him out. 'You're a potter; you make pottery, is that right?' The head bobbed up and down again. 'That's interesting. And where do you work?'

'Here in Sant'Antonio. I live out on the Volterra road. It's only a ten-minute walk.' He waved vaguely up the road and a young waitress, interpreting it as a call for service, came over and gave him a smile and a friendly wave.

'*Ciao, Danny. Vuoi un caffè?*'

He gave her a big smile and answered in reasonable Italian. '*Un caffè latte, per favore, Virginia.*' As the girl went off, he looked across at Amy. 'My Italian's nothing like as good as yours. I heard you talking to that lady the other night and I thought you *were* Italian.' Heartened by her answering smile, he finally got to what he was trying to say. 'You see, Martin let me help myself to clay from the old quarry and I was hoping you'd let me carry on. It's really high quality, you see.'

The penny dropped and Amy realised that she was in the presence of the person who had been digging at the top of the field. She gave him a big smile. 'Of course you can, Danny. Tell me, what kind of stuff do you make?'

He looked mightily relieved. 'Thank you so much. I make all sorts, really. At the moment I'm making wall plates – you know, plates to hang on the wall – and a friend of mine in Volterra sells them. But I also do mugs and jugs and, like I say, all sorts.'

'That sounds fascinating. I'd love to see them some time.'

He pulled out his phone and passed it across to her. 'You can scroll through. These are my latest batch. They're deliberately asymmetrical to accentuate the fact that they're handmade.'

While the waitress returned with his coffee, Amy scrolled through the photos. The dishes were beautifully made and painted with intricate designs ranging from fleurs-de-lis to wild flowers and tiny, delicately drawn animals. She admired them before handing him back his phone.

'So tell me, Danny, what brings an American here to Sant'Antonio?'

He gave her a little grin. 'Love. The love of my life lives here.'

She smiled back at him, secretly a bit envious of his obvious infatuation. 'Well, good for you. It's a lovely place.'

'It sure is.'

'Did you know Martin well?'

He did that bobbing nod thing again. 'Sort of. He wasn't an easy guy to get to know. He kept himself to himself and he always seemed busy.'

'Doing what?'

There was a long pause before he shook his head. 'I don't really know. Writing stuff, I think, but it was probably with pen and ink. I don't think he had a computer. He was one of those technophobes – you know, people who hate modern-day gadgets – and he didn't even have a phone. If I ever wanted to talk to him, I had to go round and bang on the door.'

'And you don't know what he was writing? Was it a book, or was he a journalist or an academic?'

'I just don't know.'

'Nobody seems to know. Talk about a man of mystery…!'

Chapter 9

At half past seven on Monday morning Amy made her way up the road from the hotel to the house and arrived just as a van drove in through the open gates and parked on the gravel. A sign on the side of it indicated that it belonged to Angelo Rossi, allegedly the best plumber in Sant'Antonio. She was so pleased to see him, she almost kissed him instead of shaking his hand. He was probably aware of the effect his arrival could have on desperate clients so he didn't look surprised at her enthusiastic welcome as he climbed out of the van.

'Good morning, Signora. I'm Angelo Rossi. I believe you have some work for me.'

'Signor Rossi, you can't image how pleased I am to see you. Do come in.' She unlocked the door and ushered him into the house.

When he was safely inside, she closed the door behind him. Remembering Rosa's advice, she even considered locking the door to keep him in there but decided to draw the line at that.

'So, what exactly would you like me to do, Signora?' The plumber was probably about the same height as her, strongly built with spectacularly tattooed forearms and a straggly ponytail – his hair not nearly as lush as Danny the potter's. His T-shirt had been washed so often she could only just make out the last letters of his name and part of a phone number on it but he had a friendly face. He looked around. 'Quite a bit of modernisation and refurbishment, I imagine.'

'Yes, definitely. I'll need a central heating system and I also need you to take a look at the kitchen, the toilet, the washbasin, and see if you could create a new bathroom upstairs. I don't think anything's been touched in here for decades.'

Signor Rossi smiled. 'My compliments, Signora. You speak impeccable Italian. I was rather concerned when I heard you were English. In fact, I've been wondering if I was going to need my new phone app that allegedly translates what I say into English.' He grimaced good-naturedly. 'I tried it last week with some English tourists who asked me the way and I have a feeling they may still be going round and round in circles.'

Amy grinned back, led him through to the kitchen, and offered him a cup of tea, apologising for not having a coffee machine. While she waited for the kettle to boil she explained to Signor Rossi about her mother being from the north of Italy and how they had always talked Italian together. He nodded sagely.

'I thought I could detect a northern accent. If I didn't know, I would have taken you for an Italian from Lombardy or Piedmont. You certainly don't sound English.'

'Thanks. All I need is a bit more practice, but it seems to be coming back pretty well.'

She indicated that he should sit down at the table and dug out the biscuits she had bought. As she did so, the plumber gave her his initial impression.

'From a very brief preliminary glance at your kitchen, I get the feeling that we might be talking about a fairly major job here.'

Amy nodded, concentrating on locating two clean cups. 'I'm sure you're right.'

'Maybe I could take a look around while you're so kindly preparing the tea?'

Amy nodded again and he took off on a tour of the property. Five minutes later the tea was ready and she could still hear his footsteps on the floor upstairs. She went to the bottom of the stairs and called up to him.

'Your tea's ready, Signor Rossi.'

She heard his footsteps as he clumped down the stairs. When he came back into the kitchen, he sat down and picked up the cup. Raising it to his lips, he took a sip and looked across at her.

'Is this the way you English always drink tea, with milk?'

'Yes, is it all right? I'm sorry, I forgot that here in Italy you tend to drink tea without milk.'

He gave her a grin. 'To be totally honest, Signora, this is the first cup of tea I've tasted for twenty years.' He took another sip. 'And it's... drinkable.'

She chuckled at his lukewarm response. 'Please don't feel you have to drink it if you don't like it. I promise I'll get a proper coffee machine before you start work here. It's just that I don't trust the electrics.' She pushed a packet of biscuits across the table towards him.

He took one and studied it carefully. 'English?'

She shook her head. 'Italian. I bought them in the supermarket down the road.'

Reassured, he took a bite and then gave his report on the house. 'Yes, there's a lot to be done, but nothing insurmountable. I have another small job I must do this week. I can't put that off any longer, I'm afraid. But, seeing your fairly urgent need, I could start next Monday.'

He took another sip of tea and looked hopefully at the biscuit packet. Amy nudged it closer to him and thanked him profusely. From what Rosa had said, she hadn't been expecting him to be able to start anything like so soon.

'That would be wonderful, Signor Rossi, but are you sure you can fit me in at such short notice? Like you say, there's a lot of work to be done, you know.' The last thing she wanted was for him to make a start and then disappear off to some other job and leave her high and quite literally dry as a result.

'It's the least I can do. Martino was a good man and a good friend. Any friend of his is a friend of mine. And friends need to help friends.'

Amy was impressed. Martin Slater's popularity really had been extensive. 'That's lovely to hear. Thank you so much.'

'In fact, I have a proposal for you, Signora. I have a good friend who's a builder. His name's Lorenzo Pozzovivo.' Amy immediately recognised the name Rosa had mentioned. 'He and I often work together and he also knew Martino very well. The three of us used to go fishing together. If I tell him what needs to be done here, he might be able to organise things so that he could join me for a week or two. He could fit a new kitchen for you and create a bathroom upstairs. Two if you like. I'm afraid we're looking at a fairly major replacement of your whole plumbing system.' He took another biscuit and nibbled it pensively. 'And I couldn't help noticing that your electrical system is not only ancient, it looks positively dangerous.'

'I rather got that impression myself. I don't suppose you...'

'My cousin, Emilio, is an electrician; in fact he's a very good electrician. If you like, I could ask him to come along and take a look?'

'That would be wonderful, Signor Rossi. Hopefully it won't be too expensive.'

Absently, he helped himself to another biscuit and chewed it while clearly doing some mental arithmetic. His eyes closed as he calculated. It took a remarkably short time before he opened them once more and glanced in surprise at his empty fingers. Amy offered more sustenance.

'Another biscuit?'

He shook his head regretfully and patted his stomach. 'Thank you, Signora, but I'd better not. Now, I'll do a formal calculation for you later this week, but don't worry, we'll make sure you get a good price.'

Amy nodded in agreement. She didn't really have much choice and she knew the work had to be done. This would give her more time to decide on her future and whether to sell the house or hang onto it.

'Thank you. Tell me, how long do you think it will all take? I've got a few weeks' back holiday entitlement to use up and it might be a good idea if I'm around to make decisions. I'm at the Corona Grossa at the moment and I can stay on there until you tell me it's okay to move in here.'

'I would hope to get most of the work done before the end of the month, but you should be able to move in before then if you like. There may be a few days when you'll be without power or water, but, as you say, there's always the hotel.' He had a sudden thought. 'If you like,

I have a little electric stove with two hotplates I can lend you. At least you can have some hot food until your new kitchen's done. I'll bring it with me next week. Now, I must go. It's been very good to meet you. Thank you for the English tea. I must tell my wife about it.'

Amy noticed that most of the tea in his mug was still there and decided to run the risk of fusing the whole house and take a chance and invest in a coffee machine before the work started.

Chapter 10

On Wednesday morning, Amy was sitting outside the hotel with a coffee, checking her emails and sending a message to Lucy to ask whether she felt like coming over for a holiday. It had been a busy couple of days, dedicating herself to administrative matters, starting at the bank. The people there had been remarkably helpful although they had told her they were unable to open a bank account for her until she had completed a number of other formalities. Prime amongst these was to get herself an Italian fiscal code, an essential item for all financial transactions. They confirmed that the substantial sum of money mentioned by the lawyer was sitting in the bank waiting to be passed on to her as soon as she had opened an account.

Deciding to strike while the iron was hot, on Tuesday Amy had driven straight to the tax office in Pontedera where she went through the unexpectedly straightforward process of getting a fiscal code. After that she went to the power company and spent a far more wearisome half hour queuing in a stiflingly hot room before changing the account from Mr Slater's name to hers. Her final visit was to the phone company, where she had received the information that her new phoneline and broadband wouldn't be available for another few weeks, so in the meantime the hotel was the closest place she would be able to find a decent Wi-Fi connection. As for her mobile, that didn't work inside the massively thick stone walls of the house and she had been feeling a bit isolated both from friends and from work. But she was now starting to meet new people here in Sant'Antonio, and one of these put in an appearance at the café on Wednesday morning.

'Ciao, Amy.'

She looked up to see Rosa Grosseto. This time she had left Coco the dog at home.

'Ciao, Rosa. How's things?'

'Fine. Can I get you anything?'

Amy pointed to her cup and shook her head. 'No, thanks, I'm sorted. Time for a chat?'

Rosa raised her hand towards the waiter who was lurking by the door. No words were spoken but he nodded in acknowledgement. Rosa pulled up a chair and sat down. Amy closed her laptop, sat back and looked across at her. 'You would appear to be a regular here.'

'I come in most days for my caffeine fix. I saw the plumber's van outside your house the other day. Did you lock him in like I said?'

Amy smiled and recounted what had transpired on Monday morning and Rosa nodded approvingly. 'That's excellent. I'm delighted they're all coming so quickly but it's like I said, everybody liked Martin. Remember, if you're stuck for a bed for the night any time, we've got spare rooms.'

Amy thanked her and they chatted. Rosa was a mine of information on everything from where to buy kitchen and bathroom furniture to local bureaucracy. 'Have you been to meet the mayor yet?' Amy shook her head. 'I would, if I were you. After all, his office is just across the piazza and his house is only a few hundred yards away.' She caught Amy's eye. 'He's an important person round here, and he knows it. He's a career politician and we're all convinced he'll be running for parliament before too long. It wouldn't hurt to keep him sweet.'

Amy nodded. She had been meaning to call into the Municipio to inform them that the house was once more occupied. 'I'll do that. I suppose I'll have to start paying my taxes as well.'

'You know what they say, there are two certainties in life – death and taxes.'

When Amy had finished her coffee and her email to Lucy, she decided to call into the town hall on her way back to the house. She went across the square to the Municipio, walked in through the glass doors and followed the sign to Reception. A young man – probably still in his early twenties – behind the desk told her the mayor was busy, but if she wanted to wait, he would take her through as soon as he was free. The man was very helpful, talking to her about all sorts of technical issues like refuse collection and access to the municipal dump. He also gave her details of local clubs and societies and the town's Facebook page, where she could find information about upcoming events.

However, when she gave him her address, the funniest thing happened. The hitherto helpful young man suddenly turned into a disinterested civil servant who abruptly went off and left her. As she watched his retreating back she found herself wondering just what on earth this was all about. Somehow either her name or the address of l'Ospedaletto had sparked off a negative reaction in him and she couldn't understand what it might have been.

After a short while a woman emerged through double doors on the other side of the entrance lobby and left the building. Reluctantly – or so it seemed to Amy – the receptionist, who had since returned to his desk, picked up the phone. A moment later, he indicated with a dismissive wave of the hand that the mayor would see Amy now, but he didn't even bother getting off his seat.

The mayor's office was even larger than the notary's. The air conditioning was running and the mayor was in his shirt sleeves. He rose to his feet and held out his hand.

Amy shook it, and sat down opposite him. He was about her height, olive-skinned and with thick black hair. She was mildly surprised to see that he didn't look much older than she was. He had a business-like air about him and his desk was piled high with files. She introduced herself but, unlike the man behind the counter at reception, this resulted in a hint of a smile.

'Welcome to Sant'Antonio, Signora Sherwood.'

Amy smiled back. 'Thank you. I just wanted to come in and introduce myself and to let you know that I've taken over Martin Slater's house and I'm going to start renovations next week. I arrived last Friday and I'm staying at the Corona Grossa for now.'

He caught and held her gaze. 'Thank you, but we already know that.' Amy was quite taken aback. She saw a twinkle in his eye and realised he had enjoyed surprising her. Also, it was clear he wanted her to know that little escaped the mayor's attention.

'It was a great pity about Signor Slater. He was well-known here in Sant'Antonio and he was well-loved. Was he a close relative of yours, Signora?'

Amy shook her head. Pretty obviously there was little point in beating about the bush. In all likelihood the mayor already knew the situation, so she told him the truth.

'No, we weren't related. In fact, I never met him.'

She glimpsed something on his face confirming her suspicion that this information wasn't new to him.

'How strange that he should leave you his house, if you didn't know him.'

'Indeed, although I believe he might have known my mother.' Just exactly how well was the big question, but she kept that to herself. 'Alas, she died recently and so I haven't been able to ask her about him.' The more she thought about it, the more she felt sure her mother was the key.

She went on to explain about only recently receiving news of Mr Slater's death. As she spoke, she definitely got the feeling the mayor already knew this, too. In all probability he and the notary, along with the local priest and maybe the doctor, knew all there was to know about the inhabitants of Sant'Antonio.

After a brief conversation lasting only a few minutes, he glanced at his watch. 'I hope you enjoy your time here in Sant'Antonio. If there's ever anything I can do for you, please don't hesitate to contact me.'

Taking this as a sign that the brief interview was over, Amy rose to her feet, shook his hand once more and headed back into the hall. She gave a friendly smile and a wave of the hand to the man behind the counter but he ignored her completely. Still mystified, she went out into the heat and returned to the house.

As she approached the house, she saw a man in tattered jeans and a blue T-shirt standing on the terrace outside the front door. His clothes were barely managing to contain the pressure of the muscular body beneath them. He was tall, he was dark and he was very, very handsome. She stopped and took a deep breath. He really was gorgeous.

It didn't need the name written on the door of his truck for her to realise that this must be Lorenzo Pozzovivo, the builder described by Rosa as an absolute sweetheart. Amy reflected that there was nothing wrong with Rosa's judgement. He was probably about the same age as she was, or maybe in his mid- or late thirties, and a spontaneous smile appeared on her face as she walked up to him and stretched out her hand.

'How good of you to come. I hope you haven't been waiting long.'

He took her hand in a powerful fist but shook it surprisingly gently.

'Good day, Signora.' He was remarkably soft-spoken for such a huge hulk of a man and he looked friendly – which was just as well, as he could easily have torn her limb-from-limb if he had wanted. 'I'm Lorenzo Pozzovivo. Angelo, the plumber, told me you're in urgent need of some work. Is it the roof?'

Amy raised her eyes. She hadn't given a thought to the roof – and there was an awful lot of it. 'Is there a problem with the roof?'

Signor Pozzovivo gave her a reassuring smile. 'Nothing too serious, I'm sure, but I'd better go up and check. I could see from the road that the chimney needs some work on it and the gutters need renewing. But, otherwise, it doesn't look too bad. It'll be fine, I'm sure.'

Amy was about to usher him into the house when another van pulled up on the gravel. The driver jumped out and climbed the steps towards them. After exchanging greetings with Lorenzo Pozzovivo, he came over to Amy and they shook hands.

'I'm Emilio Rossi. My cousin Angelo tells me your house might need some work.' Unlike his cousin, Emilio was immensely tall and stick thin. A grizzly black beard concealed half his face, giving him a piratical air.

'Thank you so much for coming.' Amy was seriously impressed. Tradesmen in London didn't often demonstrate such enthusiasm.

Amy led the two men through the house, pointing out what she felt needed to be done. The electrician reached his conclusion within a very few minutes.

'I'm afraid the only thing to do is to start again. As it is, I should really advise you not to use any electrical device for fear of electrocuting yourself.' Noticing the expression of horror on Amy's face, he smiled. 'But, seeing as you already have, and you're still alive, I should imagine you're safe enough for now. Just be careful.' He glanced at her trainers. 'That's good, rubber soles. Better to be safe than sorry.'

He squatted down on his heels and pulled at one of the power points. It came out of the wall with a shower of dust. He scrutinised the wires behind it and frowned.

'Angelo tells me he's coming next week to start the plumbing work. In view of the urgency of the matter, I'll do the same. I should really have another job at a hotel in Castiglioncello, but that can wait for a week or two.'

Amy told him how grateful she was but he brushed away her thanks and said the same thing the plumber had said. 'Martino was a good man. It's the least I can do. Were you related to him? His daughter, maybe?'

This was getting too frustrating for words so all Amy could do was to shake her head and play it down – for now. 'We weren't that close but I'm delighted to hear that he was well-liked in Sant'Antonio. Thank you so much.'

After she had showed him out she went upstairs to see how the builder was getting on. She found him in the last room but one, tapping the walls. She gave him a questioning look.

'Is everything all right?'

'Yes. The good news is that I can't see any serious water infiltration around the chimney or anywhere else on the ceilings, so your roof shouldn't need a lot of work. I think the best thing to do in here would be to sacrifice one bedroom and turn it into two bathrooms. If you like, we could make one an ensuite bathroom alongside the main bedroom.'

He talked her through what needed to be done and ended on an encouraging note. 'We're not doing anything major, you know. We're not knocking any walls down. Just making a few openings and building up a new partition wall, so it shouldn't be a long job. I'll bring two men with me and, as long as you can decide what bathroom and kitchen furniture you want, I don't think it will take more than two, maximum three, weeks.'

Amy did a rapid calculation. Hopefully she would still have some holiday left. All in all, that was amazingly fast, as long as it worked out like he said.

Downstairs once more, he took his leave, promising to let her have a formal estimate by the weekend. He held out his hand to her. 'See you next week.'

'I'm very grateful that you're all able to come so quickly. I wasn't expecting it.'

His reply came as no surprise. 'It's the least we can do for Martino. He was a good man. We all liked him a lot.'

Chapter 11

That evening Amy made another new friend. She was sitting at her regular table outside on the piazza, sipping a glass of cold white wine while she listened to the haunting panpipes of a group of South Americans in colourful costumes performing out under the trees. The sun was low on the horizon and the whole area was bathed in a rich red glow. She was wondering idly what Gavin was doing right now – needless to say, he still hadn't been in touch – when she looked up to see an unfamiliar figure approaching. A tall man with short-cropped fair hair and broad shoulders was carrying a bag from which the handles of two tennis racquets protruded. He was wearing shorts and she found that her eyes were level with his suntanned thighs. She hastily swallowed the wine in her mouth, trying not to choke in the process. He might have been a year or two older than her and he was a very good-looking man. To her surprise, he spoke to her in fluent English with an American accent.

'Hi, sorry to disturb you, but I wonder if you might be able to help? You've met Danny, haven't you? He tells me you're British, but you speak Italian like an Italian and English like an Englishwoman. I badly need somebody to help me with some translating.'

She gave him a little smile. 'If I can help, I'd be happy to. Am I right in assuming you're American?'

'Sort of. I'm originally from Canada but I spent most of my working life in California until I came here a few years ago. I'm sorry if I'm disturbing you. I can come back another time if you prefer.'

'I'm just sitting here waiting to have my dinner, so you've caught me at a good time.'

'The thing is, I badly need a translator.'

'So you've just said. What do you want to translate?'

'It's a work thing. I have a film production company over here. We're based out on the Volterra road. It's only a ten-minute walk from here.'

It occurred to Amy that this sounded as though it was probably close to where Danny the potter had said he lived. Maybe the same place? She took a better look at the American. It could well be that this guy was Danny's dinner companion from the other night. She had only seen him from behind then, but the hair and the shoulders looked somehow familiar. The film company sounded interesting. 'Wow, movies. Why here, not Hollywood?'

'How long do you have?'

She settled back, indicating the chair opposite her. 'I'm all ears.'

As he sat down, the waitress appeared and he glanced across at Amy. 'Another glass of wine?' She shook her head so he just ordered a beer for himself in fairly fluent-sounding Italian. As the waitress went off, Amy queried this with him.

'Your Italian sounds pretty good to me. Are you sure you need my help?' Or, she wondered to herself, was this just an excuse for a date? And if it was, how did she feel about it? He didn't give her time to dwell on this.

'I'm sure. Believe me, I need help. My name's Adam, by the way.'

'I'm Amy. So tell me about Hollywood.'

'We're just a small operation – for now. We're growing fast, but somehow I don't think anybody at Netflix is losing too much sleep over us.'

He launched into the story of how he had ended up here. He told her he had worked his way up from doing a degree in Film Studies at UCLA to being a humble camera operator in California where he had joined one of the big film companies. Four years ago, he struck out on his own and, as his grandparents had originally been from Tuscany, had decided to settle over here. 'I wasn't sure how it was going to work out, but living and working here costs a fraction of what I'd be paying in LA and I just love it.'

'So what sort of movies are you producing?'

'Not so much movies as films-for-TV. Nothing particularly glamorous. Documentaries on climate change and global warming, for the most part.' He caught her eye. 'It's sort of a pet thing of mine. I'm afraid the world's living on borrowed time. Anyway, what about you? How long are you here for? Do you plan on settling here?'

'I'm here for a few weeks. I'm not sure what's going to happen after that. Did Danny tell you about the house? The inheritance?' She saw him nod but she didn't feel like going over the whole thing again so she changed the subject. 'Tell me how I can help you.'

'My Italian's sort of okay but I'm nothing like as fluent as you are and I've been running into all kind of complications with the bureaucracy over here. I really need somebody competent to lead me through all the small print in the multitude of forms that just keep coming. I don't suppose you'd have a few moments to come and take a look, would you? And we'd pay you well, I promise.'

The arrival of the waitress with Adam's beer allowed Amy a few extra seconds to reflect on his proposal. The idea of being involved with a movie company was an exciting one – and her mum would have approved of her earning some extra cash, even if she didn't need it now – but she only had his word for it that he was on the level. She didn't want to run the risk of ending up in a remote location alone with a strange – if undeniably handsome – man. Before she could answer, he reassured her.

'If it's no trouble for you, why not drop round tomorrow and take a look? Just come whenever you like – I'll be there most of the morning and all afternoon. I'll tell Marta at the reception desk that you're coming.'

This sounded encouraging. If there was a receptionist, it hardly sounded like Dracula's castle.

'Okay, by all means. I could call round at, say, four-ish?'

'That's great.' He drained his glass of beer and jumped to his feet. 'I'm sorry I have to dash off, but I have a tennis match. Here's my card with the address, but you can't miss it. It's just on the right, past the water tower. I look forward to seeing you tomorrow.'

Dinner that night was an open buffet and the chef had gone to town with a fine selection of hot and cold dishes. Amy helped herself to a starter of cold seafood salad and ate it slowly while reflecting on the conversation she had just had with the American. Or, rather, she found herself reflecting on the impression he had made on her. Although she did her best to convince herself to the contrary, the fact was that, whereas his friend the potter had attracted her in a non-physical way, the same could not be said about her feelings for Adam, the Canadian-American. There was no getting away from it. She had enjoyed his company and she knew she wanted more of it. No sooner had this realisation dawned than the spectre of Gavin reared its equally handsome head. Whatever her current misgivings about the future of their relationship, he and she were still in one together. Her ruminations were interrupted by her phone. It was Lucy, calling to check up on her.

'Hi, Amy, how's it going? How're you feeling?'

Amy told her about the upcoming remedial works and how she was gradually beginning to scrape some of the decades of dirt off the inside of the house. She then asked if Lucy had had time to consider her offer of coming over to join her on holiday and the answer was a resounding yes.

'I'd love to, and we can argue about who pays when I get over there.'

'Are you sure your boyfriends can spare you for a few days?'

'They'll survive. Besides, I've always had a thing for Italian men. Today's Wednesday. I've got a CPD weekend I can't wriggle out of. I'll be tied up on Monday but how would it be if I came over on Tuesday for the rest of the week? There's a flight that gets into Pisa at two and a flight home on the Sunday afternoon. Could you pick me up? I'm dying to see you and to see the wonderful house.' Her tone became a bit more serious. 'And I can give you all the gossip. There's lots of it.'

Amy pressed her for more information but Lucy told her she would have to wait. Amy was still wondering about this later on when she had another visitor. This time it was Alfredo Lucchese, the notary. He stopped by her table and she asked him if he would like a glass of the cold white wine. He glanced at his watch.

'That's very kind of you, but I'm having dinner with the mayor at nine o'clock so I'll have to rush off.' He grinned. 'Mr Mayor doesn't like being kept waiting.'

'Well, you're very welcome to sit here and wait if you like.'

He sat down opposite her and she was soon telling him about the building works due to start on Monday. He didn't appear surprised that the tradesmen were making an effort to help her out so quickly.

'Martin made a lot of friends during his lifetime. I'm sure you'll find that he's sorely missed by a lot of people in the town. You maybe remember that he left money to a lot of local charities. That's the way he was: very generous. Are you any nearer finding out just exactly what the connection between the two of you really was?'

She shook her head. 'It's so frustrating. He must have known my mother, but I never heard her mention his name. I suppose he might have been a distant relative, but his name never came up. I just don't understand. I've spoken to a few people here and none of them can shed any light, although everybody says he was a kind and generous man. For instance I met the local potter, an American called Danny, the other day, and he told me Mr Slater allowed him to help himself to clay from his land. I've said I'm happy for him to keep on doing that. Do you know the guy?'

He nodded. 'Yes, of course. He and his partner live out on the Volterra road. I handled the purchase of the property a few years back.'

Amy smiled at him. 'He told me the love of his life lived here. What's she like?'

He smiled back as he corrected her. 'He, not she. The love of his life is another man. Ah, there's the mayor now. I'd better go. Enjoy your meal.'

Amy finished the last of her seafood salad and took a mouthful of wine, her mind turning over what she had just learned. Did this mean that Danny and Adam were a couple? It sounded like a logical combination of two beautiful people with similar artistic talents. At least, she told herself, this made it even less likely that a visit to Adam's studio tomorrow might result in an inappropriate approach by him, but she had to admit to a little twinge of regret. He was a very good-looking man, after all.

Chapter 12

The following afternoon Amy collected Max the dog and set off to do a bit of exploring of the surrounding area. She folded the back seat of her little Fiat down and Max jumped in willingly. He was clearly very excited and it took a while before she managed to convince him to sit down and not stand behind her, nibbling her ears. She took the Volterra road and, as Adam had explained, barely a few hundred metres outside of town she came upon a fairly unsightly concrete water tower, and right after that she spotted his studio.

It had probably started life as a large winemaker's cantina at the side of the road. It looked as if it had recently had a complete makeover and the repointed stonework and grey-blue windows and shutters were very smart. A sign on the façade indicated that this was the home of APTV, Adam's company. There was a car park alongside it with half a dozen cars in it, and this appeared to support his claim that she wouldn't find herself all alone with an unknown man – whatever his sexual orientation. For now she just drove past, determined to give Max a good walk.

She followed the increasingly winding road until she emerged from the vineyards and olive groves into open fields and patches of dense woodland. Just before the top of a hill, she pulled over and parked at the side of the road. Outside it was still very warm but there was definitely more than a breath of air up here, which made the conditions more tolerable. She let Max out and they set off along a white gravel track – one of Tuscany's famous *strade bianche* – which ran along the contour line around the hill, dipping in and out of thick woodland that provided welcome shade to both of them. It was quite an isolated place and if she hadn't had her canine companion she probably wouldn't have ventured here alone, but having Max to protect her – although he would probably have licked rather than bitten a would-be assailant – was more than reassuring.

She recognised chestnut trees, the ground below them littered with last year's spiny pods, and stunted oaks, all interspersed with the iconic umbrella pines and cypress trees for which Tuscany is so famous. The shade of the forest provided welcome relief from the heat of the June sunshine. The views down the valley and across to the faint blue line of the distant coast were spectacular, although the heat haze prevented her from making out any details.

They gradually circled the hill, with Max covering two or three times the distance she did as he ran in and out of the trees, retrieving sticks. On the way back to the car she met another human being. Considering that the beaches were little more than half an hour away and no doubt heaving with people, it came almost as a shock to see somebody coming towards her. It was an elderly gentleman who was obviously feeling sociable, as he stopped to chat while Max wandered over to greet him, and he tipped his hat politely in Amy's direction.

'Good afternoon. It's too hot for them now. You'll need to come back early in the morning.'

Amy was momentarily stumped. What was he talking about? Then she spotted the small wicker basket in his gnarled old hand and it all became clear. He was a mushroom hunter. She thanked him for the advice and asked if she could take a look at what he had found.

'Two small porcini and that's it. It's very early in the season but yesterday morning, quite unusually, I got almost a kilo. I put it down to all this climate change stuff. But I left it too late today.'

He proffered the basket and she peered down to find two beautiful porcini mushrooms, each the size of a baby's fist. A wonderful aroma of the forest wafted up to her and she resolved to come back and try her hand at doing a bit of mushroom-hunting of her own one of these days.

At four o'clock on the dot, she and a calmer Max walked in through the glass doors at the entrance to Adam's studio. A dark-haired woman was sitting behind a stylish curved counter over to one side. She looked up as Amy walked in, smiled as she saw the dog, and stood up.

'Are you Amy? I'm Marta. Adam's expecting you, but he didn't tell me the name of your companion.' She spoke Italian with a local accent.

'His name's Max but if you'd prefer, I can leave him in the car. We've just had a long walk. I'm sure he'll sleep.'

'Not at all. Adam loves animals and so do I.'

'He's very friendly and if you give him food he'll be your friend for life.'

Marta emerged from behind her desk and proceeded to make a fuss of the Labrador before leading them along a terracotta-tiled corridor to a large room with a huge, glazed arch occupying most of one wall looking onto a rocky garden, built in a series of steps up the hillside. As he saw them, Adam jumped to his feet and came across to greet them. In return Amy felt a little shiver of attraction go through her, irrespective of what she had heard from the notary.

Marta made the introductions. 'Here's Amy, and her friend's called Max.'

'Hi, Amy and hi there, Max.' Adam crouched down and stroked the dog's ears before straightening up and waving Amy towards one of a pair of sofas by the window. She felt she had better explain.

'He belongs to Signora Grande and I've started taking him for walks. You're sure you don't mind my bringing him?'

'I'm delighted to see you both. Thanks for coming. What can I get you? Afternoon tea, seeing as you're English, or coffee, or a glass of wine, maybe?'

'To be honest we've just been for a walk so something cold would be good. Plain water's fine.'

Adam glanced across at Marta. 'Two mineral waters it is please, Marta, and a packet of biscuits for Max.'

'Actually, if you've got a bowl or an old pot with some water that's probably more what he needs.'

'A bowl of water *and* some biscuits, please. We must look after our guests.'

He sat down opposite Amy and they chatted until Marta returned with the refreshments. Max slurped up the water willingly, making a right old mess of the terracotta floor as he did so, but Adam waved away her apologies. When Amy told him about her plans to upgrade Mr Slater's house, he looked up with evident interest.

'L'Ospedaletto's a lovely old place, but it definitely needs modernising.'

So Adam, too, had been inside Martin Slater's house. 'Yes, indeed. You knew him?' Was there anybody in the town who hadn't known the mysterious Mr Slater?

'I knew him well. We were good friends. So how come you're renovating Mart's house?'

'He left it to me in his will.'

'So you must have known him well?'

Amy shook her head. 'No, that's the thing – I never met him. I have no idea why this man I've never even heard of should have decided to leave me this gorgeous house.'

'That sounds strange. Are you sure you've no idea?'

Amy hesitated. The idea that she might be Martin Slater's daughter was still little more than conjecture and she didn't feel like sharing it for now, particularly with somebody she barely knew. However, what Adam said next shook her to the core.

'You want to know what I think, Amy? I think he might have been your father.'

Amy was stunned. 'Whatever makes you think that? Did he say something?'

'Yes, in fact, he did.' Amy sat up and took notice as he continued. 'You see, he and I got to know each other pretty well. When I first arrived here four years ago, I only knew Danny. Then I met Mart and we just clicked. We were both sort of on our own over here, both outsiders, and we both used to live in Canada. I was born in Canada but I left Vancouver for the States when I was twenty-one and I lived in LA for ten years. I suppose that, and living here in Italy, has knocked the corners off my Canadian accent.'

Amy found herself wondering what he meant by 'sort of on our own'. If he was living with Danny, why would he say that? Doing a quick bit of calculation, she tried to work out his age. He looked as though he was a bit older than Danny, maybe four or five years or so. He'd told her he'd been in Tuscany for four years so that would make him...

He must have read her mind because he helped her out. 'I'm thirty-five.' His smile broadened. 'Which makes me a whole lot older than you, but, don't worry, I'm not going to ask your age. We Canadians are brought up to be polite.'

She found herself smiling back at him. 'I've just turned thirty-one but thank you for your tact.'

'I had you pegged for twenty-five. Anyway, Mart and I used to play tennis together most weeks. The fact that we have floodlights on the courts was down to him. He was very generous. Even though he was twenty-five years older than me, he was red-hot, and he beat me more times than I beat him. By the way, the tennis club courts are on the far side of town if you ever want to play. I'd be delighted to give you a game.'

'Thanks, but I haven't played since school. So, go on. What did he say about me?'

'It was only once. It was winter of last year, maybe eighteen months ago now, and he'd just been diagnosed with the degenerative heart condition that killed him. I took him out to dinner at the Vecchia Cantina – that's a great little restaurant about ten k's from here – and let him pour his heart out.' His tone softened. 'He didn't have anybody, you see. I suppose I was just about his closest friend. It's sad, really.'

Amy could feel the tears welling up for this unknown man, but she was powerless to do anything about them. She just nodded and Adam carried on.

'When we came back to his place after the meal, he brought out a bottle of Jack Daniel's and we both drank far too much. That was the one and only time he ever mentioned he had a daughter, but he'd never seen her. I remember telling him he was crazy and he should try to make contact with what would have been a grown woman by that time, but he wouldn't hear of it.' He caught her eye. 'That's something else about us Canadians. To us – at least, most of us – a promise is a promise.'

'A promise made to whom?'

'To the mother of his child. I never got any more out of him but it sounded as though she'd made him swear to stay away from her and her child.'

Amy felt a tear run down her face and she didn't reply for quite a while. The sofa beside her creaked and for a moment the thought crossed her mind that Adam might be coming to comfort her, but it was a more familiar and less fragrant body that tried to climb onto her lap. She looked down into a pair of worried brown eyes and couldn't help smiling.

'Thanks, Max, but it's all right.' She persuaded him to sit back down again and as he settled onto the floor at her feet she ran the back of her hand across her face and looked up at the Canadian. 'Sorry about that, Adam. It's sad to think of anybody having to go through the last months of a terminal diagnosis on their own. I've just been through pretty much the same thing with my mum, and hearing you talk about it brought it all back to me.' She pulled a tissue out of her pocket and wiped her eyes. 'Sorry about that. Maybe we should talk business.'

He must have seen that she needed to change the subject as he got up without a word and went back to his desk, returning with a sheaf of papers. He sat down alongside her and passed them across. Glad to have something else to take her mind off the possible significance of what he had just told her, she shuffled through the sheets. Most were on Italian Ministry of Cultural Affairs headed paper, or from the tax authorities, and all were convoluted and verbose. After her experience over the past few days, she was no stranger to Italian bureaucracy, so after a minute or two she turned towards him to offer reassurance.

'This is mostly just boilerplate stuff. If you can give me or email me copies of everything, I should be able to get through them pretty fast. I'll fill in what I can and I'll highlight where you need to add stuff. The good news is that I don't see any threats to close you down or make you pay exorbitant sums of money so, like I say, it's just a series of bureaucratic hoops to jump through. Nothing unusual there – we are in Italy after all, and they're legendary for their bureaucracy. I'll be happy to help you with it.'

An expression of considerable relief crossed his face and for a moment she got the impression he might even be about to lean over and kiss her. She caught her breath but, instead, he just gave her a broad smile.

'That's great to hear. Thank you so much. Give me your contact details and I'll send it all across to you.'

On her way back home later on, her mind was filled with two main thoughts – could it be that Martin Slater had been her father, and how would she have reacted if Adam really had tried to kiss her?

Chapter 13

Back at the hotel, Amy quickly completed translations of the papers Adam had given her and sent them back to him with a note confirming her initial impression that he didn't need to be too concerned about the contents. Some follow-up action was needed for some of them and she repeated that she would be happy to help out if required. She spent a lot of the evening thinking about Adam and what he had said. As far as Martin Slater was concerned, it was looking more and more likely that he and her mother must have had an affair, but without proof she was unwilling to entertain the thought that everything her mother had told her had been a lie. Could it really be that her real father hadn't been an officer in the Marines, tragically killed on active service as told by her mum, but a totally different man? It would, of course, explain the amazing bequest, but until she could get concrete proof, she refused to let herself believe it.

She also allowed herself a few minutes to think about Adam. She couldn't deny the frisson that had gone through her when she'd seen him up close in his office, but she knew deep down that she would do well to dismiss any romantic ideas. First, he appeared to already be in a relationship, and second – and most importantly – she was already in a relationship herself, however precarious, with Gavin.

Although the farmers were crying out for rain, it was unseasonably hot – no doubt to the delight of people on the beaches down on the coast – over the next couple of days and nights. The hotel didn't have air conditioning but she was pleased to find it was still cool enough in her room with the window open, for her to be able to sleep all through the night, albeit just covered by a single sheet. What was interesting was that she fell asleep both nights thinking not of Gavin, but of Adam.

On Saturday morning, after taking Max for a walk in the fields, she plucked up enough courage to venture down to the cellar to take a better look around. All went well at first, but not for long. She was sifting through a pile of old junk and lifted an old china chamber pot when there was a sudden movement beneath it. She found herself confronted by a black and yellow snake, barely a foot long, clearly annoyed at losing the roof over its head. She dropped the pot, which smashed on the ground, before she scampered back up the stairs as fast as she could.

She was still thinking about the snake an hour later when there was a knock on the door. She opened it to find Rosa, holding a basket, with Coco the dog.

'Rosa, how nice to see you. Do come in.' Amy stood aside and the dog slipped past, followed by Rosa.

'Ciao, Amy. It's good to see you again.'

Amy stroked Coco and then pointed towards the sofa.

'Come and sit down. Can I make some tea or coffee? I'm afraid the coffee's only instant for now, but an all-singing, all-dancing coffee machine is being delivered tomorrow.'

'A cup of English tea would be wonderful, thank you. I hope you don't mind me popping round, but it's the only way to get in touch. Martin used to say he was perfectly happy without a phone. He did almost everything by letter. I still can't understand how he managed.' Rosa sat down on the sofa and put the basket on the floor at her feet. 'Do you like peaches? We've got three trees in the garden and there's a limit to the amount of jam I can make.' She removed a bag from the basket and handed it to Amy. Inside were a dozen gorgeous ripe peaches and the aroma wafting up from the bag was enticing.

'How wonderful. Thank you so much. I'm afraid the garden here's a bit of a wasteland.'

'Martin used to enjoy gardening but it doesn't take long for it to get out of hand.'

Amy went through to the kitchen, filled the kettle, and switched it on. As usual, the lights dimmed as she did so. She remembered the electrician's words and kept her fingers crossed that the electrics would hold up for another few days. While the kettle heated up, she went back to the living room and found Rosa standing at the open French windows, peering out into the garden.

'I remember coming here a few summers back. Martin invited us round for a glass of champagne to celebrate England winning some cricket match or other. It was a fine evening and we were all out in the garden. It's been let go terribly since then. I suppose he did nothing to it in his last year or so. You'll have your work cut out.'

'Have you got a big garden where you live?'

'Big enough. I'm always finding things that need doing.'

Just then, the kettle reached the boil and switched itself off with a loud click. Amy went back to the kitchen and made the tea and then she and Rosa sat and chatted. After a while it turned out that Rosa had come around with an invitation to lunch the next day.

'Vincenzo so likes his roast on a Sunday. Do say you'll come. It'll just be us and a few other friends. I'm sure they'll all be so terribly pleased to meet you. Do come.'

Amy realised that she would probably do well to try to get to know a few more local people. 'That's very kind, I'd love to.'

'Excellent. Vincenzo said to tell you he can promise you some good wine. He knows his wines and he likes them.'

'That sounds wonderful. I've been drinking the local wine and it's really good. I found a couple of dozen bottles in the kitchen cupboards and I met Signor Montalcino the other day. He's the man who rents the fields belonging to this property, and he pays the rent in wine. He's told me he's got two hundred litres of back rent for me and I can have it any time I want. I'll bring a couple with me.'

'Lucky you.'

Barely half an hour after Rosa had left, Amy had another visitor. It was Signora Grande and she had brought Amy's four-legged bosom buddy with her. Unlike the Labrador, she was looking worried.

'I wonder if I could ask a big favour of you, Amy. I've just had a call to say that that my sister in Livorno has had what sounds like a stroke and my son's coming from Pistoia to collect me and take me to see her. I don't suppose you could look after Max for me. I'll be back tonight.'

'I'm so sorry to hear about your sister, I do hope it isn't too serious. Of course I'll look after Max. In fact, I'll take him for a walk now.'

She and the boisterous Labrador had a pleasant, if hot, walk and returned to the welcome shade of the old house. Amy gave Max a drink and a couple of biscuits – which disappeared down his throat in seconds. After he had stretched out on the cool floor and appeared to be fast asleep, she left him and went upstairs. She decided to have a go at clearing Martin Slater's study before the tradesmen came in on Monday. Gradually clearing the worst of the clutter, she couldn't help thinking back to the spring when she had found herself doing the exact same thing in her mother's house. It was sobering to reflect that both her mum and Mr Slater had died so relatively young and she spared a thought and a tear for her mother as she worked. She hadn't always seen eye-to-eye with her, but they had still been very close and she knew she owed her a great debt of gratitude for managing to bring her up all on her own. She was still coming to terms with her mum's death now, even though months had already passed.

The floor of the study was littered with boxes, books, piles of paper and files. There were even pieces of a suit of armour and a rusty dagger in a tatty leather sheath. She had just about reached the far side of the room, her hands dusty and her fingernails black, when she made a discovery. Shifting stuff on one of the lower shelves – very gingerly after coming face-to-face with a whopping great hairy black spider – she saw something sticking out of the stone wall behind. She pulled half a dozen big books out of the way and found that what she had spotted was a dial, protruding from the front of a solid metal safe firmly cemented into the thick stone wall. Fascinated, she knelt down in front of it.

It wasn't very big – probably no bigger than an average briefcase. There was no keyhole, just the brass dial, with numbers around the rim. She screwed up her eyes and peered at the numbers as she twisted the dial in both directions to see if it opened. After a bit, she tried using her ears. She turned the dial a few more times, listening closely to hear if it made any more significant clicking sound on one number rather than another, but to no avail. Frustratingly, it remained firmly locked.

She sat down on the chair and racked her brains for a solution. It didn't take long.

'The letter!' She found herself shouting out loud. She ran back downstairs, startling the comatose dog, and together with him hurried out of the door and ran like a mad thing back to the hotel, with Max bouncing along excitedly beside her. While he sniffed around her room and wandered out onto the balcony to admire the view, she dug into her suitcase and pulled out the envelope that the notary had given her. She retrieved the letter and looked again at the riddle Mr Slater had set her. As soon as she read the first couple of lines, she realised she had to be on the right track. The words *key* and *safe* leapt out of the page at her.

> *My dearest Amy*
>
> *Initially this may puzzle you, but you will find that these are key questions. Keep them safe.*
>
> *1) On what day was your mother born?*
>
> *2) On what day were you born?*
>
> *3) Your mother has a brooch in the shape of an animal. How many diamonds are there on the brooch?*
>
> *4) The pub opposite the church where you were christened – how many bells on the sign?*

She set about answering the questions in her head. Her mother had been born on the ninth of October and her own birthday was the thirtieth of March. The pub was the Seven Bells and the only complication was the brooch that she realised was still buried in one of the cardboard boxes back at the flat in London. For a moment she toyed with the idea of calling Gavin and asking him to go round and look for it but, as he still hadn't bothered to contact her, she didn't really feel too much like talking to him and decided against it. Still, she reckoned from memory that there were between fifteen and twenty little diamonds on it, so it should be possible to make it work. Armed with the letter she and Max hurried back to the house.

Upstairs in the study, she dropped to her knees in front of the little safe and wondered what to do. How many numbers would it need? She started with 9 30 15 7. She carefully spun the dial so as to compose the numbers, but nothing happened. She tried again, using all the numbers in third place from sixteen to twenty, but still without success. She tried inserting the month of her mother's birth as well as her own, but still to no avail. Frustrated, she sat back on her heels and considered her next move. She read the letter again very carefully and suddenly realised something she had missed. The first word of the riddle was *initially*. Maybe this meant that only the initial digit of each number counted? She tried once more, this time just with the numbers 9 3 1 7. Again no joy, so she tried substituting a two for the number of diamonds and as she clicked on the final 7, the door sprang open.

She had done it.

She leant forward and reached into the safe. As far as she could see, all it contained was an old-fashioned cardboard box file. Amy pulled it out and then peered inside the safe, even running her fingers around the interior in case anything was left behind, but found nothing. Picking up the file, she got to her feet and went over to the desk.

Sitting down on the chair, she switched on the table lamp and opened the lid of the box. The first thing that caught her eye was a wad of banknotes. They were green one-hundred-euro notes and a quick count revealed that there was a total of twenty thousand euros there. Although she dealt regularly with seven- and eight-figure sums in her working life, she had never handled so much cash before and she felt almost awe-struck. Mr Slater's generosity knew no bounds. She set the money carefully aside and checked out the rest of the contents of the box.

There were some odd keys, a British passport in the name of Martin Thomas Slater, a collection of old cheque book stubs held together with a rubber band, and a copy of his will. A quick check revealed that this was exactly the same as the one she had received from the notary. Beneath them, held together by a bulldog clip, was a clutch of other documents. She flicked swiftly through them and saw that they all appeared to be relating to the house, insurance, guarantees for household items and so on, along with a load of old invoices and bills. And then, underneath everything, she found a sealed envelope addressed to *My dearest Amy*. With shaking hands, she slit the envelope open and took out two sheets of paper.

The first bore the heading of a private clinic in Geneva, Switzerland and, although Amy had never seen one before, it was clear that it was the DNA profile of Martin Thomas Slater. The other document was a single typewritten letter. It was dated the thirteenth of January the previous year, not many months before his death.

Amy read the letter closely, word by word. As she read, she found herself having to keep stopping every so often to unclench her fingers, such was her state of nervous tension. When she reached the bottom of the page, she went back and read it again, and then again, until she had absorbed it all. Only then did she drop it back onto the pile of documents on the desk and sit staring blankly out through the window. Teardrops began to form and run down her cheeks. She had never, ever, in her whole life felt so totally bemused, stunned and perplexed.

My dearest Amy

I imagine this will come as a considerable shock to you and I apologise for not being able to tell you in person, but your mother made me swear never to contact you during my lifetime. As the doctors tell me my life will now come to an end within a few months, I'm finally able to tell you what I have been waiting all my life to say. I just wish it could be to your face.

Amy, I am your father. (I'm attaching a DNA test that will support my claim.)

You are the product of the relationship your mother and I had while your father was away on active service in the Marines. I never met him but I'm sure he was a good man and I have carried the burden of guilt for what we did throughout my whole life. I was much younger then, more irresponsible, more selfish, but I loved your mother very dearly. I can still remember the thrill that ran through me the very first time I saw her. To me she was the most beautiful woman in the world and I can honestly say it was love at first sight. I truly believe she felt the same way about me, but your father's death hit her very, very hard. She was struck by an insurmountable feeling of guilt that changed her whole being. Although we had agreed to break the news of our relationship to him as soon as he returned from abroad, the news of his death changed everything. From that moment on, your mother refused to see me ever again and, as I say, she made me promise never to contact you.

I was left with no choice other than to respect her wishes and move away. I gave up my job teaching history at Bristol University and went to Canada. I lived and worked in Edmonton for some years until I was lucky enough to write a bestselling book. There are copies of Far From Home on the shelves of my study if you ever want to read it. Although fictionalised, I can tell you that I drew heavily on my own personal heartbreak when writing it and deliberately wrote under an alias so as to avoid any possible embarrassment for your mother.

When my subsequent books sold even better and I realised I was able to make a living from my writing, I desperately wanted to return to the UK but, instead, I settled for Italy. Much as I felt the urge to return to England and to see you, I knew I had to stick to the agreement I had made and keep my distance, hard as it was. At least I was in nearby Europe and not separated from you by the ocean. I spoke reasonable Italian, so I came to Italy and settled here in this wonderful historic building. Here, after so many unhappy years, I finally found some contentment, although, without you and your mother, it was never all I could have wished for.

I have many regrets in my life, and I am acutely aware that my actions have brought unhappiness to those I loved as much as to myself, but the greatest by far is that I have never spoken to you, held you in my arms. I gave your mother my solemn oath and I had no choice but to stick to it. All I can now do is to ensure that you are well provided for and hope that, now you know the truth, you will be able to think well of me. I do so hope your own life has been, and will continue to be, much happier than mine.

With all my love, my dearest Amy, from the father you never knew.

Martin Slater

She was still sitting there, weeping softly, when she was roused by the unmistakable sound of Labrador paws on the wooden floor. She looked around and saw Max standing at the study door behind her, his head cocked to one side, his expression troubled. As they made eye contact he trotted across to her side and laid his big hairy head on her thigh, his unblinking eyes staring up at her. She reached down to scratch his ears.

'You know you shouldn't be up here, don't you, Max? Dogs live downstairs, not upstairs.' The reprimand would have carried more weight if her voice hadn't been croaky and she hadn't had to stop partway through to blow her nose.

In spite of her words, he just kept looking up at her and then sat down and raised a big heavy black paw and laid it on her thigh in a canine gesture of solidarity. She caught hold of it with her free hand and held it tightly. And the tears started once again.

It was quite a considerable time later before she roused herself and headed back downstairs for a sorely needed glass of wine.

Chapter 14

Rosa and Vincenzo lived less than five minutes' walk away. It was still very hot on Sunday, but at least now a good breeze had started blowing, and the branches of the trees above Amy's head were being whipped about by it as she made her way to their house. As a result, the air felt fresher and cooler. Rosa and Vincenzo lived in a large modern detached villa. The front garden had been meticulously looked after, the house itself was newly painted and it all looked very smart. Amy could hear a hubbub of voices inside as she rang the bell. A few seconds later Rosa appeared, looking flustered. She greeted Amy with kisses to the cheeks and ushered her inside where her husband welcomed her and handed her a glass of what looked like Prosecco.

'Welcome, Amy. So glad you could come.' He took the bottles of Signor Montalcino's wine off her and set them down on the table. 'Thank you so much for the wine, but you shouldn't have.'

She grinned at him. 'It's the least I can do. If somebody had told me only two weeks ago that I would actually have wine made from grapes on my own land, I would have laughed at them. It still feels like a dream.'

The lounge was a charming room with French windows that opened onto the garden. The property boasted a magnificent expanse of lawn that would not have disgraced an English garden, ringed by some fine shrubs and ornamental trees. Amy found herself wondering how much time, work and, above all, water it needed to keep it looking like this. Maybe they had a well. Her reflections were interrupted as she spotted the notary outside admiring the plants.

She hurried out to Alfredo and saw a smile of recognition appear on his face. As before, he was impeccably turned out in a dark suit, polished black shoes, collar and tie.

'Signora Sherwood, how lovely to see you again. All going well?'

Amy smiled back at him as she shook his hand. 'Do call me Amy, please. Everything's fine, and the builders are starting work for me tomorrow. There's an awful lot to be done.' She hesitated, glancing around to see if they were being overheard, but was pleased to see there was nobody within earshot. 'I wanted to see you to tell you there's been a pretty monumental development.'

She watched his face as he registered what she went on to tell him about her discovery. His expression gradually changed from amazement to delight and then to uncertainty. There was real sympathy in his voice when he responded.

'Signora... Amy, how amazing, but how sad that you never had the chance to meet him. He was a charming and generous man and he was well-loved.'

Amy could hear the emotion in her voice as she replied. 'Thank you. That's so reassuring to hear, but I do so wish I could have known him. All my life I've believed that another man was my father but, tragically, I never knew him either. He was killed just before I was born. Now I find myself with two fathers and I never knew either of them.' There was a catch in her voice and she had to stop and collect herself before continuing. 'But knowing he was well-loved here means a lot to me.'

He reached over and placed a comforting hand on her arm. 'I know this must have all come as a massive shock to you but I can tell you this. I'm sure Martin would have been delighted to have such a charming, talented daughter. You can take comfort in the knowledge that he would have been very proud of you.'

It took Amy a full minute to pull herself together. Finally, she mustered a little smile. 'Well, at least I now know that there's a real link between me and Sant'Antonio. Ever since I arrived here I've felt it, and it's reassuring to know that it wasn't just an illusion.' A thought occurred to her. 'Do you think I should make this news public?'

'It's completely up to you, but I can guarantee you an even warmer welcome in Sant'Antonio when you do. Like I say, people here thought very highly of him.'

Just then, Vincenzo appeared carrying a tray of drinks. Amy hadn't started on her fizz yet so she just thanked him while the notary reached for a glass of mineral water. Vincenzo nodded towards Amy and addressed himself to the lawyer.

'Alfredo, I'm glad you've met our new arrival. It's about time we had some new blood in the town. I'm sure Martin would have been pleased to know that such a lovely young woman had taken over l'Ospedaletto.'

Alfredo Lucchese caught Amy's eye for a second before replying. 'Yes, indeed. I'm sure she'll be a great asset to the town.'

Amy hesitated and then decided she had nothing to lose – and maybe even much to gain – by revealing what she had just discovered. She took a big mouthful of the very good wine and owned up.

'Thanks, Vincenzo. In fact only yesterday I found out that my links with Sant'Antonio are stronger than I'd thought.' And she told him about the letter in the safe.

He looked delighted for her and, to her surprise and considerable embarrassment, he set the tray down on the grass, reached out and hugged her to him, bestowing a couple of smacking kisses to her cheeks before catching her by the hand and dragging her back into the lounge. When they got there he immediately pulled out a chair and proceeded to climb up onto it remarkably nimbly, brandishing an empty glass in the air as he did so. Amy stood behind him, worried he might fall off, but he turned out to be steadier than she had thought.

He produced a coin from his pocket and proceeded to bash it against the glass hard enough to turn all the heads and even bring his wife running out of the kitchen. Fortunately, the glass didn't break.

'Dear friends, I have some absolutely wonderful news. This lovely young lady, for those of you who don't know her, is Amy. And she's just discovered she's the daughter of our very own sadly missed Martin.' There was a flutter among the audience and murmurs of surprise. Amy suddenly found herself the centre of attention and the colour rushed to her cheeks again. 'Ladies and gentlemen, we have a Slater in the town once more. Isn't that amazing?'

As Alfredo helped Vincenzo down from his chair, Amy was immediately surrounded by friendly locals, shaking her by the hand, kissing her on the cheeks and enquiring about how she had only now discovered she had a father. It was eminently clear that Martin had been a popular and well-loved member of Sant'Antonio society and she felt pleased and proud for him.

By the time they filed through into the dining room and Amy had told and retold her story time and time again, she felt quite drained. She found the card with her name on it and took her place at table. She was at the top end, with Vincenzo on her right and a good-looking woman on her left who might have been in her mid- or late fifties. Her name card indicated that she was called Domenica, but Amy hadn't met her before. Rosa's empty seat was directly opposite and when her head emerged from the kitchen Amy could see she was perspiring. There were eleven mouths to feed around the table so she had her work cut out. She gave a wave of the hand to the assembled guests. 'Do sit down, everybody. So glad you could come.'

Seeing Rosa hurry back into the kitchen, Amy excused herself and slipped out to join her.

'Can I make myself useful?' It was a lovely big room, with modern kitchen equipment. The enormous table was covered with plates as Rosa served up her own mix of antipasti. There was wonderful aromatic *finocchiona* salami scented with fennel, cured ham and slices of juicy, orange-fleshed melon and a selection of bruschetta slices. Coco, the Labrador, was lying in her basket in the corner and Amy was very impressed. She felt sure Max would have been far too excited to stay out of the way. The previous day he had provided welcome canine support to her as she came to terms with her father's letter, and when Signora Grande had returned with the news that her sister was recovering, Amy had felt really sorry to say goodbye to him.

Rosa put up a few token protests and then let Amy take over the task of adding fat green olives and slices of avocado to the plates. For her part, Rosa hauled a series of roasting dishes out of the ovens and checked the progress of the meat and vegetables. By the time she had finished doing the basting, Amy had prepared the starters.

Rosa and Amy loaded the plates onto a couple of trays and took the starters into the dining room. Amy set her tray down on a side table and returned to her seat so that Rosa could serve everybody personally. As she sat back down again, she felt a hand tap her wrist. It was Vincenzo.

'That was very kind of you, Amy. Thank you.'

'My pleasure.'

She chatted to him for a while and then to the woman on the other side of her and learnt that she, too, had known Martin Slater well.

'So you're Martin's daughter. I saw quite a bit of him. I'm Domenica.'

'And are you a resident of Sant'Antonio? Born and bred?'

'I've been living here now for quite a few years, but I'm originally from Pisa. And you, what have you been doing up to now?'

She and Amy chatted throughout the meal and by the end Amy felt sure she had made another friend.

The antipasti were followed by broad flat *pappardelle al cinghiale* and although Amy deliberately only took a small portion of the pasta, the taste of the rich wild boar sauce was wonderful. After this came roast pork accompanied by little roast potatoes flavoured with rosemary, and then panna cotta to finish. It was an excellent meal and by the end Amy felt as though she was truly settling into the town that was fast becoming her new home.

That evening, sitting outside the restaurant with an iced coffee, Amy was trying to work out if she actually needed any more food, when she got a call back from Lucy. Amy had called her the previous night as soon as she had digested the contents of the letter in the safe, but had just got her friend's voicemail. She had tried a couple more times but it had been clear Lucy was tied up.

'Hi, Amy. Sorry you missed me yesterday. We've been on that CPD weekend I told you about in a hotel in deepest Norfolk and they took our phones away. What's new?'

Amy told her all about the wall safe and the letter and she could hear how pleased her friend was to learn that that her paternity hunch had been right.

'That's amazing – he really was your father! And did he say he was a writer? At least he wasn't a gangster like the man in the restaurant said.'

'Quite, and not just any old writer. I checked out the books he's written. He wrote under a female pen name. Have you ever heard of Danielle Stonehouse? I know the name, but I've never read any of her stuff.'

'Wow, she's a household name; I've read a couple of her books and they're real tear-jerkers. Are you telling me she's a man? How amazing! She writes wonderfully slushy emotional stuff: some contemporary, some historical romances. The last one I read was a family saga set at the time of the Renaissance. And so that was your dad...'

'I'm still trying to come to terms myself with the fact that he was my father.' Even just referring to him in these terms felt weird.

Lucy wasn't Amy's best friend for nothing. She must have picked up on something in her tone. 'What's the matter, Amy? Aren't you pleased?'

Amy wasn't sure how to answer. 'Yes, of course I'm pleased, but there's no getting away from the fact that I never knew him. The more I learn about him, the more he sounds like a fascinating, lovely man and yet I'll never get to meet him, to talk to him...' Her voice broke and the tears that had been sparking in her eyes all day finally started to run down her cheeks. 'I never got to see him, to sit on his lap, to hug him. If only...'

As always, Lucy was only too keen to help out. 'But you've got the next best thing. You've got the memory of a man who was widely admired and loved. Imagine if you'd discovered he was Jack the Ripper.'

In spite of herself, Amy found herself smiling. 'You're right, Luce, all I have is his memory but at least the memories are good.'

'That's the spirit, Amy.' Lucy was clearly determined to shake her friend out of her melancholy. 'So what are we going to do to celebrate? I wish I was able to come over sooner, but at the very least, we need to open a bottle of champagne when I get there on Tuesday night. I'll buy one at the duty free.'

'Don't bother bringing wine with you, I'm swimming in the stuff here. I was too shell-shocked to celebrate last night and today I was invited for a huge lunch with some friendly neighbours. Tonight I'm going back to the house to get everything ready for when the builders come in tomorrow morning, so I'll probably just have a glass of the local red and a quiet night in.'

But that wasn't how it worked out.

A bit later on Amy went back to the house and up to the study where she picked out a mint edition of *Far From Home* by Danielle Stonehouse and brought it back downstairs. She was sitting on the old sofa, trying to summon up the courage to make a start on the book and thinking about pouring herself a glass of wine when there was a knock at the door.

Standing there outlined against the setting sun was a tall man holding what looked like a bottle of champagne. It was Adam.

'Hi, Amy, is this a bad time?'

She could feel a broad smile appear on her face. 'It's a great time. Do come in. Can I offer you a glass of wine?'

He held up the bottle of champagne. 'If you have the glasses, I have the wine – and it's straight from the fridge.'

'That's very kind but there was no need to bring a bottle. I've just learnt that I've got hundreds of litres of wine due to me in back rent. Anyway, come in and take a seat and we'll open your lovely champagne.'

She went off to the kitchen and with a struggle managed to locate a couple of clean wine glasses in a cardboard box on the floor. She had rescued these, along with a selection of plates, mugs and cutlery, from the old kitchen cupboards which were to be among the first things to be demolished when the builders arrived the next day. The rest of the cupboards' contents had ended up in the huge pile of rubbish outside. She took the glasses back into the living room.

'Sorry I couldn't find any champagne glasses. Hope these will do.'

Adam opened the bottle with a minimum of fuss and with just a slight hiss. He filled the two glasses and passed one across to her. She perched on the end of the sofa and held up her glass.

'It's a happy coincidence that you've brought champagne. My friend Lucy was just telling me I should open a bottle.'

'Really? Is it your birthday?'

'Far more than that. I'm celebrating the fact that what you told me was right. I now know for certain that Martin Slater was my real father.' She went on to tell Adam all about the letter in the safe and he beamed at her.

'So you *are* Martin's daughter.' He clinked his glass against hers and drank deeply. 'Cheers. I'm really happy for you. He would have been very proud of you, I know.'

Amy just managed to stop herself from crying all over again, but it was a close-run thing.

'Thanks, Adam. I'm glad he had you as a friend.'

'I was glad to know him. And without him I wouldn't have met you.' As if realising that might have sounded a bit too personal, he set his glass down and produced a white envelope from his pocket. 'Here, I came to pay my debts. Thanks so much for translating those documents. We didn't discuss how much you wanted so, for now, I've paid you on the same scale as the last time I had a translation agency in Rome do some stuff for me. If it isn't enough, just say so.'

Amy shook her head and waved the envelope away. 'Keep your money. I was happy to help. And I'd be happy to do any more if it's needed.'

'Are you sure?' His brow furrowed in concern. 'I told you I'd pay you...'

She gave him a reassuring smile. 'Seriously, no. I did it as a friend, and now that I know that the man you were close to was my real father, that's all the more reason for me not to accept your money. Let me know if you want any more help. Maybe filling in those forms for the tax people?'

'Definitely, but they're not due for months. I'm afraid I'm going to be away for a couple of weeks. I'm off on Tuesday at the crack of dawn – filming in Brazil – but maybe you could drop by one day when I get back.' He corrected himself. 'No, you'll have the builders here and you'll need to be here for them during the daytime, so why don't we meet up one evening after they've finished?'

'Yes, that's probably the best solution, if you don't mind.'

'But first, if you can spare the time, I'd love to see you again. I promise to take you out for dinner to that restaurant I was telling you about, where I went with Mart… your father, but I'm tight for time before going away. But at the very least, might you be free for an *aperitivo* tomorrow night? I could meet you at the Corona Grossa. I want to thank you for helping with the translating, but also we need to celebrate your discovery of your true identity. I should really take you for a good meal but, like I say, I won't have much time.'

'That would be great, but are you sure you won't be too busy getting ready for your trip?'

'It'll be a bit of a rush but I'll be okay. Maybe if we make it early. How does six thirty sound?'

'Well if you're sure, that's fine by me, thanks. I would have invited you here but with the builders starting in the morning it'll be a while before this place is habitable.'

She felt a little pang at the thought that she wasn't going to see him again for two weeks and by that time she wouldn't have much holiday left. But at least she had tomorrow night's quick drink to look forward to. There was no getting away from it: she had to accept the fact that the little ripples that shot through her every time she saw him were signs of attraction and she was looking forward eagerly to seeing him again. The big unknowns hanging over her head remained whether Adam was likely to have any interest in her as anything more than a friend and then, of course, there was the question of Gavin. Although he had been back in the UK for a week now, she still hadn't heard a word from him. Normally she was the one who called him, but she had been deliberately maintaining radio silence – not even calling him to tell him about finding the letter in the safe – to see how long it took him to remember to call her. The answer to that one was: a long time.

She and Adam sat and chatted for a while and she found she could relax in his company. As they talked she studied him surreptitiously and she liked what she saw. Apart from looking good, he was friendly, articulate and she instinctively felt that she could trust him. She had dated a number of good-looking men in the past and had quickly realised that not all of them were as trustworthy as they should have been. Whether that description extended to Gavin remained to be seen, but she had her suspicions.

After a while Adam pointed at the book on the table. 'I see he let you in on the big secret. I think I was just about the only person here that he told.'

'Why all the secrecy? Somebody here the other day told me they thought he was a gangster.'

Adam laughed. 'There were all sorts of theories doing the rounds but he wasn't allowed to tell a soul – a clause in the contract with his publishers meant that he had to keep his true identity a secret in case the fact that the books were written by a man affected sales.'

'I see. I wonder if that still applies now he's dead? I'd better keep the news to myself until I get in touch with the publishers – but I'll read at least one of his books first.'

As the clock neared eight o'clock she knew that she wanted to keep him here longer and started thinking of food.

'I was out for a big lunch today so all I've got for dinner here are some biscuits and a questionable slab of cheese, but you're very welcome to stay and share them with me if you like.'

He smiled. 'That sounds enticing, but I'm just on my way down to the pizzeria to meet up with some guys from the tennis club to decide on the summer tournament. I'm afraid I can't back out of it, much as I'd like to.' Apparently unaware of the wave of disappointment that had run through her, he finished his champagne and stood up. 'But I look forward to seeing you tomorrow at six thirty.'

She accompanied him to the door. 'Thanks for the champagne.'

'Thanks for doing the translations. You have no idea what a great help that's been. See you tomorrow.'

'*A domani, Adam.*'

Chapter 15

Amy made sure she was up and dressed well before seven o'clock on Monday morning. After grabbing a quick cappuccino and a brioche at the hotel she hurried across to the house. Just as she got there, she was delighted to hear a vehicle follow her into the drive. It was Signor Rossi, the plumber, true to his word. Even better, barely two minutes later, the roar of a truck engine told her that Signor Pozzovivo and his two men had also arrived.

Keen to make up for inflicting English tea on the plumber the other day, she set about making coffee for all of them with her fancy new machine. She had only just finished one lot when there was a knock on the door. It was Signor Rossi's cousin, Emilio the electrician, nostrils flaring as he smelt the coffee. His presence also reduced her fears of the coffee machine causing a major power outage.

The rest of the day was a confusing sequence of decisions to be made on the hoof. Still, she told herself, having to decide where to position a power point was a whole lot less stressful than doing a twenty-million-pound forex deal. She refused to venture into the cellar and told the electrician to install lights and sockets wherever he thought fit. The memory of the snake was still fresh in her mind. The good news was that the men all agreed that the only snakes around were harmless grass snakes, so that was one less thing to worry about. In fact, according to Lorenzo, the little yellow and black snake might well not have been a snake at all but a young slowworm. Snake or not, harmless or not, Amy knew that she had no desire whatsoever to find any more of them so she stuck to her plan of staying well clear of the cellar.

In the course of the day the coffee machine barely stopped as she ensured that the tradesmen were all happy. By the end, she had finally managed to get them to start calling her Amy instead of Signora and she was calling them all by their first names. This at least made it easier to distinguish the lanky electrician, Emilio Rossi, from his tattooed cousin, the plumber Angelo Rossi. It was just after four o'clock when she closed the door on the last of them and hurried around to Signora Grande's house to pick up Max for his delayed daily walk. Both of them greeted her warmly and she and the Labrador had a quick walk in the fields, which cleared her head and blew the dust out of her lungs. After having skipped lunch, she was beginning to feel hungry – and filled with nervous anticipation at the evening to come. Was the *aperitivo* a date?

She went back to the house to lock up for the night and stood at the door looking inside. The floor she had spent days cleaning was now a dusty mess all down the middle where the builders had carted out the old kitchen and bathroom furniture. To the right of the fireplace, plugged into an extension lead on Mr Slater's… her father's old coffee table, were the electric kettle, coffee machine and the little cooker lent to her by Angelo the plumber. This had two hotplates and would be her only source of hot food if she were to decide to move in any time soon. The kitchen itself was now just an empty shell waiting for Lorenzo Pozzovivo and his men to replaster a couple of walls prior to fitting the new units. Electric cables and water pipes protruded from the walls, ready to be connected once the builders had finished their work.

The consensus was that she would be without hot water and power from the middle of the week for four or five days, so she resolved to stay at the hotel until then. Lucy was arriving the next day so it made sense to stay with her at the hotel until she left again. After that Amy could move into her first ever house – and what a house! It promised to be magnificent once it was finished. Of course, that then begged the question of what to do with it. She felt sure she should be able to sell it for a lot of money if she wanted, but the longer she stayed here in Sant'Antonio, the closer she felt to the community and she knew she would miss the place and all the new friends and acquaintances she was making. Alternatively, she could keep it as a holiday home but, as she knew only too well, the constraints of her high-pressure job would probably only allow her to snatch a few days off here and there.

She spent ten minutes washing the cups and checking that she had enough coffee, milk, sugar and biscuits to feed the workmen, whose appetite for coffee rivalled Max's appetite for food. By her reckoning, Emilio the electrician had had seven cups of strong coffee in the course of the day and she wondered how he would ever be able to get off to sleep. She dried all the mugs and returned them to the box that would be their temporary home for the next week or two until the new kitchen units arrived.

All the time her mind was working, digesting the developments of the past few days. The discovery that a completely different man was her real father was exciting, but it threw up as many questions as it answered. Prime among these was what she should think of her mother, who had, after all, lied to her throughout her whole life.

It couldn't have been easy for her mother to bring up a child single-handed on just a military widow's pension – or had she? Maybe Martin Slater had contributed. Looking back on it, Amy couldn't remember any particular financial hardship – although her mother had always been careful with money – so he probably had. Considering his reputation for generosity here in the town, she felt confident that he would have provided financial help for his daughter, even if her mother had banished him forever. Not for the first time, she wiped away a tear as she thought of the frustration he must have felt throughout his whole life, but then, of course, things must have been tough for her mum as well.

Amy knew she hadn't been the easiest of children, especially during her teenage years. She had loved her mum – there could be no doubt about that – but she was the first to acknowledge that their relationship had never been a warm, cosy one. Somehow her mum had always been too unemotional, too withdrawn, and now, of course, she knew the real reason why. Not only had she lost her husband, but she had taken the decision to expel the father of her child from both of their lives and that must have taken its toll. If the letter in the safe was right, it had been her choice to sever all links with him, out of a sense of shame or guilt, and the result had been devastating, forever stunting her emotionally.

Amy knew that her mum had been a deeply religious woman – at least she had been after the death of the man Amy had been brought up to believe had been her father – and she had also been very stubborn. But, even so, surely she should have come clean and told her only daughter the truth as she entered adulthood? Amy now found herself in mourning for three parents, two of whom she had never met. She gave a deep and heartfelt sigh and headed for the hotel to change in readiness for her drinks with Adam.

After a quick shower, she stood in her room for a minute or two, trying to decide what to wear for the *aperitivo*. In spite of the glamorous name, she knew that this wasn't going to be a James Bond-style black tie and evening gown event where they would be sipping vodka martinis, shaken not stirred. It would probably just involve sitting at a table in the piazza outside the hotel like she had been doing most evenings since arriving here. On the one hand, she wanted to look good but, at the same time, she had no intention of throwing herself at him. First, that wasn't the way she was made. She had never been a particularly ostentatious person and she hadn't brought a dress with her that could be described as even mildly scandalous. Secondly, there was the unresolved question of Adam's relationship with Danny and she would look pretty foolish if she tried to act as a seductress, only to find that he wasn't interested. And third, of course, was Gavin. Whatever his defects, she was still in that relationship and it wouldn't be fair on him.

In the end she opted for one of her favourites, a light pink linen blouse and a pair of white jeans. Checking herself out in the mirror before leaving the room she decided that she would do. At least she was clean and she looked presentable. She went downstairs just as it was striking the half hour and found Adam waiting for her in the bar. He gave her an appreciative look and held out his hand. 'Wow, you look great.'

She was completely unable to stop her cheeks from flushing as she shook hands with him and she hastily pointed towards the open doors. 'Shall we go outside? It's a beautiful evening.' She didn't remark that he was also looking very good in a light grey polo shirt and faded jeans. She could have done, but she didn't.

Outside they sat down at her usual table and Giuliano came over to see what they wanted to drink. Adam didn't hesitate.

'It has to be champagne, doesn't it? This is a celebration, after all.'

Amy shook her head. 'It's been a long day and if I have more than a glass of wine I'll probably fall over. Besides, that would mean you have to drink the rest of the bottle and I imagine you don't want to get hammered if you've got to get up at the crack of dawn tomorrow. Instead, I would quite like an Aperol spritz.' She glanced up to see if Giuliano had understood her order, even though it had been delivered in English, and she saw him nod.

Adam also nodded. 'Okay, you're the boss.' He ordered a beer for himself and once the restaurateur had disappeared inside, he repeated his earlier comment. 'You do look great, you know. Martin would have been so pleased.' He leant towards her. 'You have his eyes.'

Amy swallowed hard as she stared back into his eyes at close quarters. 'I wish I'd known him. Tell me, did he have a special someone?'

'I'm afraid that's one area where I can't help you. We never spoke about women but I would be surprised if he didn't have somebody. He was a good-looking guy, as well as being charismatic.' He waited until the drinks had been placed in front of them. 'But to my knowledge, he never had a live-in girlfriend.'

The conversation drifted away from her father and Adam told her all about his upcoming trip to Brazil, which sounded pretty scary, trekking off into the wilds of the Amazon rainforest. She warned him to be careful, particularly to look out for snakes or those fish which could strip a man to the skeleton in two minutes. She wasn't totally sure of her facts but she remembered hearing about something like that in a documentary. He promised to take care and then he got her to tell him about her job. In the end, although she had intended not to mention it, she told him about her scare when she had collapsed in the kitchen, and he was quick to offer advice in his turn.

'The doctors were right, you know, Amy. You can't take your health for granted. However much you enjoy your job, you've got to learn to take it easy.' He then went on to make the suggestion that had been running around in her head ever since arriving in Sant'Antonio. 'Why don't you give up the day job and move over here? I'm sure you can find something to do and it's a great place to live. Remember, your health has to be your number one priority. To be perfectly honest, that's part of the reason I moved away from Hollywood. The pressure there is non-stop.'

They carried on chatting about less contentious subjects and all too soon he finished the last of his beer, gave her an apologetic glance, and stood up. 'I'm sorry, but I need to make a move. I promise I'll take you for that meal when I get back from Brazil.'

'Well, you just look after yourself. Stay away from those creepy crawlies.' She stood up as well and when he came over to say goodbye, she caught hold of his shoulders and kissed him on the cheeks. He didn't recoil and, in fact, he looked as though he enjoyed the contact. She certainly did. Armed with that impression, she stepped back and finally found the courage to bring up the subject that had been playing on her mind all evening. 'How's Danny going to cope while you're away?'

A look of surprise spread across his face. 'Danny? He'll be fine. He's got Pierpaolo to look after him, after all.'

She watched him walk off across the piazza and there was one thought going round and round inside her head.

Who the hell was Pierpaolo?

She didn't know what to think. Nobody had mentioned the name Pierpaolo to her before, so who could he be? Maybe this Pierpaolo was Danny's love of his life? If that were the case then what did this mean as far as Adam was concerned? Did he have a significant other and who might that be? She had never liked uncertainty and these questions continued to nag at her all evening, even as she enjoyed a generous helping of the chef's delicious lasagne made with spinach, mushrooms and aubergines. As she ate, she kept reminding herself that she was still in a relationship with Gavin – assuming he could eventually summon up the energy to contact her.

Chapter 16

Around mid-morning the following day she drove down to Pisa to collect Lucy from the airport, but first she had a lot of stuff to buy for the house: sheets, towels and new pillows, pots and pans, kitchen utensils, some decent glasses and a vacuum cleaner. This way, at least, she knew she would be able to get by when she finally moved in, although it occurred to her that if she decided to sell the place, she was going to have all this stuff on her hands. Still, that was a problem for further down the road.

Lucy's plane was on time and Amy was delighted to see her friend again. Even though little more than a couple of weeks had passed, so much had happened and she spent the whole drive back to Sant'Antonio trying to relate all the events, discoveries and new friendships that had presented themselves. For now, she made no mention of Adam, not because she didn't trust Lucy not to say something to Gavin, but because she really didn't really know what to say.

Back at the house, Lucy was totally blown away by how beautiful it was but, predictably, she was even more impressed with Lorenzo Pozzovivo. Amy had to remind her that not only was he married with two little kids, he also didn't speak a word of English, but it was still a struggle to drag her friend away. Fortunately, the sight of the big black dog and the prospect of a walk in the sunshine with Max did it, and Amy led both of them up the hill to the tumbledown shed where they sat down side by side, admiring the view, with Max sprawled at their feet. Conversation lagged for a minute or two and Amy began to realise that Lucy had something on her mind, so she glanced across at her friend.

'You mentioned gossip. What's the news back in the big city? Added any more conquests to your list?'

'No, not really... It's not that.' Lucy was now looking downright uncomfortable. 'You know I told you I'd joined the gym? It's the one in the basement of the squash club just along from the office. You know the one.'

'Of course, that's where Gavin plays squash.'

'Erm, yes, about that... The thing is, I saw him there last week.' Amy saw her take a deep breath. 'There's a two-way mirror – or should that be a one-way mirror? – between the gym and the bar. People on the bikes or treadmills can see out, but the people in the bar can't see in. Well, I was on one of the bikes, pedalling like a maniac, when I saw Gavin.' She reached across and caught hold of Amy's hand. 'I wanted to call you and tell you last week but I thought it would be better face-to-face. You see, he was with another woman.'

'When you say "with"... maybe she was his playing partner.'

Lucy shook her head. 'He was wearing normal clothes and she was all glammed up, looking as though she was ready for a night out. When she came up to him she kissed him and he ran his hands... well, let's just say he put his hands where he shouldn't have.'

'I see.' Amy sat back against the wall of the shed with a sigh and felt the whole thing shake. Very cautiously she shuffled forward again until she was leaning on her hands with her elbows on her knees. 'And there's no way you could have been mistaken? Wrong man, different sort of kiss, or whatever?' She glanced sideways and saw Lucy shake her head. 'Right, I get the picture.'

She sat there for several minutes, trying to digest what she had just heard. Assuming it was true – and she had no reason to doubt her best friend's word – the idea of Gavin cheating on her didn't come as a complete shock. He was a good-looking man and she had always known he had a flirty nature and it was probably this, as much as anything else, that had prevented her from taking the next step in their relationship. Something had stopped her from suggesting they move in together – although his almost constant presence in her flat and his use of her as his maidservant had been the next best thing, at least as far as he was concerned.

The news that he had been with another woman was still a slap in the face but somehow, deep down, she had almost been expecting it. All those trips away to romantic places, dinner assignations with unspecified clients, late nights and weekends away, had sometimes made her wonder if something might have been going on, but she had chosen not to confront him. Now it looked as though she had no alternative.

She felt a movement at her feet and a big black paw suddenly landed on her lap as Max did his best to offer support. Just like when she had been sobbing over the letter from her father, he must somehow have worked out that all was not well with her and he was doing his best to cheer her up. In fact it worked, and she found she could answer Lucy in a reasonably unemotional voice.

'Thanks, Luce, you're a good friend. It can't have been easy telling me that.'

Lucy gave her hand a little squeeze. 'That's what friends are for, Amy. Better that you hear it from me than from somebody else or, even worse, that you just carry on blissfully ignorant of what he's been doing behind your back. What are you going to do?'

By this time Amy had made up her mind. 'I need to talk to him, have it out with him and, as far as I'm concerned, dump him as soon as I can. To be honest, I've been having doubts about the relationship for some time now so it almost makes things easier for me really.' She produced a little smile for Lucy's benefit. 'But you're here on holiday and I'm on holiday and I'm not going to let Gavin ruin that. I think what I'll probably do is fly back to London one day next week and confront him.'

'And then what?'

'And then I'll get on the plane again and come back here to finish my holiday. Hopefully by then I'll be able to move out of the hotel and into the house. The builders reckon it should be habitable – although not finished – by the middle of next week.'

'And then what?'

Amy hesitated before she replied, still doing her best to sound positive. 'I'm not really sure. One thing at a time: first a great holiday with you, then go and see Gavin, finish off the house, and then I'll have time to sit down and start thinking about the rest of my life.'

The next few days passed in a flash. Amy and Lucy made coffee for the builders – no easy feat after the water had been disconnected and power was only available via a long extension lead – walked in the hills with Max, had a series of excellent meals and visited a number of the surrounding places of interest. Beautiful as their surroundings were, as far as Amy could gather, the highlight of

Lucy's week was on Wednesday afternoon when Lorenzo the builder removed his shirt while he dug a hole. Amy almost had to pin her friend down to prevent her from jumping on him. He was doing a great job and the last thing she wanted was for him to be distracted.

On Thursday she and Lucy drove the twenty kilometres down to the pretty little seaside town of Castiglioncello with its fine sandy beach. They paid for rental of two sun loungers and a parasol for the afternoon and Amy had her first ever swim in the Mediterranean, or more precisely the Tyrrhenian Sea, finding the water remarkably clean and a most agreeable temperature. The biggest ice cream cone she had ever seen completed the holiday feel of the day and she returned to Sant'Antonio feeling mildly debauched. Having a place like that almost on her doorstep was a rare treat.

Another treat came the next day. On Friday they drove inland to Volterra to see what the Discover Tuscany website described as a 'medieval town with its own special charm' and it lived up to its billing. This historic walled town, perched on a hilltop amid a sea of gently rolling hills, was delightful. They parked alongside a remarkably well preserved two-thousand-year-old Roman amphitheatre and were surprised to discover that this wasn't the oldest part of town. Lucy's phone told them that Volterra had been an important centre belonging to the Etruscans – the predecessors of the Romans – three or four centuries before Christ, and the old walls and gates were still standing. The Middle Ages had seen the creation of a plethora of fine stone buildings in the *centro storico*, ranging from the twelfth-century Duomo to a fortress built by the famous Medici family. The town was a historical gem.

Although Amy was familiar with northern Italy, she was unprepared for the sheer variety and antiquity of the buildings here in Tuscany, and she was as impressed as Lucy by everything they saw. After stopping for a snack lunch of focaccia bread filled with fresh goats' cheese and grilled aubergines, they set off to look at the shops in the afternoon. It was while they were admiring the pots and dishes in one of numerous shops selling pottery and objects made of the local alabaster that she spotted a familiar face. Inside the shop, sitting chatting to the shopkeeper, was Danny from Sant'Antonio. She turned to Lucy.

'I know that guy. He's a potter and he lives in Sant'Antonio. Feel like coming in to meet him? He's American.'

As they walked into the shop, an old-fashioned bell above the door started ringing and attracted the attention of both men, as well as an aged poodle with a pink neckerchief around its neck, who wandered across to say hello. When Danny recognised Amy he jumped to his feet and came over to greet them.

'Amy, hi. Great to see you.'

Amy introduced Lucy and they chatted while the poodle sniffed Amy's jeans with interest. She hoped this was because of some lingering aroma of Max, rather than grime. Danny pointed out a number of the items on display which he had made and he introduced them to the shop owner, whose name was Mario. Amy had secretly been hoping to find that this might turn out to be Pierpaolo and she wondered how she might be able to find out more about that mysterious man, or, indeed, about Danny's relationship with Adam, but the subject didn't come up. Mario, who had a fine head of glossy black hair that cascaded down to his shoulders, was Italian but it turned out that he had spent ten years of his life living and working in St Ives in Cornwall and he even spoke English with a bit of a West Country drawl. He insisted that they sat down and had cups of coffee with him and they were there for a quarter of an hour chatting, while Lucy bought a charming faux-medieval fruit bowl to give to her parents and Amy bought half a dozen mugs to replace the battered ones back at l'Ospedaletto.

Amy did, however, get a step nearer to discovering more about the Adam, Danny, Pierpaolo triangle when Danny offered to show her around his potter's studio back at Sant'Antonio. She accepted with alacrity and they arranged that she would call round on Sunday afternoon after she'd taken Lucy back to Pisa to catch her flight home. The arrival of an elderly German couple a few minutes later made Amy think they should get out of the way of these potential customers, so they bade farewell to both men and left. She was pleased with her purchases and delighted that Sunday's appointment might mean that the opportunity to quiz Danny more closely had presented itself.

That evening, as a change from the Corona Grossa, Amy took Lucy to a pizzeria tucked away in a little piazza behind the old medieval market at Sant'Antonio. Rosa had told her about the place and that they had tables outside in the market square. Amy had been here in Sant'Antonio for two whole weeks now but still hadn't had an authentic Italian pizza and Lucy sounded equally keen to try the real thing. This would also allow them to tie the meal in with a walk for Max first and he could snooze under the table while they ate. The breeze was still blowing and it promised to be very welcome on a warm night like this.

At seven o'clock she and Lucy collected the happy Labrador from Signora Grande and they set off on a leisurely circular tour of the little town. The first ten minutes of the walk were a struggle of wills between Amy and the dog, who almost choked himself to death tugging at the lead and almost pulled her arm out of its socket in the process. It took a while but they finally came to a compromise that relieved the pressure on her arm while still letting him lead the way.

They had an enjoyable walk and Amy saw much of the little town that was new to her, including the medieval church and the gruesome gallows right beside it where convicted criminals had been executed in years gone by. The pizzeria was opposite the old market and the tables extended out into the shade provided by the ancient timber roof supported on massive brick pillars. The floor was made up of flagstones and it couldn't have felt more different from London. When they got there Amy recognised a couple of familiar faces sitting among the diners. Over to one side were none other than Rosa and Vincenzo. As they spotted Amy, they waved and then, strangely, their table started to move across the ground all by itself, emitting a nerve-jangling screeching noise as the metal legs scraped across the stone.

The reason for this soon became apparent. Coco the Labrador had just seen her brother Max and had decided to come across to say hello, oblivious to the fact that she had been tied to the leg of the table. In consequence, the heavy table had followed her. Amy hurried over and introduced Lucy to them. While the dogs sniffed each other and wagged their tails and the table was returned to its former position, they chatted for a few minutes before Amy politely refused their kind offer to join them. She didn't want to impose herself on these friendly people and, as Lucy spoke no Italian and they spoke no English, it would have been hard going. Wishing Rosa and Vincenzo *buon appetito*, she gently prised Max away from Coco and they followed the waiter to a table on the far side of the restaurant.

She noticed that most people around them were drinking beer with their pizzas, so they did the same. Lucy ordered a *quattro stagioni* and Amy just went for a simple *pizza margherita*. As she sipped her drink, enjoying the perfect temperature and the picturesque surroundings, she reflected on her good fortune. Interestingly, the fact that her boyfriend had almost certainly been cheating on her barely caused a ripple in her happiness.

After the scare of her collapse and hospitalisation, life had changed for the better so abruptly, and it was all thanks to a man whose existence had been completely unknown to her until a few weeks ago. Just as she had spent her life wishing she had known the man she had been brought up to believe to be her real father, she now also wished she had known Martin Slater. From everything she was hearing about him, she felt sure she would have loved him just as he – quite evidently – had loved her. She still had to make a start on *Far From Home*, telling herself she hadn't yet because she had been so busy, but she knew deep down that it was almost certainly because it was going to be an emotional read.

Lucy must have read her mind. 'This place is amazing, and I'm not just talking about this restaurant. Sant'Antonio and Tuscany feel like a whole different world. Your fabulous house, the surrounding countryside and don't let's forget your four-legged friend – you're so incredibly lucky. And all thanks to a man you never met.'

'I know, Luce, and that's down to my mum. I've been doing a lot of thinking about her. The fact of the matter is that she lied to me all her life. If she hadn't been so stubborn, I could have met my real father. She had no right to deprive me of that.'

Ever pragmatic, Lucy was upbeat. 'I can't imagine what you're feeling but think of it this way: you never knew him but you also never knew the man your mum told you was your dad. It would be far worse if you'd grown up alongside a man you loved, only to discover that he wasn't what he seemed. Nothing should stop you continuing to love the memory of that man but, at the same time, nothing should stop you loving this unknown man who's turned out to be your real father. And the same applies to your mum. None of this should change the way you feel about her. Okay, so she didn't tell you the truth, but try putting yourself in her position. Guilt is a powerful motivator, and as the years went by and the dust began to settle on the upset surrounding your birth, she understandably didn't want to put you or herself through the heartbreak that would have ensued if she'd told you the truth. Sleeping dogs and all that, Amy. It's only human.'

Amy's eyes strayed for a few seconds to the black shape lying stretched out across her feet beneath the table. Lucy was right. Her mum had taken the cowardly, but eminently understandable, way out. Why should she have wanted to risk stirring up a hornets' nest? She had clearly decided it was better to leave well alone and Amy couldn't help feeling sympathy for her. She certainly hoped her own life would prove to be less complicated. Any further reflection was interrupted by her phone telling her she had a text message. She looked down at it and was surprised when she saw who it was from. She glanced up at Lucy.

'A text from Gavin. It's only taken him two weeks!'

The message was hardly a declaration of undying love.

> Hi Amy. Hope you're okay. Any idea where my blue shirt with the white collar is? I can't find it anywhere.

Unsure whether to laugh or cry, she read it out to Lucy and saw her wince.

'What're you going to do? What about a reply suggesting he looks under the bed of his other girlfriend?'

Amy shook her head. 'No, I won't reference her until I can look him in the eye. When the builders come in on Monday I'll check to see if it's okay to take a day out. I don't think there are too many big decisions still to be made, so I'll hop on a flight one day next week and go and have it out with him. For now, I'll just acknowledge the message.' She sent him a reply in a similar style to his.

> All well here. No idea about the shirt.

Their pizzas arrived barely five minutes later and Amy was glad she hadn't opted for a starter first. The plate was big but the pizza was even bigger and actually spilled over almost onto the table cloth. It looked and smelt wonderful and she suddenly felt stirring at her feet and a big black nose landed on her thigh, nostrils flared.

'No, Max! No food from the table.'

He was adopting an expression of desperate starvation, even though Signora Grande had told her he had eaten only a couple of hours previously. Forewarned that Labradors would happily eat until they explode, Amy was determined to harden her heart. However, as he had been remarkably well-behaved this evening – once they had got the walking on a lead thing sorted out – she compromised by opening a little packet of bread sticks and passing one down to him.

'There, but that's all. Is that clear?' Of course it wasn't, and by the end of the meal he had emptied the packet of grissini, but she couldn't complain. She'd been worried he might start barking or try to emulate Coco and set off across the floor with the table in tow. Instead, he snoozed most of the time with his heavy head resting on her toes. It felt rather nice. There was a lot to be said for a dog as a companion rather than her current – albeit almost certainly not for much longer – boyfriend.

The meal was excellent and the conversation lightened. Soon she and Lucy were chatting happily about Volterra, the house and Sant'Antonio. Inevitably the subject then moved back to Gavin and how Amy saw her life panning out. She had been doing a lot of thinking about this over the past few days and she had almost managed to persuade herself that Gavin's alleged infidelity might actually turn out to have been for the best. At least it had served to make her take stock and consider the doubts and reservations she had been having about him. That didn't make the bitter pill of his presumed deceit much easier to swallow, but it helped. As for the future, she finally gave in and told Lucy about Adam.

'The thing is, Luce, I've met a guy.' Seeing her friend's eyes light up, she held up her hand. 'Nothing's happened between us and it could well be that nothing will happen.

Apart from anything else, there's a question mark over his relationship with Danny that we met in Volterra today.'

'What sort of question mark?'

'It could be that they live together, maybe along with another guy called Pierpaolo.'

'And when you say "live together"... I got the impression that Danny and his shopkeeper friend with the poodle are probably less interested in women and more interested in men. What about you?' Seeing Amy nod, she continued. 'So are you saying that your new man might be gay or bi as well?'

Her voice tailed off and Amy was quick to clarify. 'Like I say, nothing's happened between us, but it was just something that I heard.'

Lucy smiled at her over the rim of her beer glass. 'You don't want to believe everything you hear. Go with your heart.' She took a mouthful and carried on. 'Well, go on then, tell me all about him. What's he look like? What does he do? How come I haven't met him yet? Have you been hiding him from me?'

While Lucy finished her pizza, Amy gave her a brief description of Adam and told her about his job and his trip to Brazil. By the time she had finished, Lucy was looking convinced.

'He sounds like the perfect man for you. It's easy: you wait until he comes back from Brazil and then all you've got to do is to snog him and start tearing his clothes off. You'll soon know one way or another whether he's gay or not.'

Amy was in the middle of a mouthful of beer and this sparked her off in a coughing fit which resulted in her canine companion actually getting up and putting his head on her thigh and giving her a worried look. She collected herself and patted him on the head.

'Thank you, Max, but I'm okay. Here, I've got a little piece of pizza crust left over. Want it?'

He did.

Chapter 17

They set off for Pisa quite early on Sunday morning so that Lucy could see the Leaning Tower before her flight home. Amy herself had only glimpsed it briefly on the day Lucy arrived so the two of them spent a couple of hours wandering around the *centro storico* and the incomparable Piazza dei Miracoli. This broad grassy space in the town centre was home not only to the tower but also the twelfth-century Duomo and the Baptistery, and even now in early June it was crawling with tourists. Neither Amy nor Lucy felt like climbing the tower, which really did lean quite frighteningly, and, instead, they went into the cathedral and admired the statues, paintings and architecture of this medieval gem, before heading into town for a quick snack lunch and then to the airport.

Amy felt quite emotional saying goodbye to her best friend but she promised to be in touch later in the week when she came over to have her showdown with Gavin. Lucy told her she planned on hitting the gym – or that might have been her male friend at the gym – pretty hard over the next few days after all the lovely Italian food and promised to send on any gossip or developments. By the time Amy got back to Sant'Antonio it was almost three o'clock, the time she had promised to go and see Danny's pottery studio, so she drove straight there.

The first discovery she made was that the studio was about a hundred yards further along the road from Adam's office so it looked less likely that they did in fact live together. In case that hadn't been conclusive enough evidence, the first person she met when she knocked on the door of the studio was a slim, olive-skinned man probably around her age, with a mane of bleached blond hair and a diamond stud in his nose. As he saw Amy, his face lit up.

'*Ciao, sei Amy, vero? Benvenuta.*' And just to add to the greeting, he put his arms around her shoulders and air-kissed her spectacularly somewhere around the ears with a resounding smacking noise of the lips as he switched to excellent English. 'Danny told me you were beautiful, but he didn't say how beautiful!' Reverting to Italian, he put the fingers of one left hand together, kissed them and then launched them in her direction in the traditional Italian expression of aesthetic appreciation. '*Bellissima!*'

He waved her in through the door and into a large room with a glazed archway looking out into the back-yard, not dissimilar in style to Adam's office. Here she found Danny, once more wearing his clay-splattered smock, and he gave her a cheerful wave.

'Ciao, Amy, come in, come in. I'm just glazing some dishes and then I'll talk you through the whole process.' She saw him put a tray of his wall plates, all painted with an intricate pattern of grapevines and leaves, onto the last empty shelf inside a business-like industrial kiln. He closed the door, fiddled with a few knobs until an orange light lit up, and then turned towards her. He came over to greet her less theatrically than his partner. 'Thanks for coming. You've met Pierpaolo, haven't you? He's the reason I'm here in Sant'Antonio.' Just in case Amy still hadn't got the message, he pulled up his sleeve and revealed a tattoo of what looked like a pair of cherubs on his upper arm, with the initials P and D intertwined below. 'What did I tell you about my one true love?'

Amy shook his hand and smiled at both of the men. That settled one of the questions going through her head. She toyed with the idea of asking the other question and then decided to wait for the answer to emerge spontaneously in the course of the afternoon. She didn't want to sound too interested in Adam. As promised, Danny then walked her through all the different stages leading up to the production of a completed piece of glazed pottery. She was fascinated to see the raw earth transformed into a malleable, plastic medium that he then worked skilfully with his hands, flattening, rounding and crimping.

He asked her if she would like to have a try and, dismissing the famous pottery scene with Demi Moore and Patrick Swayze from *Ghost* from her mind, she accepted the clean apron Pierpaolo offered her and then spent an unexpectedly happy half hour making mud pies. At least, she felt sure that's how her mother would have described it. By the end she had produced two roughly oval plates, both a bit bigger than dinner plates and which, if you didn't look too closely, were almost flat in the middle, although the edges looked decidedly dodgy. Danny assured her that this would only add to the rustic charm of the items although she wasn't so sure. These were then put safely to one side to begin to dry before being fired in the oven while Danny took her through the rest of the process including painting, glazing and finally firing them.

'This means you have to come back and see us next week when they're bone dry and hard and ready to paint and glaze. What sort of pattern are you going to put on them?'

The idea had been growing in her mind as she made the dishes. 'I thought a series of tiny black Labradors. I want to give one to my neighbour, Signora Grande, as a present for letting me take her lovely dog for walks. He's great company and she's a sweetie. Do you know her?'

Pierpaolo shot her a grin. 'Know her? She's my auntie.' Seeing the surprise on Amy's face, he carried on. 'Everybody knows everybody here in Sant'Antonio. I bumped into her the other day and she told me that having you to take Max for walks has been a blessing for her. Max was my uncle's dog and since his death a few months back she's really been struggling. I bet if you offered to take him off her hands full-time she'd be relieved and delighted.'

This rather stopped Amy in her tracks. The idea of having the big friendly dog as a permanent companion was immensely appealing but, of course, when she went back to London there was no way he'd be able to come with her. Apart from the fact that she lived in a third-floor flat with no balcony or terrace, it wouldn't be fair to leave him cooped up all day on his own while she went back to working all hours again. Or would she? She remembered only too well what the specialist had told her about trying to take life a bit easier and this had been playing on her mind over the past couple of weeks. Was she really ready to trade down to a more boring, but less full-on, job?

'You should do that, Amy. Come and live here full-time and take over Max.' Oblivious to her reservations, Danny sounded enthusiastic. 'You've got all that land where he could run around and, as a woman on her own, having a guard dog would make a lot of sense.'

'Yes, but...' She thought back to the conversation she had had with Gavin. He had, of course, been dead right: she would be bored stiff within a matter of weeks if she were to just give up the day job, move here to this admittedly lovely place, and sit around doing nothing all day. 'It's complicated. I have a job back in London that I love doing and I'm not the sort of person who could just sit around drinking wine and spending my days taking the dog for walks, nice as that sounds for a few weeks.'

Danny nodded. 'You need to get yourself an occupation. Try something new. That's what I did when I gave up the day job.'

'What was it you did?'

'I worked for the New York Stock Exchange. I gave it up two years ago.'

'Well, well, that's a bit like me. I'm in foreign exchange. Why did you give it up to come here?'

'I already told you, and the reason's here alongside me.' He gave Pierpaolo an affectionate hug. 'Best thing I ever did. You can't imagine the pressure there was in that job.' He stopped and corrected himself. 'In fact, if you were in forex, you probably can. I'd probably have had a coronary by now if I'd stayed on.'

Amy caught his eye. 'This sounds horribly familiar. I didn't have a heart attack, but I had a sort of collapse a few weeks back, and everybody's been telling me to try and take life a bit easier.'

Danny reached over and gave her arm a little squeeze. 'And you need to listen to them. Trust me, Amy, life's too short.' He released his hold on her and surveyed the dirty marks he had left on her skin. 'Sorry about that. I need to wash up and then why don't we go and sit in the garden and have a drink?'

Pierpaolo took her arm and led her through to an ultramodern kitchen composed almost entirely of stainless steel, where she washed the clay off her hands and arms. Unlike the chaotic and messy pottery studio, this place looked as though it had just come from the pages of *Vogue Maison*. There wasn't even a teaspoon left lying on the polished worktops. She surveyed it critically, having decided that the units for her new kitchen should be simple smooth gloss white, and decided that steel was too clinical, too sober. She definitely wanted something a bit more inviting but she envied them a room without a trace of dust to be seen anywhere – unlike l'Ospedaletto.

Pierpaolo handed her a perfectly ironed hand towel to dry herself and took back her apron in return. 'What shall we drink? We have cold beer and wine in the fridge or my homemade lemonade – made with our own lemons. Or would you prefer tea? I bought some English Breakfast tea specially for you.'

'That was sweet of you, but it's too hot for tea. I think if you don't mind I'd like to try your homemade lemonade.'

They sat outside in the shade of an ancient olive tree whose trunk was the thickness of a post box and which, according to Pierpaolo, had been in existence for over two hundred years. He told her how he had grown up just outside of Sant'Antonio before going to UCLA to study design art. Amy was fascinated.

'And did you meet Danny over there?'

He shook his head. 'No, I met him here two summers ago. He'd just thrown in his job and he was staying with Adam.'

'And where does Adam live?'

'He has a beautiful apartment above his studio. You've been to his office, haven't you?'

'Yes, but not to his apartment.' Although it sounded inviting. 'And what do you do now? Do you and Danny work together in the pottery studio?'

He shook his head. 'No, that's Danny's thing, though I do help out if he needs a hand. I'm a graphic designer. I do all my work on the computer screen.' He laughed. 'It keeps my fingernails a lot cleaner than Danny's.'

A minute or two later Danny reappeared, showered and changed into a clean T-shirt and shorts. He picked up a glass of lemonade and toasted Amy. 'Thanks again for letting me help myself to your wonderful clay and for coming to see us. Don't forget, you need to come back next week to paint and glaze your dishes.'

'That's very kind, thanks.' Amy took another mouthful of the excellent lemonade and risked bringing up the subject that had been on her lips ever since she had walked in. 'Any word from Adam?'

Danny shook his head. 'No, but I wasn't expecting to hear anything. He's way out somewhere in the depths of the Amazon rain forest and he told me before he set off that he was likely to be incommunicado for most of the time.'

'Oh, I see.'

He must have picked up something in her voice and he shot her a little smile. 'Are you missing him?'

Amy wasn't too sure how to answer that so she just kept it vague. 'He's nice. I'm looking forward to seeing again when he gets back.'

Pierpaolo giggled. 'You English, you love the word "nice", don't you? If I wasn't already spoken for, I'd think him more than nice.'

Danny gave her a meaningful look. 'My brother likes you a lot, you know.'

Puzzled, all Amy could do was stare at him. 'Your brother? Who's your brother?'

'Adam, of course. Didn't you know?'

Amy shook her head, feeling distinctly silly. 'Ah, I see. I had no idea. I just thought you were friends.' That answered her other query most satisfactorily. She reflected on what he had just said. 'What makes you think he likes me?'

'Because he told me so, of course. And Pierpaolo and I totally agree with him; we like you too.'

Pierpaolo giggled again. 'But maybe not in the same way.'

Amy thought it better not to pursue this topic so she moved the conversation along. 'So why did he come over to Sant'Antonio?'

Pierpaolo answered. 'Fate. He told me he came over looking for somewhere in Tuscany a bit off the beaten track and when he got here he liked what he saw. And when I saw his brother two years ago I liked what I saw, too.'

Danny shot him an affectionate glance. 'Funny the way things work out, isn't it?'

Chapter 18

On Monday the builders all returned as promised and Amy queried if they could spare her if she took a day off to go to London, but she didn't specify what it was that was drawing her back to the UK. They told her that seeing as the electricity and water would be reconnected on Wednesday evening, the most sensible thing would be for her to fly over the next day or Wednesday and come back on Thursday so that by then she should be able to move straight into the house. They warned her they would still be finishing off, but they all agreed that she should be reasonably comfortable. The idea of moving in was very appealing so she took their advice and booked a flight to London on Wednesday afternoon, with a return flight the next day. She told the people at the Corona Grossa that she would be leaving them and she resolved to bring over some 'nice' – that word again – clothes, as Adam would be returning at the weekend.

She had been doing a lot of thinking about him since talking to his brother and Pierpaolo. It now seemed pretty clear that he liked her and that he didn't share his brother's sexual orientation. The trouble was that by her reckoning she should have just two weeks' holiday left when he got back this weekend, and that wasn't going to give them much time to get to know each other.

The big unknown, of course, was what would happen after that. There was no way she would be able to keep seeing him once she returned to her job – if she actually did return to her job. This was something else that had been occupying her mind for some time now. Should she take the massive decision to give up her job and settle here in Italy? On the one hand, this would resolve the whole taking it easy question and, at the same time, it would keep her closer to Adam. However, considering that he was a man she had only just met and that she had spent no more than a couple of hours in his company altogether, there were an awful lot of unanswered questions. So all she could do for now was to relegate that to the back burner while she sorted out the next most important thing on her agenda: Gavin.

On Wednesday afternoon she drove to Pisa airport and left her hire car there. The flight was only ten minutes late and she arrived back at her flat just after seven. Gavin wasn't there but it came as no surprise to find the laundry basket overflowing with his shirts that he had brought round and dumped, and she felt her hackles rise. Taking a few deep breaths, she picked up her phone and called him, but it just went to voicemail. Unsure exactly what to say, she didn't leave a message and sat down for a think. It would have been nice to make herself a cup of tea, but of course there was no fresh milk, so she settled for a double espresso, and as she sipped it she decided on her plan of action. The fact that he wasn't answering his phone was probably because he was either playing squash, in the gym, or in a meeting, although the only meetings he tended to have after five o'clock in the afternoon normally involved cocktails and expense account meals. She knew she needed to speak to him face-to-face so as she had a key to his flat, she decided she would go round there and wait for him.

Finishing her coffee, she dug out a big black rubbish sack and filled it with all his dirty washing. There was no way she was going to spend her one night back in London doing his chores. Hitching this over her shoulder, she took the short fifteen-minute walk to his place. As she had expected, he wasn't in, so she went to the bathroom to dump his washing.

It was here that she made her first discovery.

She told herself afterwards that she hadn't been deliberately studying the contents of his waste bin but there, lying on top of the other rubbish, were a couple of crumpled tissues bearing the unmistakable marks of where somebody had used them to wipe away make-up. There were traces of a ruby red lipstick as well as mascara and, unless this was a whole new side to him that she hadn't come across, the finger of suspicion pointed only in one direction. He had had female company.

She went through to the bedroom and continued her tour of inspection. She didn't need to look too closely. As she walked into the room, the scent of an unfamiliar perfume was unmissable. When she flicked back the sheets, the scent became even stronger and she dropped the sheet in disgust and turned on her heel. Her instincts were telling her to get out and just forget about him although, having come all this way, she felt she needed to have it out with him once and for all, just so that she could get some kind of closure. She sat down on the sofa and turned on the TV, resisting the temptation to help herself to a glass of his vodka. She was halfway through a documentary about the shrinking ice caps when she heard his key in the lock, and she stood up to face him as the door opened.

'Amy, hi, I didn't know you were coming back. You should have said.' Even without the evidence she had already accumulated, she would have known that the expression on his face was one of guilt.

'Hello, Gavin.' For a moment it looked as though he was about to come over to kiss her but something on her face must have registered, and she saw him falter and then stop halfway. She pointed towards the bathroom. 'I brought you your dirty shirts. I'm going back to Italy tomorrow so there's no way I can do them. Why don't you ask your new lady friend or, here's a radical thought, why don't you wash them yourself?'

'New lady friend?' She could see he was doing his best to feign ignorance, but she knew him well enough by now to see through it.

'Whoever the woman is whose perfume is making your bedroom reek.' She caught his eye and held it. 'And don't try telling me your mum's been to visit.'

'No...but... look, Amy, you must understand...' He stuttered to a halt. Even he must have realised that the evidence against him was overwhelming.

She had told Lucy that she wanted to look him in the eye when she accused him, and there could be no question now that his face had given him away. She headed for the door, deliberately skirting around him. When she got there, she turned back, doing her best to keep her voice level.

'Your dirty washing's in the bathroom. I'm going back to Italy tomorrow and I want you to go round to my place tomorrow night and remove anything else of yours that's in there. When you've finished, just post the key through the letterbox. I don't want to see you or hear from you again. Is that understood?'

'Amy, look, it doesn't have to be like this…'

He was interrupted by a soft tap at the door and she saw him blanch. Her hand was already on the handle so she turned it. As the door opened, she was confronted by what had to be the owner of the lipstick and the perfume: an attractive blonde with ruby red lips and a penchant for short skirts and high heels. Amy produced a smile as she brushed past her.

'Hi, I'm Amy, and you're welcome to him.'

Once she was back outside in the open air again she stopped and took a few deep breaths. Although she had come here expecting to have it out with him and to end things, his obvious indifference to the years they had known each other hit her hard and she could have found it very easy to burst into tears. But, instead, she just stood there and collected herself, determined not to let his behaviour make her cry. She'd done what she'd set out to do, and he was out of her life.

That immediately brought up the question of what sort of life it was going to be, and where? Was she really capable of turning her back on what had had the makings of a very successful and lucrative career, or would that be crazy? What was waiting for her if she went back to Italy to live? Yes, there was maybe Adam, but she could hardly plan her whole life around a chance encounter with a man she barely knew. So many questions but her head was still buzzing from the Gavin incident that she felt incapable of making sense of them all. Once her pulse had returned to something approaching normal, she pulled out her phone and called Lucy. The sound of her friend's voice was welcome and they agreed to meet up in a nearby restaurant.

When they met up a few minutes later Lucy took one look at the expression on her face and enveloped her in a bear hug. 'You've done it?'

Amy nodded into her friend's shoulder and for a moment almost gave way to the tears again but just about managed to hold it together. 'Yes, and I even had the pleasure of meeting his lady friend.'

Lucy stepped back and stared at her in horror. 'You didn't catch them at it like rabbits?'

Amy couldn't help smiling at her choice of words. 'No, no rabbits, thankfully. She arrived just as I was leaving.'

They went inside and Amy gave her a blow-by-blow account of the events of this evening but Lucy wasn't going to let her wallow in a sea of regret. She caught the waiter's eye and ordered a bottle of Prosecco and then gave Amy her advice.

'You knew what you had to do and you did it. That chapter of your life has now ended and you're far better off without him. You know that, don't you?'

'You're right, Luce. Much better.'

'Good, right, I'm glad we've got that sorted. Now tell me what your plans are – short term and long term.'

Amy was saved from having to give an immediate answer by the arrival of the waiter with the wine. She waited until he had opened it and filled two glasses before attempting a reply to Lucy's question. 'I'm flying back to Italy tomorrow and I've got another couple of weeks' holiday in which to make up my mind. I like my job and I reckon I could go a long way in the company – assuming I can squeeze that leech Christian out of my office first. If I sell the house in Italy for a good amount, that plus the money from my father and my savings mean I could buy myself a really nice place here in London. On the other hand, I can see the attraction of the more relaxed lifestyle of living in Tuscany and I'm sure the specialist at the hospital would approve. The house is beautiful, the little town's lovely and I've met some nice people. I must admit, there's a part of me that's tempted to give up on London and move over there.'

'When you say you've met some nice people, is there one in particular?' Lucy already knew the answer to this and she gave Amy a lurid wink. 'Have you managed to work out the dynamics of your friend Adam's relationship with the potter?'

Amy related what she had learnt at Danny and Pierpaolo's house on Sunday and saw Lucy beam.

'Excellent. And when's he coming back from South America?'

'This weekend, I believe.'

'Well, if you want my advice, you need to find out once and for all just how much this guy means to you, and how much you mean to him. You don't have much time. Invite him round to your place for a meal, take him on a tour of the house ending up in your new bedroom and then let nature take its course. I'm sure you'll find that'll help crystallise your thinking'.

Amy grinned back at her. 'Are you talking about rabbits again?'

'What else?'

'I'm not that kind of girl, Luce, you know that.'

'Well, get him drunk and get him to tell you the story of his life. How old did you say he was?'

'Thirty-five.'

'You need to find out how come a good-looking thirty-five-year-old man hasn't got a significant other. Maybe he's got webbed feet or something.'

Amy found herself giggling in spite of everything. 'I can hardly ask him to take his shoes off on a first date.'

'If you'd followed my original plan he'd have had to take his own shoes off.'

Chapter 19

It was wonderful for Amy to return to Sant'Antonio on Thursday afternoon and find the house nearing completion. The modern radiators and boiler had been installed, the new furniture in the downstairs bathroom was already fitted, and the bath fully functioning, although the tiling was still to be done. The lights now worked and she was able to make herself a cup of tea without them dimming ominously. The kitchen was taking shape and the builders had promised her it would be operational early the following week. Upstairs both bathrooms were finished and somebody had even put a fresh coat of paint on the walls of what would become her bedroom. That evening she drew a full tub of hot water, threw in half a bottle of bubble bath and sank gratefully into it, the bubbles almost covering her face. By the time she came out, she felt like a new woman.

That night she made up the bed in the main bedroom with the new sheets and covers, and when she lay down, it took her some time to fall asleep. Although part of her was still thinking back to the demise of her relationship with Gavin, her thoughts were mainly of her father. She wondered how many times he had lain here in this very same bed, thinking of the woman he had loved and the daughter he'd never seen. When she compared her current situation to his, it paled in comparison. Her split from

Gavin had been inevitable and, for that reason, less painful than it might have been if she had delayed doing anything until months or even years down the line. Her uncertainty about whether to return to London and her job or to chuck it in and stay here seemed so insignificant, as did the conundrum of whether Adam would turn out to be the man of her dreams or just a friend. She still had choices, while her father had had none – her mum had seen to that. The tears she hadn't shed for Gavin rolled down her cheeks as she drifted off to sleep. But this time they were for another man.

She slept remarkably well in spite of being alone in the big echoing house. Even a gust of wind in the middle of the night that rattled the windows and made one of the shutters bang noisily failed to unsettle her. She felt comfortable here and that wasn't just down to the efforts of the tradesmen; she knew that it was because it gave her a feeling of proximity to her real father. She got up, leant out of the window and secured the shutter, but this time when she returned to bed there was a little smile on her face.

Next morning dawned sunny but it was a hazy sun, and for the first time she spotted dark grey clouds on the skyline that didn't bode well for later in the day. Still, she couldn't complain as she had seen virtually no rain since arriving here and she knew how badly it was needed. One very positive surprise was the arrival just after eight of a Telecom van with an engineer who assured Amy she would have a fast Internet connection up and running by lunchtime. After making coffee for the builders and thanking them for all their efforts, she went across the road to collect Max for the walk he had missed yesterday.

Both he and Signora Grande looked delighted to see her and she was equally happy to see both of them.

She and the bouncy Labrador set off up the hill and partway through the vines she bumped into Signor Montalcino doing a recce of his vineyard and she stopped to chat. She had warmed to him the very first time she saw him. He was probably in his seventies and with a near permanent smile on his weather-beaten face, and he passed on the welcome information that he had delivered four fifty-litre containers of wine and they were now safely locked in her cellar. She decided not to tell him that she was still scared of going down there and resolved to ask the builders to bring some of the wine upstairs when the kitchen was finished. Mind you, if she was only here for another two weeks, she was going to find it hard to drink two hundred litres in that time. Still, that was the sort of problem she was more than happy to live with.

It started raining just after lunch and the downpour continued for the rest of the day and well into the night. The rain was torrential and the fields and roads were soon running with water. She checked upstairs and all around the house and was greatly cheered to find everything dry and the new gutters and downpipes working well.

Local radio was already listing a series of disasters ranging from the bank in the square being flooded to bridges washed away, and even some poor soul drowned in a swollen river. Looking out of the window as it was starting to get dark, Amy was quite shocked to see a roaring torrent running down from the vineyards, just past the end of her garden. Fortunately, however, l'Ospedaletto was safely out of its way.

The storm blew itself out in the course of Friday night and she awoke on Saturday morning to find it was another lovely day. Putting on her trainers she set off up the hill with Max and they were both soon very muddy. Max kept disappearing into the vines and reappearing two-tone: black on top and a milky chocolate brown on his lower half. Although she stuck to the tracks, the clay built up underneath her shoes, making it slippery underfoot. After all the rain, the sky was a clear blue and she could see for miles and miles, northwards to the Apennines and, for the very first time, she thought she could even just about make out the shadowy outline of what might have been Monte Amiata, far to the south. The dog got himself into a real muddy state and Amy decided that, much as he might hate it, before she gave him back to Signora Grande, today was going to be bath-time for Max.

She reached the shed where she often stopped for a rest, but the plank that served as a seat was still sodden after the downpour. Instead, she stayed on her feet and leant back cautiously against the rickety wall, watching the vines shake as the dog trawled through them looking for game. Although Labradors are retrievers, Signora Grande had told her that Max had never received any training as a gun dog, but there was obviously enough of the instinct in his DNA to make him never tire of chasing anything he came across. That morning the only other animal he came across was his friend Coco. As the two came rushing out through the vines together, Amy spotted Rosa climbing up towards her. She gave her a wave and glanced down at the dogs.

'Ciao, Coco, how come you're looking so clean while Max looks like a choc ice?'

'Give her time.' Rosa reached the top behind her dog and mopped her brow. 'She'll probably roll in the mud before long. Whew, it's hot again. It was so nice to have a cool day yesterday for a change. How's the building work coming along?'

She came and rested her back against the wall of the shed. Amy waited anxiously but, although it creaked, it didn't give way. Both of them could feel the warmth of the morning sun on the timber behind them as Amy answered. 'Another few days and all the building work should be over. They've worked their socks off. They've been fabulous.'

'And the lovely Signor Pozzovivo?'

'Lorenzo's a sweetie. He doesn't talk a lot, but then, he doesn't need to, does he? Actions speak louder than words and all that.'

'Lorenzo, eh? First-name terms with our local sex idol, eh?'

'I'm on first-name terms with the plumber and the electrician as well, so don't read too much into it. Besides, Lorenzo was showing me pictures of his two little kids the other day. I rather think he's already taken. Thanks again for lunch the other day. It was super and I really enjoyed meeting your friends. I got on really well with the lady sitting beside me, Domenica. She told me she knew Martin Slater – my father, but it still sounds weird to me to call him that – and it's clear she liked him as well.'

'Everybody liked Martin. Mind you, come to think of it, Domenica probably knew and liked him more than most.'

'You think she and he might have been...?'

'More than friends? Yes, I suppose they might have been. I saw them together quite a few times but, like I told you before, I don't think there was ever anybody really special in his life – apart, maybe, from your mother. Feel like telling me what really happened when you were born? How come he and your mum never married? But please don't feel you have to tell me anything. It's none of my business.'

Amy smiled at her. 'There's not much to tell, really.' She gave Rosa a brief outline of what she had learnt and read sympathy in the other woman's eyes – for her, but also for her mother and father.

'Don't be too hard on your mother. We all do things we regret. I can imagine the impact losing her husband must have had on her life and I can understand the guilt she must have felt. Poor thing, so alone. And poor Martin, cut off from the woman he loved and the child he never knew.' She reached across and caught hold of Amy's hand. 'But at least it's all out in the open now and you know the truth.'

By tacit agreement they changed the subject back to the ever-safe topic of the weather. Rosa pointed down the hill towards l'Ospedaletto.

'I hope you didn't have any flooding as a result of yesterday's rain?'

Amy was glad to return to something more mundane. 'No, not a drop. What about you?'

Rosa shook her head. 'Nothing, I'm pleased to say, but you maybe heard about the bank. Pity they didn't pump some money out of it while they were at it. I heard on the local news that a number of lower-lying places were flooded when the river burst its banks. The weather's all extremes over here, I'm afraid.'

Amy spent Saturday morning doing her best to tidy the house. She knew it was pretty pointless as the builders would be back on Monday, but she was spurred into it after washing the dog. In the absence of a bath for him, she used several buckets of warm water and a soft brush out on the gravel drive in front of the house. The dog stood shivering miserably throughout the whole procedure, and only cheered up when she finished. She had a feeling that his first instinct after a bath would be to shake himself thoroughly and then run off and roll in the grass. Seeing as her garden was currently an overgrown, muddy mess, she did her best to wipe him dry before shepherding him into the house. As a result, the house soon smelt of damp dog and his wet paws spread the builders' dust all over the living room.

After drying Max as best she could, Amy bit the bullet, picked up the mop, and washed the terracotta floor from front to back. She threw the windows open to allow fresh air to come in and change the atmosphere and finally, by lunchtime, the house as well as the dog looked and smelt clean once more and she was able to deliver him back to Signora Grande in pristine condition.

That evening she finally found the courage to open *Far From Home* and start reading. She only read for an hour before the tears in her eyes forced her to abandon it for the night. The story was almost autobiographical – an illicit affair, an unwanted pregnancy and what looked like being a lifetime of regret as a result. It was beautifully written and what struck her forcibly was that he had chosen to write it through the eyes of the child, now an adult, gradually discovering the truth. Most poignant of all was the dedication:

To Amy, with all my love.

She had just got up to pour herself a glass of wine when she heard knocking at the door. This was the first time she had had a visitor after dark and she was thankful for the electrician's suggestion that he install a security light outside. She glanced through the shutters and saw that her visitor was Danny and she hurried to open the door to him.

'Hi, Danny, come in. I was just pouring myself a glass of wine. Want to join me?'

He shook his head. 'Thanks, Amy, but I have to scoot. We've only just got back from Florence and Pierpaolo's making a risotto and he'll murder me if I'm late. I just came to tell you not to worry.'

Amy was momentarily stumped. 'About what?'

'About Adam… or didn't you hear that he's disappeared?'

Amy felt an icy cold stab in her stomach. 'What do you mean, "disappeared"? I hadn't heard.'

'It was on the news. We heard it in the car. He and his crew were filming in the Amazon rainforest and they've gone missing. They should have got back to their base camp on Wednesday night but there's been no sign of them. People are saying they might have been killed by armed guards protecting illegal timber operations or kidnapped by a remote tribe, but I came to tell you that I'm not worried. He's been in worse scrapes than this and he always gets out. I just wanted you to know.'

'Well, thanks, Danny, I'll try not to worry.'

'That's the spirit!' He glanced at his watch. 'Now I really have to go. Ciao.'

He blew her a kiss and disappeared into the dark, leaving her standing there helplessly. Finally she locked the door and wandered back to her wine glass, doing her best to analyse the thoughts running through her head. The shiver of apprehension that had run through her at hearing Danny's news had served to reinforce just how much of an impression his big brother had made on her in such a short time.

She had lost her mother, two fathers and Gavin. Could it be that she was now also going to lose Adam?

Chapter 20

Monday morning brought the builders back to finish off. The walls were painted and the place began to look like a home again. Amy spent a lot of her time making coffee and, in between, she carried on with the task of cleaning the house. Diego, one of Lorenzo Pozzovivo's men, tiled the bathrooms and kitchen, while another painted the replastered walls, so that by the time Wednesday came, everything essential inside the house had been done.

At the end of what was their final working day here at l'Ospedaletto, Amy produced a huge chocolate cake but confessed that she had bought it from the baker's because she needed to experiment with her new double ovens a few times before risking making a cake of her own. She served this to them with glasses of Signor Montalcino's wine and sent them off with slices of cake for their families. She thanked the two Rossi cousins, Angelo and Emilio, as well as Lorenzo and his men, for doing a fantastic job so amazingly quickly and she told them she was going to throw a party to celebrate completion of the work. Although her original intention had been to organise a 'do' for everybody including her new neighbours and friends this weekend, she told them it would have to be next week so as to give herself more time to prepare.

In fact, it wasn't really that she needed much more time to get the house ready for visitors but because she wasn't feeling much like celebrating. She had spent every day since the weekend scouring news reports in different languages in the hope of getting more information about Adam and his film crew. It had rapidly emerged that there was very little news apart from the fact that they had been expected back at their base about a hundred kilometres upstream from Manaus the previous Wednesday and were now a full week overdue. A Brazilian journalist who had been working with them was quoted as saying that the area where they had been filming was very remote and people had gone missing there before. He was unable to say whether this had been due to malignant forces, dangerous animals or inhospitable terrain, but nothing more had ever been heard of them.

This information hadn't brought her any comfort.

She had found herself thinking about Adam a lot, remembering little things like the colour of his eyes, the sound of his voice and the clothes he wore. The more she thought about him the more she realised how little she knew about him. They had spent so little time together and yet here she was, missing him as if she had known him for years. After she finally closed the door on the last of the tradesmen, she slumped down on the sofa and stretched her legs, feeling satisfied that the work was finished but also feeling melancholy, partly at the disappearance of Adam, and partly at the thought of her father. She hoped he would have approved of what she had done to his house.

Although she had been dining alone at the house for the past few nights, tonight she felt the need for human companionship, so she picked up Max from Signora

Grande and took him for a good long walk around town before heading for the pizzeria again. It was almost full and the atmosphere animated, and she only just manged to find a spare table. As she was making her way across to it, she spotted two familiar faces at the far end of the old covered market. One was Domenica, the woman she had met at Rosa's party and who had allegedly known Martin Slater better than most. With her was a young man whom Amy recognised immediately. It was none other than the young man from the town hall who had suddenly changed from helpful to rude. When Domenica spotted Amy she beckoned, and Amy had no option but to lead Max over to say hello.

'Ciao, Domenica, it's good to see you again.' As the young man concentrated his attention on making a fuss of Max, Amy wondered idly whether he was a relative, friend, or even toy-boy. Domenica was still a very attractive woman, after all, even if the young man was probably half her age. When he glanced up from the Labrador, his expression was far from welcoming, but Amy was determined to rise above any petty jealousies. 'Hello, again. You were very helpful to me when I came to see the mayor.'

This at least forced him to say something and he managed it with an attempt at good grace, but she could see it was an effort.

'Good evening.' Not the longest utterance in the history of the world but at least he shook hands with her, although he didn't stand up. Domenica shot him a sharp look and introduced him.

'Ciao, Amy. Let me introduce you to my son, Rolando. He's taking me out tonight for my birthday.'

Amy wished Domenica a happy birthday but the atmosphere was definitely strained so she soon left them and headed across to her own table. A friendly waitress arrived to take her order and Amy chose a *pizza ai frutti di mare* which would presumably have lots of lovely seafood on it. She also decided she was in need of a large beer tonight. She badly wanted to talk to somebody so she pulled out her phone and called Lucy.

She started by telling her that Lorenzo Pozzovivo was now no longer coming around to her house every day and Lucy, who still hadn't got over the shirtless trench-digging incident, sighed longingly. Amy then told her about the curious scene she had just witnessed here at the pizzeria with Domenica and her son. Lucy sounded as puzzled as she was feeling.

'Any idea what was bugging him?'

'I have no idea.' Amy related the events at the town hall when she had given her address and he had suddenly changed. Lucy couldn't understand it any more than Amy could.

'And he was all sweetness and light until you gave him your name and told him where you were living? Maybe he had a run-in with your dad, but everybody's been saying what a nice man he was. Weird...'

'I've been meaning to speak to his mother one of these days as she told me she knew my father – possibly very well. Maybe her son doesn't like me because she had an affair with my father and that broke up her marriage or something like that. At the very least if I sit down and talk to her I should be able to learn more about him even if she doesn't know what's got into her son. Maybe he was just pissed off about something completely different. Maybe they'd just had a fight. I'll try to find out where she lives and I'll go and knock on her door one of these days.'

She then went on to tell Lucy that there was still no news about Adam, and Lucy was as optimistic and supportive as ever. 'Try not to worry. His Jeep's probably broken down and he's having to hike out of the forest.'

'I believe they were travelling by boat.' Remembering the piranha fish, Amy added the obvious proviso. 'They certainly couldn't swim back or they'd be eaten alive. Mind you, if they tried to trek through the jungle they'd run the risk of being killed by a poisonous anaconda or attacked by a tiger.'

Lucy giggled. 'Anacondas aren't poisonous and there are no tigers in South America, Amy. Try not to worry, He'll be fine, you'll see.'

Amy had long known that Lucy's knowledge of the birds and the bees was encyclopaedic, but she hadn't realised that it extended to reptiles and mammals. But this helped. A bit.

–

Amy had been calling in on Danny most days in search of news, but to no avail, and by the time she went round on Thursday morning to paint the plates she had made, she could tell that even Danny's optimism was wearing thin. He told her he had been in regular contact with the Canadian embassy in Brazil, who had promised to keep him informed of any developments, but Adam and his team had been missing for over a week now and every day that passed increased the chances that something serious had happened to them.

Amy painted a host of little black Labradors on the now bone-dry, hard dishes but her mind was in the Amazon rainforest and the results were a bit of a mess. Danny assured her that they would look fine when the final glaze had been baked on – repeating that the imperfections would just add to the rustic appeal – although she had her doubts. When she had finished, he made her a coffee and they sat outside under the olive tree and Danny started talking quite nostalgically about his big brother.

'I keep telling him to find himself a job which isn't so dangerous. A couple of years ago he was locked up in an Iranian prison for weeks, then he was held hostage by rebel forces in Eritrea, and only last year he got bitten by a rabid dog in Nigeria. Although he had had all his injections, he had a very nervous wait for several months until they gave him the all clear.'

'Why does he do it, Danny?'

He gave her a little smile. 'If I had a dollar for every time I've asked him that, I'd be a rich guy. He just tells me it's the job. He loves what he does, I get that, but I don't see why he has to risk his life for it.' He shot her a glance. 'Sound familiar?'

It did. 'When you love what you do, I suppose you just have to accept the risks in any job… even forex.'

'Have you decided that that's what you're going to do? Are you going to carry on trying to kill yourself in a stressful job until you succeed?'

'I hope not. I certainly don't want to kill myself. No job's worth that.'

'Have you thought any more about what I said, about maybe jacking in the high finance job and settling for a more relaxed life over here?'

'Only every day for the last few weeks!' She looked up at the perfect blue of the sky and down again at the sunshine dappling the paving slabs at her feet. 'I love it here in Sant'Antonio. I love l'Ospedaletto, I've made some great friends, like you, Adam and Pierpaolo for example, and in so many ways it would make a lot of sense for me to move here.'

He grinned back at her. 'And that way you could be close to Adam, couldn't you?'

'Assuming he comes back.'

'He'll come back, he always comes back.' She could tell that he was trying to sound positive for her sake. 'And when he comes back, Pierpaolo and I both agree that you're the best thing that could possibly happen to him.'

'You do?'

'Definitely. Up till now he's been solely focused on his job. He needs to slow down and take life a bit easier, just like you do. You're made for each other.'

At that moment his phone started ringing and, when he answered, she immediately saw the relief on his face. He murmured a few times and repeatedly said 'Thank you' and finished up with the words, 'So is he coming straight back now?' He nodded and thanked the person at the other end of the line once again before the call ended. Dropping the phone onto the bench beside him, he reached across, caught hold of Amy and hugged her to him, spilling her coffee onto her shorts as he did so, but she didn't mind.

'Adam?'

'Yes, just like I said, he's reappeared. Apparently he and the other two members of his team along with their local guide had to hike for days and days through virgin jungle. I bet he's got some stories to tell!' In spite of the delight in his voice, Amy could see tears of relief glistening in his eyes and she felt the same way herself.

'What happened? I thought they were travelling by boat.'

'That's what he told me, too, but I presume something must have happened to it. The guy on the phone from the Canadian embassy in Brazil was a bit short on detail. Anyway, understandably, Adam and the others are sleeping it off for twenty-four hours and then he'll be on a flight back here, arriving Sunday afternoon.' He beamed at her. 'Didn't I tell you he'd be okay?' He glanced down. 'Sorry about your shorts, shall I get a cloth?'

'Don't worry about it. They needed washing anyway.' She drained the last dregs of her coffee and leant back, feeling a smile on her face as she stretched her legs. 'Well, that's a bit of good news.'

He laughed. 'Pierpaolo's right, you English and your understatement. It's not only good news, it's absolutely fabulous news. We'll need to celebrate when he gets back.'

Amy jumped to her feet. 'Definitely. Why don't the three of you come round to my place on Sunday night and I'll see if I can get my new kitchen to start paying for itself?' She waved away his protests. 'Be sure to tell Adam when you talk to him. Seven o'clock on Sunday, okay? See you then.'

Chapter 21

It took Amy a long time to get to sleep that night as her mind turned over and over all sorts of thoughts. In particular, she found herself thinking about her mother. She remembered the bitterly sad time at the hospice where her mum had spent her final days, during which Amy had burst into tears more times than she could recall Every day she had got up late and every night she'd gone to bed at nine o'clock, but she had still felt exhausted, drained by her emotions. Her mother's death had reduced her to a state of near desperation for some time, but now, as the months passed since it had happened, she felt she was finally able to come to terms with the loss and start looking forward, not back. The discovery of her real father – even if she had never seen him – somehow helped. And, to a great extent, this new-found optimism was the best possible gift her father could have given her. It just hurt so bitterly that he had been prevented from ever meeting his daughter.

The news that Adam was alive and well came as a welcome relief, but she couldn't help mulling over what Danny had said about him and his job. She and Adam were more similar than she had thought and the upshot of this discovery wasn't heartening. What if she were to give up her job in London and move here to be with Adam, only to find that he insisted on carrying on with what sounded like a very risky occupation? Thinking about it, that was exactly what her mother had done when she had married a soldier. She had presumably entered into that relationship with her eyes open, realising that there was a chance that every time her man went on active service he might not come back. And, of course, that was exactly what had happened. Was she herself prepared to enter into a similar relationship?

Of course this was all pie in the sky for now. She liked Adam and she felt pretty sure he liked her – and certainly his brother appeared to confirm that. But that was as far as it went, at least for now. There was every chance that he would return from Brazil to tell her that he had no intention of settling down with her or any other woman. Maybe there already was another woman, unbeknown to her or even to his brother. The fact was that so much about Adam was still a mystery and she gave herself a mental reality check. She barely knew him and yet here she was hypothesising about a future together when they barely had a present.

Next day she carried on cleaning, looked on as her new washing machine was installed, and then took Max for another walk, her mind still elsewhere. After a salad lunch, banishing thoughts of her mother or Adam, she turned her attention to the man she now knew to be her real father. It occurred to her, not for the first time, that she had no image of him apart from his passport photo, but this was so stern and expressionless that it could have been of anybody. Adam had told her that she had the same colour of eyes as her dad, and various people had told her that he had been a good-looking man, but she really needed a decent photo.

Because of his reputed mistrust of technical things, she knew there was little point looking on the Internet. She had already tried, starting with his publishers, but there had been no photos of him at all, no doubt because they didn't want the truth of his identity to leak out, seeing as he had been a man writing as a woman. It occurred to her that he might have some photographs hidden away amongst all the papers in his study, so she went upstairs to look. His desk had been moved to one side to allow the plumber and electrician to work and it was still covered with a dust sheet. She pulled this off, sat down in his chair, and started looking through the drawers.

She was there for almost an hour and by the end of it she had found only three photos of him. All of them were of a man in his fifties or sixties, nothing earlier. One was of him in tennis gear receiving a trophy of some sort, one was of him at a formal dance in a dinner jacket, and there was only one of him relatively close up, sitting out on the terrace alongside the house. She sat and studied it carefully, starting with the eyes, which were, as Adam had said, the same grey/blue colour as hers. He had chestnut brown hair, not dissimilar to hers, and he had broad shoulders and strong forearms. He was wearing a plain white shirt and her eye was suddenly drawn to an object lying on the bench beside him. It was, without question, a woman's handbag. Presumably this meant that the photo had been taken by the owner of the handbag, which implied that at least on one occasion he had had female company here at l'Ospedaletto. Alas, there was no clue as to the identity of his female companion.

She got up and was about to leave the study when her eye was drawn to a slim cardboard folder squeezed in between three or four tall books on the bottom shelf of one of the bookcases. She pulled it out and opened it to find that it contained a couple of dozen photographs. She glanced through them and got a shock. They were photos of her. She sat back down on the chair and sifted through them, quickly finding that they were in chronological order, starting when she must have been seven or eight. The first photos were of her school nativity play and she still remembered how excited she had been when the teacher had chosen her to play the part of Mary holding a doll dressed up as baby Jesus. There were three photos taken at different moments of the performance, presumably with a telescopic lens from some distance as the rows of heads of the audience partially obscured the stage. Her father must have sneaked in at the back, so as not to be seen by her mother.

These photos were followed by others – a couple of her at school prize-giving as a teenager, one of her in black-and-white, clearly taken from the local newspaper when she had received her Duke of Edinburgh's Award, and the final handful were of her graduation day. Once again, these had been taken from a discreet distance and she could imagine him skulking around, desperate to see his daughter while making sure her mother didn't spot him. It was tragic and she felt the tears once again on her cheeks. It was a considerable time later that she stirred and went downstairs again, still clutching the three photos of her father. She propped these on the shelf beside the fireplace and stood for a minute or two studying them before letting herself out and heading across the road to see if Max wanted a walk. Needless to say, he did.

As they walked up the hill, she called Lucy to give her the news about the photos and she heard immediate interest and sympathy in her friend's voice.

'That's amazing, Amy. Poor man, having to creep around like a criminal.' The exasperation in Lucy's voice was the same as Amy herself had been feeling. If only her mother had realised the hurt she had caused. 'But at least it means he did see you – even though he never got near you – so he must have had that satisfaction at least.'

'I suppose that's something.'

'So, when does Price Charming arrive back home?' Amy had called her the previous day on the way home from Danny's studio to give her the big news about Adam.

'I'm not sure, but very soon.'

'Well, don't you forget what I told you to do. Think rabbits, Amy.'

'I've got enough trouble with snakes in my cellar, thank you.'

'Is that a metaphor?'

'Luce, please!'

'Well, promise me you'll at least try to wear something appealing.'

Amy knew full well what sort of clothing Lucy had in mind. 'I'll wear something nice, I promise, but I don't intend throwing myself at the poor man.'

'You've only got another week over there. You can't afford to waste time.'

Next day, Signora Grande told her that she was once more going to see her sister and Amy was delighted to look after Max all day. She bundled him into the car and they spent the morning walking in the woods. While he ran happily about, chasing after the sticks and pine cones she threw for him, she tried looking for mushrooms. After a lot of searching, to her surprise and delight she actually found some. In a little glade among sweet chestnut and oak trees, she came upon a little family of porcini. Daddy porcino was the height of a tumbler with a beautiful brown cap, sponge beneath, and a blemishless cream-coloured base. The other two were carbon copies, just a little smaller. She squeezed them into a plastic bag and returned to the car in triumph.

She spent the afternoon cleaning the house while Max snored on an old rug by the empty fireplace. That evening, after taking him for another walk in the vineyard, Amy was checking her laptop for recipes involving porcini mushrooms and wondering whether it might be prudent to get the view of an expert before possibly poisoning herself, when there was a knock at the door. Max raised his head but clearly couldn't be bothered to make the effort to get up and see who it was. So much for him as a guard dog. Amy opened the door and got a surprise. It was Domenica, not accompanied by her surly son.

'Ciao, Domenica. How nice to see you again. Do come in.'

'Ciao, Amy. I hope I'm not disturbing you.' She sounded very hesitant and Amy was quick to reassure her.

'Not in the slightest. Come on in. Would you like a glass of wine, or a cup of tea, coffee?'

Domenica shook her head. 'I don't want to take up too much of your time.'

She was still looking and sounding very uncertain so Amy ushered her in and pointed to the sofa. 'I've got bags of time. Come and have a seat.'

Domenica was more casually dressed than the previous night at the restaurant, but still very elegant. There was no doubt about it, she was a very good-looking woman. Had she and her father been an item? Amy's suspicions deepened. Although, she reminded herself as she hung the coat by the door, it was no business of hers whether

her father had had a relationship with any woman. When she returned to the sofa, she saw Domenica stroking Max distractedly with one hand while she stared around in wonder. She looked back at Amy as she took a seat beside her.

'Wow, you've done so much.' She gave a little smile. 'And I'm delighted to see you've put in radiators. I almost froze to death in here on many an occasion. Martin's internal thermostat was at a different setting from the rest of us.'

Amy smiled back. 'I'd already worked that out. This place must have been like a fridge in winter. I'm not sure even Max would have liked it.' She poked the dog gently with her foot and glanced down at him. 'Now lie down and leave Domenica alone.' She was pleasantly surprised to see him do just that. As she returned her attention to her guest, she could see that she had something on her mind.

'Um, Amy, I've been putting off coming to see you but I can't put it off any longer. We need to talk, you see.' Amy saw her take a deep breath. 'It's about Martin and me...'

Her voice tailed off miserably and for a moment Amy thought she might be about to cry, so she decided to give her a hand. 'Were you and he close?'

Domenica looked up in surprise. 'Yes, but how did you know?'

Amy gave her a gentle smile, deciding not to name her sources. 'I guessed.'

Domenica looked up, straight into Amy's eyes. 'I loved him, Amy. I loved him so very dearly.' And this time she did start crying.

Amy wasn't sure what to do so she jumped to her feet and went along to the kitchen where she dug out a bottle of Signor Montalcino's lovely red wine and two glasses. When she returned to the sofa, Domenica was wiping her eyes with a tissue while Max sat to attention at her feet, looking worried. Amy filled two glass and pressed one of them into Domenica's hand.

'Here, have a drop of this.'

Domenica took a mouthful as instructed and then gradually resumed her story. As it unfolded, Amy listened in rapt amazement.

'I met Martin, your father, twenty-four years ago now. I suppose it was love at first sight – at least as far as I was concerned. We became close, very close.' She paused for another sip of wine. 'And then I got pregnant. I had a son, Rolando. You met him last night…' Her voice tailed off again and Amy jumped in to help out.

'But you and my father didn't marry?'

Domenica shook her head and blew her nose, but when she replied, it was in a stronger voice. 'No, Martin didn't want to.'

'You were the mother of his child and still he didn't want to marry you?' Suddenly Amy's opinion of Martin Slater took a nosedive. The outrage in her voice must have got through to Domenica, who was quick to explain.

'It was complicated, Amy. You see, the thing was that he never stopped loving your mother.' She sniffed and wiped her eyes with the back of her hand but managed to carry on. 'Please don't think too badly of him. It's not as awful as it sounds. He was completely open and honest with me from the start. He told me he cared for me a lot, but his heart irrevocably belonged to her and to his daughter back in England. I honestly believe it frustrated him as much as it did me, but it was something he was powerless to control.' She looked up from her hands for a moment. 'Martin was always very generous. He bought me my house here. He arranged for royalties he got for his books every month to be paid direct to me and this produced more than enough to keep me and Rolando. It still does. I can't complain about the way he treated me – at least as far as money's concerned.' Her eyes met Amy's and the misery was all too clear to read. 'The only stipulation was that we couldn't marry or live together. He told me about the daughter he'd never met but, as he couldn't be with her, it wasn't right he should be with Rolando.'

Amy didn't know what to say. All this time, since learning the truth about her father, she had been putting the blame for their separation on her mother's inflexibility, but now it sounded as though her father had been equally pig-headed. She rolled her eyes in disbelief. Two people whose lives had been blighted, if not completely ruined, by a refusal to put the past behind them and move on. She was still trying to put her thoughts into words when Domenica continued.

'Amy, Martin told me he wrote you a letter. Did you find it? He said it would be in the safe and you'd know how to open it.'

Amy nodded. 'Yes, thanks, I found it. It explained so much but I'm still struggling to understand how two people could be so pig-headed.'

'Love does funny things to people.' In spite of the way she had been treated it was only too obvious that Domenica was still in love with this strange and troubled man.

They talked for a good long time and, by the end, Amy felt she knew her enigmatic father a lot better and she was developing a lot of affection – and pity – for this kindly woman who had been dealt just about as poor a hand by her father as her mother had dealt him. It beggared belief. Then, suddenly, something clicked in her brain.

'Domenica, you're going to think I'm totally stupid, but I've only just realised something now. Your son, Rolando, is my half-brother.'

Domenica nodded and smiled. 'I wondered how long it would take you to work that out. I'm afraid I gave you a lot to take in.'

Amy sat back and took a couple of deep breaths. All her life she had thought of herself as an only child and now, suddenly, at the age of thirty-one she found she had a brother – all right, not a full brother, but they both shared the same father. Domenica was right. It certainly was a lot to take in.

'And Rolando, how old is he now?'

'He's twenty-one.' She looked up from her hands. 'Look, Amy, that's another thing I have to say to you. I have to apologise for him. You saw how rude he was last night but maybe after what I've just told you, you can begin to understand why.'

'Of course. He sees me as the person who blighted your life and, by extension, his. Oh, Domenica, I'm so sorry. I knew nothing about all this but I feel awful. Do you think you could persuade him to come and talk to me? I'd love to try to clear the air between us and get to know my little brother.' She shook her head in wonderment. 'First I discover I have a father I didn't know I had, and now I find I have a brother.' She caught Domenica's eye. 'It's taking a bit of getting used to. But, please, do you think you could speak to him? Tell him I'd love to get to know him.'

'And I'm sure he'll love you when he gets to know you, but he's had this immense chip on his shoulder ever since I told him the truth a few years ago. From that day on he refused to speak to Martin. He can be very stubborn.'

'*He* can be stubborn? I think we both know who he inherited that from. Would you and he like to come here for dinner one evening? I really would love to patch things up between us. By the way, we can keep this secret between us, if you like. Nobody else needs to be in on it, but I really would like to get to know Rolando.'

She read relief on Domenica's face. 'That would be perfect. I've never told anybody and I'd definitely prefer it if we keep this to ourselves. Considering how fast news travels here in Sant'Antonio, I've been amazed that we managed to keep the secret for so long. As for dinner, that's very kind of you. I'll do my best to persuade him to come. None of this is your fault; he has to realise that. The trouble is that Rolando could never understand Martin's behaviour. I tried time and time again to explain it to him, but to no avail.'

'I don't blame him one bit.' Amy reached across and squeezed Domenica's arm. 'I'm not so sure I understand it either.' Anxious to change to a more cheerful subject, she jumped to her feet. 'Do you know anything about mushrooms?'

Domenica looked at her in surprise. 'Not a lot. I can recognise porcini and a couple of others that are good to eat, but I steer clear of any other types just in case.'

'Terrific.' Amy dashed to the kitchen and dug out her porcini and brought them back for inspection. Domenica's eyes lit up.

'What lovely mushrooms and so early in the season. Yes, these are porcini all right. What are you going to do with them?'

'I was just trying to work that out when you arrived. Any suggestions?'

'Is it just you or are you expecting company?' Seeing Amy hold up a single finger, she continued. 'Personally I love a starter of raw porcini, sliced and drizzled with lemon juice and olive oil. Follow that by cutting the larger ones into pieces the size of the segments of an orange, dip them in egg and flour, and then lightly fry them.'

'Super, thanks. I'll try that tonight.' Another thought occurred to her and she pointed at the photos of her father on the shelf alongside the fireplace. 'I've been looking for photos of my father but all I've found are these three. I don't suppose you have any I could take a look at or copy, have you?'

Domenica nodded. 'I have lots. I'll have a sort through and next time we meet up I'll bring them with me.'

'Thank you so much. That'll be one night next week when you come to dinner, hopefully with Rolando.'

'I'll do my very best to get him to come. Let me check with him to see which nights he's free and I'll give you a call.'

After exchanging numbers, Domenica headed for the door but stopped before she got there. 'If you don't mind me asking, what are you planning on doing? Are you going to move here to Sant'Antonio or are you going back to England?'

Amy shrugged helplessly. 'I've been trying to make up my mind for weeks now. I love this house and the town, but I also love my job. It's a tough decision.'

'I can imagine. Is there anybody over there in England that you need to get back to? A partner or husband?'

Amy shook her head. 'Not now.'

'And what about over here? A little bird tells me that you might have made a conquest.'

Amy couldn't help smiling, yet again marvelling at how efficient the bush telegraph was here in Sant'Antonio – although she had a feeling its source was likely to be Pierpaolo, who knew everybody. 'Your little bird might be a bit premature. I've met some very nice people, one man in particular, but I've no idea how it's all going to develop.' She decided against naming Adam, but she needn't have worried.

'We were all very pleased to hear that he's safe and well. He goes to some terribly dangerous places, doesn't he?'

All Amy could do was keep smiling.

Chapter 22

Amy went shopping on Saturday in readiness for her dinner party the next day and when she returned, she was met by an apologetic-looking Signora Grande with Max at her side.

'Good morning, Amy, I don't suppose you could do me another big favour, could you? My sister's been taken back into hospital and I'm really worried for her. Could you possibly take Max for today and tomorrow, maybe even until Monday? I really need to stay over to be with her and the rest of the family.'

'Of course, I'd be happy to. He and I get on really well.'

After wishing Signora Grande's sister a speedy recovery, she carried her shopping bags into the house and prepared a quick sandwich for herself while the dog sat beside her feigning starvation. Used to his ways by now she gave him a big bone-shaped biscuit from a packet she had bought specially for him this morning and decided she had better go shopping again in the afternoon for more dog food. After that, she intended playing around with the new oven and hob until she felt confident enough to cook for her guests the next day.

The afternoon passed quickly and her efforts in the kitchen were reasonably successful, once she had burnt away the new oven smell. At the end of the afternoon, she took Max out for a walk and when she got back to the house, she met Danny and Pierpaolo coming in through the gates, and Danny had news.

'Ciao, Amy, Adam's just called me from Florida. He's flown into Miami from Manaus and he's booked on a flight to Rome arriving tomorrow morning. He should be back here mid-afternoon.'

Pierpaolo gave her a cheeky smile. 'And he asked about you.'

'He did?' She could feel her cheeks colouring as if she were a teenage girl, and she hastily ushered the two men into the house, but Pierpaolo hadn't finished.

'I told Danny to tell Adam you missed him, but he didn't want to say anything.' He looked positively mischievous.

Amy shot Danny a grateful look. 'Thanks, Danny, I would prefer it if you boys try not to do any matchmaking. All right, Pierpaolo?' Danny grinned and Pierpaolo gave her a reluctant nod of the head.

She grabbed a bottle of wine and three glasses and they all sat down around the kitchen table. This was her father's old table that the builders had sanded down and waxed and it fitted perfectly into this old environment. After bringing out the batch of chocolate brownies she had made that afternoon, she asked if Adam had said anything else – not about her, she hastened to clarify, but about him and what had happened in Brazil. Danny nodded.

'We didn't talk for long, but apparently their boat hit an underwater obstruction when they were miles up a little-known tributary of the Amazon and it started to sink. They managed to get to the shore before it did, but there was no way they could fix it. They had no signal so had a seven-day march through the jungle to get back to some sort of civilisation. He didn't give any details, but it sounded pretty daunting.'

'Your brother's so brave, isn't he, Danny?' Pierpaolo had a dreamy look in his eyes.

Danny rolled his eyes. 'I know Adam all too well. Knowing they were going to have to chop their way through virgin jungle, what do you think he did? He and Sammy the cameraman filmed the whole journey, and he told me he's going to turn it into a half-hour piece, of course. We'll probably be able to see it for ourselves before too long.'

The chocolate brownies met with immediate approval and Amy had to admit that they tasted pretty good. The Labrador stationed himself at her side and fixed her with an imploring stare until she looked down and tapped his nose gently with her finger. 'Chocolate's bad for dogs, Max. Even I know that.' Taking pity on him, she got up and dug out another of his big biscuits and he subsided onto the floor with it and for the next few minutes there were sinister crunching noises at their feet.

'Have you decided to come and live here full-time, Amy?'

Danny's question came out of the blue, but at least she had had time the previous evening with Domenica to come up with a non-committal reply. 'I'm still trying to work that out. What worries me is that if I give up the job in London, I'm going to get very bored over here. I need to find something else to do if I'm to stay here, but what *can* I do?'

Pierpaolo gave her a cheeky wink. 'You could have babies for Adam. Danny and I would love to be the naughty uncles.'

Amy's cheeks flushed again but Danny came to her aid. 'Leave the girl alone, Pierpaolo. You're embarrassing her, don't be a pest.'

Grudgingly, Pierpaolo nodded. 'All right, I promise I won't mention babies again – although we really would be great uncles – but if not that, then you could always try pottery, though you'd need to up your game.'

Danny was quick to intervene again. 'Amy's dishes look lovely now they're glazed, and as a first attempt they're impressive.' He returned his attention to her. 'By the way, I meant to bring them today but with the excitement of Adam's call, I forgot. As far as an occupation for you is concerned, have you thought about getting some chickens and maybe creating your own vegetable garden? After all, you have lots of land sitting here doing nothing.'

'That's a great idea,' Pierpaolo interjected enthusiastically. 'Or you could get some horses and set up a riding stables. There isn't one around here.'

Amy shook her head. 'I'm a city girl, don't forget. No, I don't think I could make a go of it as a farmer. I need something that occupies my brain, rather than my arm muscles.'

'You'll think of something,' Danny said with conviction, but Amy wasn't so sure.

They chatted some more and the subject turned to wine, with Amy soon realising she could use these two to solve a practical problem for her. At her request, one of the last things the builders had done before going off had been to bring up one of Signor Montalcino's containers of wine. This huge, bulbous glass container in a wicker basket, that probably weighed as much as she did, was now sitting in the corner of the kitchen and she couldn't even lift it. She knew she needed to syphon the wine into bottles but she didn't have much idea about how to do it. Apart from anything else, although she had spotted a lot of empty bottles down in the cellar, she wasn't keen on venturing down there if she could help it, so she asked Danny and Pierpaolo if they felt like going down to bring a whole load of bottles upstairs.

They were happy to oblige and managed to bring a dozen cases of empty bottles up from the cellar without discovering any unwelcome reptilian squatters down there. Pierpaolo also located a length of plastic tubing that had presumably been used by her father for this very same purpose. To cap it off, Pierpaolo, the local boy, spotted a big bottle of what the label described as oenological oil. He explained to her that the locals around here added a half inch of this clear, tasteless and odourless oil on top of the wine in all the bottles once these had been filled. He assured her that a cork simply pushed partway in by hand to keep out the dust afterwards was all the seal that was necessary to keep the oxygen from the wine. In that way the bottled wine would keep for many months without the need for a proper corking machine.

He then went back to scour the cellar and returned with a couple of sturdy brown paper bags, one containing little cone-shaped corks and one what looked like coarse brown cotton wool. He told her that this was in fact natural hemp. The locals called it *stoppa* and he demonstrated how she should dip this into a bottle to remove the oil before starting to drink the wine. The *stoppa* magically absorbed the oil but not the wine and removed any trace of this simple method of conservation.

Amy was fascinated to learn about such a traditional way of doing things and vowed to get onto the task of decanting all fifty-three litres into bottles, but not until after her dinner party the following night. She had decided to make it an English meal, rather than trying to compete with Italian cuisine. Her plan was to give them cottage pie with cauliflower cheese, and to follow it up with summer pudding. She would have a go at bottling the wine on Monday and it occurred to her that there would then be the question of whether she was going to be here to drink any of it or whether she would find herself a thousand kilometres away in London. One thing was for sure: she wasn't going to be able to take any with her on the aircraft.

Danny and Pierpaolo left a bit later on and she had time to complete most of what she wanted to do before the next day. Although she was keen to see if her menu turned out all right, most of her thoughts were on the adventurer's return. By the time she went to bed, after settling Max on the rug by the empty fireplace downstairs, she felt sure she would dream about him but, as it turned out, she had other things to contend with. She fell asleep almost immediately but awoke several hours later feeling terribly hot.

Here inside the thick stone walls of the house the temperature on the previous nights had been quite bearable, but tonight she felt as though she was on fire. For one horrible moment the thought struck her that maybe she was having a delayed reaction to what she had believed to be porcini that she had eaten over twenty-four hours before – and which had been very tasty – but then the true reason for all the warmth revealed itself.

She felt movement and then a waft of far from aromatic dog breath hit her as a very happy Labrador stretched his whole body against her and gave a satisfied grunt. Amy slipped sideways until she could climb out of the far side of the bed. She walked around to where he was still lying sprawled on the bed like a femme fatale in a cheesy movie, his eyes glowing green in the moonlight as he stared up at her. Even in the shadows she could see a broad canine smile on his face.

'Max! You shouldn't be upstairs and you certainly shouldn't be on the bed. Now scoot!' He stretched luxuriously again and the end of his tail wagged lazily, but she knew she had to put her foot down. 'I said get off! Come on, dog, you need to get off.'

Heaving a deep and heartfelt sigh, Max got up, stretched again and then let her guide him back to the floor where he promptly slumped down on the rug by the bed, clearly far too tired to consider using the stairs to return to the ground floor. Amy stood there helplessly for a few moments, debating whether to get tough or not, before finally deciding – in the words of the proverb – to let sleeping dogs lie. She crouched down beside him and, as she did so, a big black paw reached up towards her. She caught hold of it and looked him square in the eye. 'Not on the bed, *capito*?'

Whether it was the linguistic cocktail or not, when she woke up next morning she was mildly surprised to find him still lying on the rug. As he saw her get out of bed, his tail started thumping on the wooden floor. She smiled down at him.

'*Ciao, bello*, did you sleep well?'

He got to his feet and came over to nuzzle her knees. She ruffled his ears before pulling on a pair of shorts and a T-shirt. After a quick visit to the new bathroom, she took Max out for his morning walk up through the fields. It was a delightful day and she knew she was really going to miss this place – and her canine companion. She had grown very fond of the big black dog over the past weeks and she would miss him if she took the decision to return to London. On a morning like this, the idea seemed crazy, but she tried to imagine how it would be in the depths of winter if she were to wake up to an empty house and the prospect of a day of doing nothing. She knew she had a low threshold of boredom and the idea of being stuck here, twiddling her thumbs, didn't appeal in the slightest. As she walked up the hill she turned over and over again in her mind all manner of possible jobs from trying to emulate her father's success as an author to growing vegetables and selling them at the local market. Needless to say, by the time she reached the top of the field, she was no closer to a decision.

She had a busy day getting ready for her guests, much of it spent in the kitchen. Partway through the morning she opened the French windows onto the garden and let Max wander outside. She kept an eye on him from time to time in case he should take it into his head to run off, but he stuck around and spent most of the day sleeping in the shade of the bushes. At the end of the afternoon she went upstairs and took a tepid shower to cool off and changed into one of the dresses she had brought over from England, reflecting that Lucy wouldn't have approved of how little naked skin she was exposing. Still, when she surveyed herself in the mirror she had to admit that she looked pretty good. What effect – if any – this might have on Adam remained to be seen.

Chapter 23

Just after seven that evening Max gave a half-hearted woof, stood up and strolled across to the front door. Amy followed him to the door and opened it to find Pierpaolo with his hand raised, just about to knock. He stopped dead and took a step back, studying her closely before kissing his fingers and giving a theatrical bow.

'*Buona sera, Signora. Come sei bella!*' She was struggling to stop herself from blushing when he turned and reached behind him, emerging with his hand on Adam's arm, tugging him forward. 'I bet the *senhoritas* in Brazil weren't anything like as beautiful as our Amy, were they?'

Adam stepped forward, an apologetic expression on his face. 'You'll have to excuse Pierpaolo. He has no manners.' She was then delighted when he came closer, reached out to catch her by the shoulders and pulled her towards him. When he kissed her – only a couple of chaste kisses on the cheeks – her knees almost gave way. Apparently unaware of the effect on her, he stepped back and gave her a smile. 'Ciao, Amy. It's really great to see you.'

Doing her best to regroup, she cleared her throat and replied in as normal a voice as possible. 'It's great to see you too. You had me worried for a while when you disappeared off the grid.' As she spoke, she studied him carefully. He was looking fit and tanned, but noticeably leaner than the last time she had seen him and he had dark rings under his eyes.

'I had me worried as well, but it could have been worse, a lot worse. Luckily Estevao, our guide, knew the jungle like the back of his hand, and he had an inbuilt natural compass. Even though we walked for days, when we emerged from the jungle we were right opposite the last village we had visited. Left to ourselves, Sammy and I would probably still be walking round and round in circles – if we hadn't been eaten by something nasty.' He grinned at her. 'Do you still have snakes in your cellar? After some of the reptiles I've seen over the past weeks, I'd be quite happy to go down and clear them out for you with my bare hands.'

She repressed a shiver. 'I might well take you up on that. I'm still scared stiff at the idea of going down there.'

'You mean you haven't inspected the contents of Martin's cellar?' Adam sounded surprised. 'He had a nose for fine wines. You'll be amazed at what you find down there. If you like I'll accompany you one of these days and I'll make sure you get back upstairs again unscathed.'

'I might need a bit of Dutch courage first. Talking of that, what can I get you men to drink? I've got beer, wine, or gin and tonic if you like.' As she headed to the kitchen to dig into the fridge for the drinks, Adam wandered around the living room, admiring the work that the builders had done. He then followed her into the kitchen and for a moment the thrill of having him all to herself was almost too much for her to bear, but the moment didn't last long.

Barely a few seconds later, Pierpaolo appeared at her shoulder. 'I know I said I'd have a beer, but I think I'll have a gin and tonic if that's all right, Amy.'

She suppressed a sigh of frustration. 'Of course, the gin's in the living room on the little table near the sofa. Here...'

She handed him out a cold bottle of tonic and some ice cubes, rather hoping that he would take the hint and disappear back into the living room, but no such luck.

Moments later Danny appeared with the two ceramic dishes she had made. Fully finished and glossy, they looked rather good and even her little Labradors around the edges looked sweet. She thanked him and was wondering how to get rid of him and his boyfriend so that she could have a few minutes alone with Adam, when Danny pointed towards the stairs and asked if she minded if he went up to take a look around. She was only too happy.

Unfortunately, as Danny turned and headed out towards the stairs, Adam opted to go with him, and a couple of seconds later Pierpaolo followed the other two, leaving her all alone in the kitchen – well, not quite alone. There was the ever-hungry Labrador sitting primly at her feet, his nose pointing into the fridge, and a look of longing on his face. She glanced down at him as she closed the fridge door.

'I suppose if you can't beat them, join them.'

Leaving the beer and the wine on the kitchen table she climbed the stairs in her turn. Behind her she could hear the click of the dog's nails on the wooden stairs but she didn't have the heart to tell him he shouldn't be following her. As she climbed, she thought for a moment about Lucy's plan A. Adam was now definitely on a tour of the house and would probably end up in her bedroom, but in this scenario he would be accompanied by two other men and a Labrador. This probably wasn't quite what Lucy had

had in mind. Despite her frustration, Amy felt a smile forming on her face.

She found the three men at the end of the corridor at the door of her father's study, all of them looking serious. Adam turned towards her as she came up to them. 'This was where he worked. It was his inner sanctum. He only brought me up here once.'

Amy nodded. 'Apart from the new radiator, I've kept it exactly as it was. It makes me feel a little bit closer to him somehow.'

Adam reached out and took her hand for a moment, giving it a little squeeze. 'That's a lovely thought. It's such a pity you never met him; he was a great guy.'

Although the feel of his hand in hers was good, Amy relinquished it and turned away, knowing she was about to burst into tears. She walked back down the corridor, surreptitiously wiping away the tears that had sprung to her eyes. By the time she reached the top of the stairs again, she was able to turn back and address them in a reasonably even voice.

'Take your time and have a look around by all means. I'm going to get the antipasti ready. Drinks are on the kitchen table when you've finished your inspection.'

Her culinary efforts were well received – at least that was what the three men told her – and by the time they reached the summer pudding and ice cream everybody was looking happy – in particular the dog, who had stationed himself alongside Pierpaolo and had received a steady stream of titbits from the table, in spite of Amy's protests. Adam had told them more about his ordeal in the jungle – and it really did sound like it had been an ordeal – and Amy found herself thinking once more about the risks of his job. Could she see herself hitched to a man who might go off somewhere and never return? The thought was too sad for words. Mind you, he probably wouldn't want to have a girlfriend who did nothing but work all the time either.

It was only ten o'clock when he stood up and stifled a yawn. 'Sorry, guys, but I think I need to get some sleep. I've no idea what time my body thinks it is.' He came around the table to Amy and she jumped to her feet. 'Sorry to be a party pooper, but I'm worn out.'

'I'm sure you must be. Come on, I'll walk you home. Max needs a walk, and a breath of air will do me good.' She glanced across at Danny and Pierpaolo. 'If you two want to stay here, please do.' Sadly, they didn't take the hint and the four of them – plus the dog – ended up walking back together through the darkened streets to Adam's house. As they walked, she made sure she was right beside him, rather hoping he might take her arm or her hand, but he didn't.

When they reached his house, once again the other two didn't follow the script and, instead of carrying on to their own house a little way up the road, they just stood around as Adam unlocked his door. Accepting the inevitable, Amy decided not to prolong the agony. She went over to him and caught hold of his hand.

'Sleep well. I'm sure you will. I'm here for the rest of this week and then I'll be going back to London. Hopefully we can meet up before I do.'

He looked down at her with a gentle smile on his face. 'Thanks a lot for tonight. I was very impressed with your cooking and with what you've done to the house. I still owe you that dinner; how about tomorrow night?'

'That would be great if you're not too tired. Give me a call tomorrow.'

He nodded and then kissed her softly on the cheeks before disappearing into his house. Amy was just turning away after saying goodnight to the other two when she heard Pierpaolo's voice. 'You've missed a trick there. You should have gone in with him.'

She turned back and pointed an accusing finger at him, smiling in spite of herself. 'I have no intention of carrying on my relationship with Adam – such as it is – under your scrutiny, young man. Tomorrow night it'll just be me and him. Don't you dare come along and suggest you join us. *Capito?*'

Undaunted, he grinned back at her. 'Has anybody ever told you you're oh so sexy when you act tough?'

Amy looked down at the dog who was sitting beside her, scratching his ear with his back leg. 'Max, kill!'

All she got back from him was a lazy wag of the tail and Danny's promise to do his best to keep Pierpaolo's curiosity on a leash.

Chapter 24

Next day, Signora Grande phoned with the news that her sister was still in hospital and not at all well by the sound of it. She asked Amy if she minded looking after Max for another few days and Amy was happy to agree. It was on the tip of her tongue to suggest that she look after him permanently, but then the realisation dawned that, unless she made a radical decision about her career, she would be leaving in five days' time, and Max wouldn't be able to come with her. She knew that being separated from him would be a real wrench. She even wondered whether she should give up the day job and stay here after all for the dog's sake but that, she knew full well, would be daft. Her final decision on whether to stay or go would very much depend on what happened between her and Adam in the course of this week and whether she could find a meaningful job over here.

Adam called her just before lunchtime. 'Hi, Amy, thanks again for last night. Sorry I had to leave early. I'm phoning about that meal I promised you.'

Just hearing his voice brought a smile to her face. 'You must still be exhausted. Are you sure you feel like going out again tonight?'

'About that, I've come back to a mountain of work, so would it be all right with you if we make it tomorrow or, better, the day after. That'll give me a couple of days to get straight.'

'Wednesday's fine.' Although that would only leave her with three days before she would have to fly back to London. Stifling the wave of disappointment that swept over her at the delay before she would see him again, she continued, 'Do you need my help with any translations in the meantime?'

'No, thanks, this stuff's all in English. I'll tell you about it when I see you.'

'It's possible I might still have Max with me on Wednesday night. Signora Grande's away for a few days. I imagine that if I feed him before we go out he should be okay. Alternatively, do you think the restaurant would mind...?'

'No problem. Bring him by all means. I'll book us a table outside on the terrace so he'll be fine.'

After he had rung off, she looked at her watch. It was half past twelve and she was on holiday so she went through to the kitchen and poured herself a glass of wine. She took it out into the garden and sat in the shade of the olive tree feeling remarkably subdued. Max, somehow reading her mood, came and slumped down beside her, his head on her feet. She was halfway through her glass of wine, her mind turning over all sorts of unknowns, when her phone started ringing. It was Lucy.

'Hi, Luce, how's things?'

'All good here. What about your man? Did he get back safely? Did you do what I told you? Did it work?'

Amy recounted the rather underwhelming evening under the constant scrutiny of Danny and Pierpaolo and she heard her friend snort.

'That's no good. You need to get him on his own. Remember, you don't have much time.'

'He's taking me out for dinner on Wednesday night. We'll be alone then.'

'Well, make sure you invite him into the house when he takes you home. Repeat after me.' She adopted a seductive voice. 'Would you like to come in for a coffee or something? That should do the trick, especially if you let your voice linger on the word "something". Okay, then when you've got him inside, you lock the door and ravish him.'

Amy almost spilt her wine. 'Luce, I've never ravished anybody in my life. I'll take it slowly and naturally. Like they say here in Italy, *che sarà sarà*.'

'Time, Amy, time. Remember that time is of the essence.'

Amy knew that only too well.

That afternoon she spent an interesting couple of hours bottling the wine, and it wasn't all easy going. First she had to wash the empty bottles and in so doing she evicted a number of sinister-looking spiders. She had never been a fan of anything with eight legs and, in particular, two or three of the spiders she discovered had extremely hairy legs and she didn't like the look of them at all. Still, she didn't like killing any animal so she assiduously caught them one by one with the aid of a glass and a postcard and took them out of the French windows and relocated them in the shrubbery, hoping they didn't have a homing instinct. As a result, it took her twice as long to wash the bottles than she had anticipated, but it soon turned out that this had been the easy part.

She remembered using a rubber tube to syphon liquid in science class at school but the plastic pipe that Pierpaolo had located in the cellar was three times as thick, two or three metres long and definitely more of a challenge. The first problem immediately became apparent. The builders had placed the huge fifty litre glass container on the kitchen floor but she knew that the end of the tube submerged in the wine had to be higher than the bottles she was filling for gravity to do its work. There was no way she could lift the container onto the table so she had to settle for dragging it close to the door to the cellar and doing her bottling on the second step down. The next problem was that in order to start the flow of wine she had to suck so hard she almost ran out of breath and then when the wine finally arrived at her end of the tube it arrived at such speed that it went up her nose, made her choke, and sprayed all over her.

She gradually got the hang of it and by four o'clock the kitchen table was covered with full bottles of wine, each with a few millimetres of clear oil on top of the liquid and a simple cork to conserve it. She was seriously concerned that this wouldn't be enough to stop the wine from going off so she went out and looked in the vines until she found Signor Montalcino. After explaining why her clothes were splashed with red wine, she told him what she had done. He reassured her that this was the right way to do it and she had nothing to worry about. Feeling pleased with herself, she returned to the house and set about storing the bottles in the kitchen cupboards. By the time she had finished and went into the bathroom to clean up, she found that the wine on her hands had dried almost a blue colour rather than red. Still, it all washed off after a bit of scrubbing and she was relieved that she wouldn't have to have her date with Adam looking as though she was wearing purple gloves.

That evening, changed into a clean top and leaving her wine-stained T-shirt to soak, she and her four-legged friend walked through the town to the pizzeria. It was another gorgeous warm night and when she sat down at table she checked on her phone and saw that the temperature in London was currently half what it was here. That, too, was going to be a shock to the system, when or if she went back.

She was just finishing another wonderful *pizza ai frutti di mare* when her phone rang and she saw that it was Dominica.

'Ciao, Domenica, have you been able to persuade Rolando to come and talk to me?'

'Hi, Amy, I've had a long talk to him – well, several long talks to be honest – and he's finally agreed to sit down and talk to you. He says he's free any evening this week.'

'That's great news. Why don't you two come round for dinner tomorrow? Would that be okay? My new kitchen's up and running now.'

'Thank you so much. Tomorrow will be fine and, Amy, don't let it bother you if he's still a bit surly. He'll soften up once he's got to know you, I'm sure.'

'Let's hope so.'

–

The following night all went well as far as the food was concerned, or at least as well as could be expected for somebody with a new kitchen. Amy decided to go with a tried and tested favourite: her go-to chicken casserole, made with white wine, leeks and mushrooms. This was to be accompanied by a selection of vegetables roasted in the oven.

As she prepared the meal that afternoon, she found herself in reflective mood. On the one hand she was nervous at how Rolando was going to react to sitting down to dinner with her, but on the other hand she was excited to forge closer links with her only living relation whose existence had been completely unknown to her until barely a handful of days earlier. This meant that when the doorbell rang at seven thirty she was feeling both pensive and apprehensive.

Domenica was on her own. She came in and kissed Amy on the cheeks before apologising, telling her that Rolando had called to say he would be a few minutes late. Amy hadn't planned on eating until eight, so she assured Domenica that was no problem, but secretly found herself wondering if this might be the prequel to Rolando crying off.

Domenica handed Amy a brown envelope. 'You asked if I had some photos of Martin. I've got lots more and some time we can go through them together, but I thought you might like to have these for yourself. I have copies, so just keep them.'

They sat down side by side on the sofa and Amy opened the envelope, tipping out a dozen or so photos. Some were obviously taken at the seaside, one was taken somewhere in the mountains as her father was dressed in skiing gear, and a couple were of him looking very smart in a dinner jacket and bow tie. One in particular stood out. It was a close-up of his face, and she could see him in fine detail, from the colour of his eyes to the gentle, loving smile on his face. Somehow the eyes reached deep inside her and by the time she slipped the photos back into the envelope again, both she and Dominica had tears in their eyes.

To change the subject and while waiting for Rolando to arrive, Amy jumped to her feet and gave Domenica a full tour of the house and got the impression she was impressed, but she couldn't miss the nostalgic look in Domenica's eyes when they climbed the stairs and inspected the newly redecorated bedrooms, bathrooms, and her father's study. In consequence Amy didn't hang about and made sure they returned to the ground floor as quickly as possible. She was relieved to find that the chicken was still bubbling away happily and the roast vegetables hadn't turned to a crisp. She opened a bottle of the local spumante, filled two glasses and saw Domenica gradually recover and start looking around the renovated kitchen.

'Martin was a very generous man but he hardly spent any money on himself or on the house. I'm sure he wouldn't recognise the place now. You've done so well.'

'It was all done by some super local tradesmen who knew my father. I'm going to invite them all for a meal some time to say thank you.' Although she was counting off the days until she would have to leave. 'In fact, I'd like to have a party for all the friends I've made since I arrived here.' She caught Domenica's eye. 'And hopefully Rolando will be one of the guests.'

They had just returned to the lounge area and were standing chatting when the doorbell rang. Amy took a deep breath, went over and opened the door.

'*Ciao, Rolando.*' She used the familiar greeting.

'*Buona sera, Signora.*' His choice of a more formal response spoke volumes but at least, she told herself, he was here.

'Do come in, please.' She carried on speaking to him in Italian as she imagined he probably hadn't spent long enough with his father to have picked up much English.

She led him over to where his mother was standing and as she reached for the bottle of fizz to give him a drink she couldn't help noticing how he was staring about with an expression on his face that was somewhere between awe and disgust. After handing him his glass she decided to take the bull by the horns and be the first to try to make conversation.

'The builders have just finished. I imagine it's changed a lot since you were last here.'

He returned his gaze to her and shook his head stiffly. 'I wouldn't know, Signora. I've never been in here.'

'Oh, I see.'

This came as a real surprise and Domenica was quick to explain.

'It's like I told you, Amy: Rolando and Martin were never close.'

'Never close?' His voice rose sharply but Amy saw him make a conscious effort to restrain himself as he stared at her. 'There was only ever one child in his life and that was you.' His eyes ran around the room again. 'It's just not right that he left this place to you and not us.'

Amy deliberately counted up to ten before replying, but before she could speak, Domenica cut in.

'Just listen to yourself, Rolando. How can you be so greedy, so ungrateful? Who do you think paid for the house we live in? Who arranged for me to have more than enough money to keep both you and me comfortable for life? Who bought me my car, or you your shiny new motorbike? Shame on you.'

He gave no response but he was still looking like thunder. Although Amy had been expecting him to be far from cordial, his outburst had shaken her and she had to measure her words when she spoke to him.

'You do know that I never met my father, don't you, Rolando? Did your mother tell you that?' In spite of her best efforts, all of a sudden the pent-up emotion began to pour out. 'At least you saw him, spoke to him. All I have are a couple of letters, a handful of photos and this house. I'll tell you this: I'd trade it all in an instant if it meant I could meet up with him, get to know him – just like you had the opportunity to do.' Her eyes had filled with tears and she turned away. A large black shape materialised at her side and gave her a supportive prod with his cold wet nose. Behind her, she heard Rolando's voice, this time less aggressive but sounding incredulous.

'You really never met him? I can't believe that.'

She concentrated her attention on the dog, who was looking up at her with deep concern in his eyes. 'Well, whether you believe it or not, it's true. Until a few weeks ago I hadn't even heard his name, and until a few days ago I didn't know he was my father.' She steeled herself before turning back towards Rolando. 'So if you feel hard done by, how do you think I feel?'

Taking heart from an expression of what might have been comprehension that appeared on his face, she ran the back of her hand across her eyes and carried on.

'He must have been a complex man and my mother was every bit as emotionally screwed up as he was. Like it or not, Rolando, I'm your sister and I would dearly like to be able to get to know the brother I didn't realise I had, but that's up to you. If you want to blame our father's behaviour on me there's nothing I can do about it but, deep down, you have to know that I did nothing wrong. Now, I've got food in the oven, so please excuse me.'

Followed by the Labrador, she headed back to the kitchen where the automatic actions of readying the meal gradually calmed her down and steadied her hands, which were shaking after the confrontation.

That morning the fish van had been in the square and she had been able to buy six fat scallops. She threw them into a pan with some pieces of smoked ham for barely a minute on either side before turning them out and serving them with a salad of wild rocket, sliced shallots and Parmesan shavings as a starter. She was just about to carry the plates over to the table when she heard a low voice beside her.

'Let me help you with those, Amy.' It was Rolando and now he was using the familiar form of the language to address her. 'I'm sorry for what I said just now. You have to understand what it was like growing up with a father who didn't want me.'

She glanced around at him. 'And you have to understand what it was like for me, growing up with no father at all.'

He had the grace to look a little shamed. 'Like I say, I'm sorry. I just didn't realise. All my life I've had this image of you living a happy life at my expense.' His expression softened. 'I now realise that you had it as tough as I did, maybe more so.'

Amy managed to produce a little smile. 'Thank you for the apology. All I can say is that I would really like to get to know you. You are my little brother, after all.'

He smiled back at her. 'And I promise I want to get to know you too… big sister.'

She felt a wave of relief. 'Thank you, Rolando, I'd love that.'

The three of them sat at one end of her father's big old table, and the scallops were pronounced delicious. The chicken was also well received and by the time they got to the cheese Amy was relieved and delighted that all had gone to plan. Signor Montalcino's wine was as good as ever and, above all, the conversation around the table gradually picked up pace and her half-brother's demeanour changed radically from confrontational to friendly. She was delighted to see Rolando begin to come out of his shell in the course of the meal and he was soon chatting freely. From time to time, she saw him laugh and when she looked at him there was often a smile on his face. Her little brother was definitely loosening up.

By the time they had finished her attempt at apricot tart and custard, Amy reckoned they had all had more than enough to eat and she could rate the evening a success – not just for the food but for the distinct thawing in relations between her half-brother and herself. The party broke up at eleven. As Amy kissed Rolando good-night, she wished him well. He thanked her and when he suggested meeting up for coffee one of these days, she was quick to accept, even as a voice in her head whispered that she wouldn't be in Italy for much longer.

She felt a wave of relief. "Thank you. I think I'd love that."

The three of them [illegible] the [illegible] of her [illegible] big [illegible] table, and the scallops were [illegible] [illegible].

The chicken was also well received, and by the time they got to the cheese Amy was relaxed and delighted that all had gone to plan. Signor [illegible] was as good as ever and, above all, the [illegible] [illegible] the table gradually [illegible] up pace, and her half-[illegible] [illegible] [illegible] radically [illegible] [illegible] [illegible]. She was delighted to see [illegible] [illegible] [illegible] [illegible] [illegible] of the road and he was [illegible] [illegible]. [illegible] [illegible] [illegible] [illegible] [illegible] and when she [illegible] [illegible] [illegible] [illegible] [illegible] [illegible] [illegible] [illegible] [illegible] [illegible] [illegible] [illegible] [illegible] [illegible].

By the time they had [illegible] [illegible] [illegible] apricot tart and [illegible]. Amy [illegible] [illegible] [illegible] had [illegible] than enough to eat and she could [illegible] [illegible] evening a success. [illegible] [illegible] [illegible] [illegible] [illegible] [illegible] [illegible] [illegible] in [illegible] between [illegible] half [illegible] and [illegible]. The party broke up at eleven. As Amy kissed [illegible] [illegible] again, she [illegible] [illegible] well. He thanked her [illegible] [illegible] [illegible] [illegible] [illegible] [illegible] [illegible] [illegible] [illegible] [illegible] quick to accept [illegible] [illegible] [illegible] her [illegible] [illegible] [illegible] she wouldn't be [illegible] [illegible] [illegible] [illegible].

Chapter 25

The following night Adam came to pick her up at seven thirty. By the time she heard his car outside she had changed outfits three times and she was still checking herself in the mirror nervously. Taking a deep breath, she went across and opened the door.

When she did so, Max realised that he was being visited by his new buddy and jumped to his feet remarkably nimbly. He rushed to greet Adam, and Amy followed behind and waited until Adam had finished making a fuss of the happy dog, who by now was stretched out on his back on the floor, tail wagging. When Adam straightened up, he shot an appreciative look at her.

'Ciao, Amy, you look great.'

He looked pretty good as well but she just gave him a big smile and went over to kiss him on the cheeks. '*Ciao, bello*. Are you feeling more rested now?'

'Much better, thanks.' He glanced outside. 'Shall we go?'

The restaurant occupied a slightly shabby stone building in a delightful little hilltop village about ten kilometres to the southeast and they were shown to a table outside on the terrace. Here they were sheltered from the setting sun beneath a rickety timber framework almost completely submerged beneath luxuriant vines with bunches of young grapes already formed and hanging above their heads. Amy kept Max on the lead but he behaved remarkably well and settled down under the table at their feet without objection. She hoped he would continue like that for the rest of the evening. Once she was sure he was behaving, she looked around and took in the panorama.

The village occupied a commanding position and from the restaurant terrace they had a spectacular view south towards the heart of Tuscany. Rolling hills, many carpeted with vineyards and olive groves, were dotted with isolated villas surrounded by cypress trees. The setting sun bathed everything in a surreal red glow and Amy breathed deeply. It was gorgeous. She looked back across the table to Adam. 'What a super location. Didn't you say you brought my father here?'

'That's right, but he was the one who introduced it to me originally. We came here quite a few times. He was like me; he liked simple places without a lot of fuss.' He grinned. 'But don't be fooled. Although it looks quaint and old-fashioned, the food's terrific – especially the fish.'

They both chose seafood antipasti to begin with, followed by mixed grilled fish. Amy was feeling a bit awkward to be here with Adam on what was to all intents and purposes a date – assuming that's what he thought it was – so to help get the conversation started, she decided to talk shop.

'Did you manage to get through all your paperwork?'

He reached into his pocket, looking sheepish. 'Erm, sort of. There's just one document that I'd like you to look at. No need to do it now. Just when you have the time.'

Amy took the handful of sheets of paper from him and gave them a cursory glance. It looked like the printout of a long and convoluted application form for entry to the prestigious Accademia del Cinema awards here in Italy. She looked up with interest. 'So does this mean you win prizes?'

He smiled back at her. 'It means we *try* to win prizes.'

'And have you?'

He gave a dismissive wave of the hand that failed to hide his expression of pride. 'One or two.'

She grinned at him. 'Go on. I'm listening.'

His eyes glowed with joy as he explained, 'Well, we were nominated for an Academy Award in LA last year. We just lost out to an air pollution feature made by a Chilean company.'

'Wow. So you almost got an Oscar?' That really was impressive.

'Almost, but not quite. Still, I have high hopes for the one we finished earlier this summer. It's set in holiday paradises like the Seychelles and Maldives, showing how half the islands are at risk of disappearing under the ocean as the ice caps continue to melt.'

'God, that sounds awful, but at least for once you weren't in a war zone. Danny told me you've been to some scary places.'

'I go where the stories are and, if you'll forgive the pun, those islands are only the tip of the iceberg. If we carry on as we are, huge swathes of low-lying coastal areas around the world will be under water. And I'm not just talking about faraway lands. It'll include parts of the US, UK, Canada and Europe. As for Africa, it's getting hotter and hotter and drier and drier, which is going to lead to famine, starvation and, ultimately, insurrection on a frightening scale.'

She listened in fascination as he told her more about what was obviously a subject very dear to his heart. As he talked, she watched him closely. The animation on his face only added to his attraction, which she had long since given up trying to deny to herself. Then, maybe feeling himself being scrutinised, he suddenly stopped and apologised.

'I'm sorry, Amy, I tend to get carried away. Anyway, if you can spare the time one of these days, maybe you could drop round and we'll go through this document together.'

'Of course.' At least this would give her a chance to spend some more time with him.

They were interrupted by the arrival of their antipasti. This consisted of a wonderful salad of octopus, mussels and prawns covered in lovely thick olive oil and surrounded by rocket leaves. Along with this were slices of bruschetta laden with chopped tomatoes, also liberally doused in olive oil. It all looked and smelt excellent. Tonight they were drinking a local white wine that was light, fruity and wonderfully crisp. It went perfectly with the seafood and she gradually found herself relaxing and she got the impression he was also loosening up.

She asked him more about his travels and he listed a number of places he had visited over the past five years, many of them sounding extremely dangerous. As she listened to him, she once again found herself wondering how she would cope if she were to be partnered with somebody taking so many risks. The memory of her mother and the man she had been brought up to believe to be her father came back to her. The idea that she might end up with a blighted life like her mother was truly scary, although her mother had had the added complication of an unexpected pregnancy to contend with.

They talked for a while before the waiter arrived to remove the empty dishes and replace them with a slab of slate that he placed on the table between them. On this there were five or six different types of grilled fish ranging from sardines to tuna steaks. Slices of grilled aubergine and courgette accompanied the fish. Along with them were skewers loaded with prawns and squid rings and a heap of fries. She looked across the table at him and smiled.

'This all looks amazing and I bet it tastes even better. *Buon appetito* and thanks again for bringing me here.'

'You're most welcome. Thank *you* for coming.'

She picked up her wine and took a closer look at him over the rim of her glass. He was a very appealing man. Apart from his good looks, from what she had learnt from him so far, he was bright, capable, courageous and kind. He had provided a shoulder to cry on and helped her get to know the father she had never met. Yes, she told herself, she could do worse. A lot worse. The trouble was that he lived here and unless she took a massive leap into the unknown, she would be back at work in London in just a few days' time. She took a sip of wine before replying.

'For what it's worth, I couldn't ask for better company either.' His gaze held hers, the warmth in his eyes unmistakable.

The meal was excellent. Finally, as she was working her way through a mountain of peach, strawberry and meringue ice cream, he said something that reinforced all her doubts and fears.

'This time next week, I'll be in Somalia.'

'I was just reading about Somalia the other day. Isn't it terribly dangerous with rebel militia groups constantly fighting amongst themselves and against the government?'

'Yes, but hopefully I won't be involved with any of them. We're going over to make a programme about the terrible drought that's been affecting people there. It promises to be pretty grim but I'm only going to be there for ten days or so.'

Amy shuddered. 'Well, you just be careful.'

He gave her a confident smile. 'I'm always careful. I'll be okay, you'll see.'

On the way home they stopped to give Max a run in the woods and a comfort break, and she took Adam's arm as they walked along a rough track. The white gravel reflected the starlight and the dark shape of the Labrador was easily visible. They didn't talk much but being alone with Adam like this felt intimate and a sense of glorious anticipation crept over her at the thought of getting him back to her house. She had no intention of following Lucy's directive to mount an all-out assault on him, but she definitely wasn't going to object if he did the same to her.

When they got back to l'Ospedaletto, she was feeling quite breathless and by the time he walked her to the door she could hardly keep her hand steady as she put the key in the lock and turned it. She glanced back towards him and waved him inside.

'Coming in for coffee?' She decided not to add Lucy's provocative 'or something'. Maybe she should have done, because his response wasn't what she'd been hoping for.

He ducked towards her, kissed her softly on the cheeks and then stepped back. 'Thanks for the offer, but I'd better head back. Some other time?'

Swallowing a hefty helping of disappointment and an unwelcome feeling of rejection, she did her best to sound unmoved as she replied.

'Of course. It's been a great evening. Thank you very much for dinner and for introducing me to that lovely restaurant. Shall I give you a call tomorrow about that award application?'

'Oh yes, thanks, that would be great. Ciao.'

He gave Max an affectionate pat – quite a bit more affectionate than the little kisses he had given her – and then he was gone.

Chapter 26

Amy didn't sleep well that night. This was for a variety of reasons, all of them rattling around inside her head. At first she found herself thinking, of all people, about Gavin, wondering what he was doing and if he had really removed all his stuff from her flat. She had heard absolutely nothing from him and if Lucy had seen anything of him at the gym, she hadn't mentioned it. The other man who occupied her thoughts was, of course, Adam. The way the evening had ended had been far from the sexually charged scenario Lucy had painted or, indeed, the more intimate and romantic vision she herself had harboured. It had all been going so well: the restaurant, the meal, their conversation, the walk in the woods. To her mind, everything had been moving smoothly towards a much more romantic conclusion.

But he had just gone off and left her.

What was the problem? They were both grown-ups and she felt sure he must have realised the way she was feeling about him. If not, it showed that he was far less sensitive than she had imagined. She was quite sure that he didn't share his brother's sexual orientation – not least as she felt sure Pierpaolo wouldn't have been so obvious in his matchmaking if that had been the case. Could it be there was another woman already in Adam's life? If so, neither he nor the other two men had mentioned her existence. Could it be that he was just so totally fixated on his job that romance didn't enter his head? Alternatively – and this was the most disconcerting of all – maybe he just didn't fancy her.

She was under no illusion as to how she felt about him. She liked him a lot and he ticked so many boxes in her head. Apart from his physical attributes, he was bright, creative, articulate and caring – his relationship with her father proved that. She couldn't help reflecting that the immediate impact he had made on her was not dissimilar to what her father had written in his letter about his first impression on seeing her mother. She knew full well that if Adam had responded as she had hoped when they had got back to her place after their dinner, she would have abandoned herself in his arms.

But he hadn't.

She spent quite a lot of the night tossing and turning, wondering why and hoping that it wasn't just a simple matter of a lack of chemistry on his part. By the time she was woken by a cold wet nose prodding her bare shoulder at seven o'clock next morning she had reluctantly come to the conclusion that this had to be the most likely answer. In all probability he didn't feel the same way about her as she did about him and that was that. And if this were the case, what did it mean as far as the big decision about whether to return to London or stay here permanently was concerned?

As she and Max walked up through the vineyard and across the fields in the blissful cool of the morning air, she did her best to tell herself that the decision to give up her job wasn't dependent upon Adam. Yes, he would have been the icing on the cake, but if she were to decide to uproot herself from London and come here to live, it needed to be for more than just one man, however desirable. If she moved here it would be for this wonderful house and all this land in which she was now wandering about, as well as the attraction of the much less stressful environment of Sant'Antonio. The other great attraction of this place was, of course, the big black dog at her side and she knew she would miss him if she returned to her old life in London. But then there was always the question of what she would do if she did settle here.

It appeared that today the Labrador had sensed that something was troubling her and, unusually, instead of disappearing into the vines, he trotted along with her and she soon found herself addressing him directly. He didn't give her much in the way of answers, but it was good to have somebody to talk to all the same.

'Look at it this way, Max. If I sell this place, I can buy myself somewhere really nice in London. The sky's the limit as far as my job's concerned, too. I know I can make it to the top and the satisfaction of doing that would be immense, wouldn't it?'

She stopped and looked down at him. He stopped as well and looked up at her while he rubbed his head against her bare leg. It was hard to work out whether he was agreeing or disagreeing.

'Yes, I know the specialist told me to take life a bit easier, and of course I have to make sure I do that. My health is the most important thing, isn't it? But I can do that, can't I? I can take things easy. I'm not stupid, you know.'

He sat down and started scratching one ear with his rear leg. It wasn't clear whether he thought she was stupid or not, but she decided that in the interests of balance she had better give him the other side of the argument as well.

'If I give up the day job and move here I'll have clean air, pretty much guaranteed sunshine, wonderful food and drink, and I've already made quite a few friends. Above all, talking of friends, I'll have you, Max.'

This time it looked as though she had got through to him as he stopped scratching, stood up and started licking her knee. She reached down and tousled his ears.

'Who needs a man when I've got you at my side? I bet if I ask Signora Grande, she'll let me keep you, and that would be good, wouldn't it?'

Tired of licking her knee, he sat down again and rested himself against her so heavily that she felt sure that if she moved sideways he would fall over. Taking this as a sign of solidarity, she carried on.

'The thing is, Max, what the hell would I do with my time if I go for it and decide to settle down over here: do a bit of gardening, go for some long walks with you and probably drink far too much wine? I need a job that gives me more than that. You have to understand that.'

This time when she glanced down at him he was licking his private parts. She decided not to get into whether this indicated how he felt about her predicament.

She spent the morning doing little jobs around the house until there was a knock at the door. She opened it hoping to see Adam and found Signora Grande instead.

'Thank you so much for looking after Max, Amy. That's been such a help. My sister's had a bypass operation and she's doing much better now, so I can take Max off your hands if you like.'

'I'm very pleased to hear about your sister, but Max has been no trouble at all. Very much the opposite. Would you like a cup of coffee?'

While Amy made the coffee, she told Signora Grande to feel free to have a wander around the house to see what the builders had done, and by the time the coffee was made, the old lady joined her in the kitchen, nodding approvingly.

'They've done so well. *You've* done so well. It's a lovely house now – I mean, it always has been a lovely house, but it badly needed modernising.' She took a seat at the kitchen table and caught Amy's eye. 'Does this mean you're going to come here to live permanently? I do hope so.'

For now, all Amy could answer was, 'I'm still trying to make up my mind.'

After lunch she called Adam and agreed to drop in at four after taking Max for another walk in the woods. She had told Signora Grande she was happy to hang onto the dog until the weekend and she had distinctly got the impression that the old lady was only too pleased to leave him with her.

This time she remembered to take a basket with her when they went walking in the woods and she was delighted to find no fewer than half a dozen decent porcini mushrooms. She was so proud of these that she took them into Adam's studio to show off when she went to see him and he looked impressed.

'You're really slipping into Tuscan life, aren't you? Next thing I hear you'll be down at the bar playing cards with the old men of the village or out in the piazza playing *bocce*.' He gave her a smile. 'So does this mean you're going to move over here permanently?'

That question again. She took a deep breath. 'Do you think I should?'

She saw him hesitate. 'I suppose that depends on you, your job and so on. It's a big decision.'

She couldn't miss the fact that he hadn't asked her to stay. 'I'm still trying to make up my mind but I haven't got much time. Today's Thursday and I need to be back in the office on Monday so that gives me two more days at the most. To be honest, I've left it so late I don't really have much choice. I can't just give them a call and say, "Sorry I won't be in next week, I'm quitting," even if I wanted to.'

'And do you want to?'

She answered honestly. 'Part of me wants to. I've grown to love Sant'Antonio and I've made some good friends here – like you and your brother, for example.' He showed no reaction so she carried on. 'I love l'Ospedaletto and I love the relaxed atmosphere here in comparison to the hustle and bustle of London, but...'

'But...?'

'But I love my job. *You* must understand that. You love your job as well, don't you? Can you imagine giving that up?'

He shook his head decisively. 'Danny's been telling me for ages to give it up, or at least to cut right back but, like you, I love what I do.' He gave her a little smile. 'Maybe if we finally win an Oscar I'll think about it.'

That sounded pretty conclusive. He had no intention of giving up what was, without doubt, a dangerous job, and she was scared stiff of hooking up with somebody who could disappear from her life in an instant – just like her first father had done. Well, she told herself, at least that removed Adam as a reason to stay here. When she got home tonight she would book her return flight.

Was she disappointed? Of course she was.

She came and sat next to him at his desk while they scrolled down through the various questions to be answered for the award entry and she enjoyed feeling him near her. It was a struggle to resist the urge to cosy up against him but she managed it. It was now looking as though she was on her way back to London and it made a lot of sense to keep him at arm's length. Besides, like the previous night, it wasn't as if he was demonstrating any particular desire for rapprochement.

It took less than an hour to go through everything with him and insert the appropriate answers on the intricate forms. When they had finally finished, she stood up and decided the best thing to do would be to go back to l'Ospedaletto, book her return flight to London, and try not to think about him. She knew it wasn't going to be easy but he had made his position pretty clear and there was no point flogging a dead horse.

He stood up as well. 'Thank you so much, Amy. That saved me an awful lot of time and effort. When did you say you're leaving?'

'It depends when I can find a seat on an aircraft, but Sunday at the latest.'

'That only gives us two days, then.'

To do what? She almost felt like screaming it at him but, again, she kept a lid on it and just nodded.

He glanced at his watch. 'I need to do something to say thank you for all the help. How about dinner tonight or tomorrow?' He stopped and gave a grunt of annoyance. 'Dammit, not tonight, I'm tied up with a conference call with the US, but let's do something tomorrow.'

'You already bought me that lovely dinner last night. There's no need to keep rewarding me; I'm not a Labrador who needs treats.' This came out sounding a bit bitter so she was quick to deflect his attention to where Max was still stretched out on the tiles, half-asleep. 'Not that I give this one any treats. He just seems quite naturally affectionate.' She resisted the urge to add, 'Unlike you'.

'It's not just to say thank you. I really enjoy your company.'

She caught his eye. 'And I enjoy your company as well, but it's probably best if we don't get too used to it as we'll be going our separate ways very soon.'

This time it was his turn to make no reply, just to nod. She reached up and kissed him on one cheek. 'Time for me to go home and think about how I'm going to cook these mushrooms.'

'Surely we could meet up tomorrow night? I'd really like that.' He looked and sounded unusually disheartened and her hard-won resolve crumbled.

'I tell you what, why don't you come to my place tomorrow night and I'll give you a porcini salad followed by fried porcini. You do like mushrooms, don't you?'

A broad smile appeared on his face. 'As it happens, I love mushrooms, but even if I hated them I would still say yes, as it'll give me a chance to spend a few more hours with you. Are you sure you feel like cooking?'

'I don't think I'll be frying too many more porcini mushrooms when I get back to London so, yes, come round to my place.' A sudden thought occurred to her. 'And while you're there you could go down into the cellar and take a look at my father's wine collection.'

'It's a date. Thanks. I'll look forward to it.'

The fact was that so would she, even though she felt sure she was on a hiding to nothing.

Chapter 27

Sunday flights from Pisa to London were all full so she managed to find herself a seat on Saturday afternoon. After booking it she sat and looked down at the Labrador, sprawled at her feet.

'I'm going to miss you, Max.' He opened one eye and the end of his tail wagged uncertainly. 'But I can't make the biggest decision of my life based on a dog, can I? That would be silly, wouldn't it?'

He didn't look convinced – but then, neither was she.

As she only had another day and a bit before leaving, she set about clearing everything away and using up the contents of the fridge, leaving just what she would need for two breakfasts and her mushroom dinner with Adam tomorrow. Once she was confident that things were more or less in order, she took Max for a walk up the hill and was delighted to run into a friend, or two friends, if she included Coco.

'Ciao, Rosa, that's good, I was going to come around and see you today or tomorrow to say goodbye.'

Rosa looked disappointed. 'Do you have to leave? Now that the house is all finished we were hoping you'd decide to stay on.'

'Unfortunately I have to be at work on Monday, but I'll try and get back here at least for a few days before too long.'

'Just a few days? That's terrible.' An expression of concern appeared on Rosa's face. 'You're not going to sell the house, are you? We would hate to lose you from the town.'

They walked across to the old shed and sat down on the bench. Amy shook her head slowly. 'I just don't know. I suppose I might sell it, but I just can't make up my mind.'

'Why not settle down here? You know we'd love it if you did.'

Amy smiled at her. 'Thanks, but I need a bit of time to think things through. You see, I have a big job back in London and it would be a massive step for me to just throw that away.'

They carried on chatting until Rosa had to head off home. Before separating, she gave Amy a big hug and kissed her on the cheeks. 'Come back and see us as soon as you can. Promise?'

Amy nodded. 'I promise.'

That evening she decided to go for one last dinner at the Corona Grossa and the first thing Giuliano asked her when he saw her was the same question Rosa had asked, and Amy gave him the same answer. She was spared from having to face another battery of questions by the arrival of a very welcome face. It was her half-brother and he came straight across to her with a smile on his face.

'Ciao, Amy, I was just on my way home and I saw you sitting here. Have you got time for a chat?'

'I definitely have.' Amy jumped up and kissed him on the cheeks and then pointed to the spare chair. 'Why don't you join me for dinner? I'm going home at the weekend and I've no idea when I'll be back next. I feel we've got so much to say to each other.'

Over a meal of cured ham and melon followed by smoked trout and a mixed salad, Amy gradually continued to bond with the brother she never knew she had. He told her about his years growing up effectively without a father, and she told him about her childhood in return. As they spoke, they both realised how similar their lives had been in so many ways. By the time Amy's panna cotta arrived, she felt she knew him much better and she sensed that he had fully relaxed in her company.

After a warm embrace, and a promise to come back soon, she walked home with the sleepy Labrador, reflecting that Rolando was another reason why she should seriously consider starting a new life over here. The trouble was that the great unknown still remained: what would she do with her time?

The hours flew by and Friday evening was soon upon her. Tonight she didn't bother dressing up particularly for Adam's benefit. She told herself that this was because she was cooking and she didn't want to risk getting splashes of hot oil on one of her good dresses, but it was also because the realisation had been sinking in that there was no point. It was all too clear that he wasn't interested in her, and that was that.

Adam arrived to a rapturous greeting from Max and a more subdued greeting from her. She kissed him on the cheeks but then hurried back to the kitchen, leaving him in the living room with his canine friend. She called to him over her shoulder as she retrieved the raw porcini salad from the fridge.

'Are you feeling brave? You offered to check out my father's wine cellar downstairs. Would you feel like doing that now?'

He came into the kitchen, closely followed by the Labrador. 'I will if you will. Why don't you come down with me and you can take a look for yourself? I promise if there are any anacondas down there I'll strangle them with my bare hands.'

She shuddered. 'Don't even joke about snakes. All right, I'll come with you, but if I run off screaming you have to promise not to laugh.'

'It's a promise.' Although he was already laughing.

She waited until he had gone down the stairs and had located the light switches. When the new lights down there illuminated the whole of the huge cellar area she took a deep breath and went down to join him. To the chagrin of the Labrador, he was left upstairs. The last thing Amy wanted was for a snake or a scorpion to hurt him, although from the plaintive whining noises filtering down to them, he wasn't best pleased to be left behind.

Adam led her the full length of the cellar until they were standing right beneath the front door. Here she saw, for the first time, that a brick wall had been built across the far corner, creating a little triangular room. Adam went over to it, opened the old wooden door and located a light switch inside.

'I thought so.' He sounded triumphant. 'Come in here and take a look at this.'

Carefully scrutinising the doorway for spiders' webs or anything else that might look sinister, Amy stepped in alongside him, instinctively grabbing his arm with both of her hands for protection. At first, she couldn't make sense of what she was seeing. The light bulb hanging from the ceiling didn't give much light and all she could see until her eyes accommodated were loads of little spots in front of her eyes. It took a moment or two before she realised that what she was looking at were shelves filled with bottles of wine on their sides, and the little spots she could see were in fact the tops of the bottles facing her. She did a very quick count and gave up trying after reaching two hundred. Suddenly conscious that she was still hanging onto Adam's arm – or more precisely his strong biceps – she released her grip on him and stepped over to investigate.

She glanced back at him. 'Are these bottles of Signor Montalcino's wine?'

He shook his head. 'No, I don't think so. All the bottles are corked. This is big-name stuff. Try checking some of the labels.'

She did as instructed and was soon feeling overwhelmed at the range and quality of the wines down here. There was everything from twenty-year-old Barolo to fine wines from Bordeaux, Rioja and even Austria, Premier Cru Meursault, Chablis and Sancerre and a whole shelf devoted to vintage champagnes. She turned back to Adam in amazement.

'Wow, there must be a fortune in wine here.'

'You can say that again. Like I told you, he knew his wines.' He caught her eye. 'His legacy to you just gets more and more impressive, doesn't it?'

She was feeling quite emotional by this stage so she just waved in the general direction of the bottles and asked, 'Red or white? Let's open one tonight and toast him.'

'Are you sure?' Seeing her nod, he made a decision. 'Red's probably best as it doesn't need to be chilled.'

She nodded. 'Red it is. It's the least I can do for him.'

She pulled out a bottle of ten-year-old St-Estèphe and blew away its covering of dust. 'How about this?'

'Looks very good to me.'

She followed him back to the stairs and this time as she climbed out of the cellar it felt less like escaping than before. So there were a few scorpions, so there might be a grass snake or a slow worm, the fact was that her father had collected an amazing selection of fine wines and left them for her. The least she could do was to find the courage to go down there every now and then and open one in his honour. But if Adam wasn't going to be around, she knew she would be doing it with gloves and boots on.

They sat down to eat at the kitchen table and the porcini salad was greeted with his enthusiastic approval. After this she then got up to fry the porcini slices but, before making a start, she opened the fridge and pulled out her new Labrador dish. On this she had laid out a selection of ham, salami and cheese. As she set it on the table, she apologised and explained. 'As I'm flying back to London tomorrow, I'm clearing the fridge, so I hope you don't mind a few leftovers.'

'Of course not. It all looks wonderful.' He pointed to the bottle of wine, which had been sitting there since he had opened it. 'Feel like trying the wine before you get the frying pan out? We probably should have let it breathe for a couple of hours or more, but it should be okay.'

He filled two glasses and handed one to her. 'Here, are you going to say a few words?'

She took the glass from him and nodded as she held it up in front of her. 'A toast to my dad. I love him even though I never met him and I'm sure if I'd met him I would love him all the more.' Her voice broke but she just managed to add a croaky, 'Cheers, Dad.'

'To your dad.' After clinking his glass against hers, Adam lifted his skywards. 'Cheers to you, Mart. You were one of the good guys.'

The wine was predictably excellent. By tacit agreement they didn't speak for a few minutes while Amy busied herself dipping the mushroom pieces in egg and flour and frying them. As she did so, she gradually regained control of her fragile emotions. Somehow, that sip of wine had brought her ever closer to the generous, loving, but complicated man who had been her father.

At the end of the meal, while they ate the fresh peach and apricot fruit salad she had made so as to use up the last of the fruit in the fridge, Adam looked across the table and asked that same question one more time.

'So have you decided that your life is going to continue to be in London? No desire to come over here and put down roots in Tuscany?'

She took a sip of wine before answering honestly. 'I genuinely don't know. Part of me likes the idea of staying here, not least because it would somehow keep me closer to my father, but the ambitious part of me tells me to head back to my job.' She gave him a few seconds to tell her he hoped she would stay but there was no response so she carried on. 'Short-term, at least, I have no choice. I'm booked on a flight tomorrow afternoon and I'll be back at work on Monday morning.'

'And that's what you want to do?'

'Like I told you, I love my job – at least, I have done up till now. Let's see how badly they've missed me over the last five weeks.' She did her best not to let the thought of slimy Christian ensconced in her office ruin a pleasant evening.

'Pierpaolo told me you had a collapse of some sort, brought on by overwork. Is that right?'

Amy smiled ruefully to herself. The love of Danny's life certainly liked a bit of gossip. 'That's what the specialist at the hospital said. But it's all right, I promised her and I've promised myself that I'm going to try to take things easier from now on.'

'What does your boyfriend think about that? Danny told me he saw you at the restaurant with a man.'

Amy suddenly realised that she hadn't told Adam about her breakup with Gavin. In fairness, he hadn't spoken about any relationship he might have either. 'He's no longer my boyfriend. We split up while you were in Brazil.'

'Was that because of your job? Did he think you were putting your work before him?' He stopped and looked across at her apologetically. 'I'm sorry, that's no business of mine. I just get so used to asking questions for my work that it's almost instinctive. Please excuse me. I didn't mean to pry.'

'It's all right, I dumped him because he and I didn't share the same values when it comes to being faithful.' She considered for a moment. 'I suppose I had been devoting a lot of time to my work, and he maybe was feeling a bit left out. But I still don't think that's a reason to leap into bed with another woman.'

'That's tough.' She saw him take a sip of wine. 'And that's my own painful personal experience talking.'

Amy's ears pricked up, but she refrained from asking for details, hoping he would say more. But all she got were a few words.

'It's a long sad story. I'll tell you some time.' She saw him glance at his watch and finish the last of the wine in his glass before standing up. 'I'd better get back, I'm afraid. The trouble with working with the US is that it's the middle of the afternoon over there and, of course, nobody thinks about the time difference. I have another Zoom meeting with Hollywood in half an hour, so I have to go.'

Amy stood up as well and, as she did so, she felt the Labrador stir at their feet. 'Thank you for coming, and good luck with the award application.'

'Thank you for inviting me, and for helping me with that damn form.'

'Any time. Be careful in Somalia, won't you?' This was all sounding a bit stilted but what else could she say? Blurting out that she liked him a lot and felt attracted to him wasn't going to help. If she did and it resulted in an outpouring of affection from him, it would make her return to London even more bittersweet. If it just resulted in him giving her a peck on the cheek and disappearing, that would do nothing to temper the sadness she was feeling at losing him from her life – or at least seriously limiting the times they would be able to meet up. His voice interrupted her thoughts.

'When will I see you again?'

She wondered if he had been thinking along the same lines as she had, but his face gave nothing away. She could only shrug her shoulders.

'I don't know. Hopefully quite soon, but I've now used up all my back holiday entitlement so it'll probably be a few months before I manage to come back over here. If you ever come to London, do give me a call and let's meet up.'

'I'll bear that in mind. Thanks again.' He reached out with both hands and caught her gently by the shoulders, pulled her towards him and for a moment she felt her eyes closing in anticipation but all she got from him were the usual pair of chaste pecks on the cheeks.

'*Arrivederci*, Amy.'

I'll see you again. But the question was when?

Chapter 28

Amy got back to London on Saturday evening still feeling downbeat. There had been tears in her eyes when she had presented the other Labrador dish she had made to Signora Grande and had given the big dog a last affectionate hug. All the way back on the plane she had been unable to concentrate on anything but Sant'Antonio and its inhabitants – all of them, both human and canine – and she knew she was going to miss them and laid-back life in the lovely old Tuscan town. And then, of course, there was l'Ospedaletto and the memory of her father, but even thoughts of him did little to cheer her. He had left her a wonderful house, but she was having to leave it. He had, by all accounts, been a lovely kind, generous man, but she had been prevented from ever meeting him. A combination of his insistence upon keeping the promise he had made to her mother, coupled with her inflexibility and stubbornness, had ruined the lives of both her parents and, looking back, had probably impacted her own. It was therefore with a heavy heart that she unlocked the door to her flat and turned on the lights.

Lying on the door mat was a jumble of mail, mostly adverts for pizza delivery services and cheap funerals. Underneath these she found Gavin's key. It appeared that he had respected her instructions to return it to her after removing his belongings. That chapter of her life, at least, now appeared to be finished. She set down her bags and wandered into the kitchen. Needless to say, the fridge was empty – all except a lone bottle of Pinot Grigio. She took it out and opened it, poured herself a glass and located a packet of cheese and onion crisps. She was just sitting down to this meagre dinner when her phone started ringing. It was Lucy.

'Welcome home, Amy. Glad to be back?'

'Hi, Luce. To tell you the truth, I have no idea. Yes, in a way it's good to be back on familiar territory and I'm looking forward to going into the office on Monday, but I can't help thinking about Sant'Antonio.'

'Anybody in particular you're thinking about?' Lucy didn't give her time to answer. 'Tell me later. I'm guessing you're sitting there all alone with an empty fridge, so why don't we meet up for a curry?'

'That sounds like a marvellous idea, Luce, but haven't you got better things to do on a Saturday night? I assumed you would be entertaining one of your phalanx of men friends.'

'I've got some news on that front. I rather think that the phalanx – good word, that – has reduced itself to one man.' Sensing Amy's heightened interest, she continued. 'I'll tell you about him over a rogan josh.'

'That's excellent news – both the man and the curry – but why aren't you with him tonight?'

'He's a pilot with British Airways and he's on his way back from Agadir as we speak. I'm meeting him at midnight.'

They met up in the Bengal Palace and Amy immediately quizzed her friend about the man in her life. It turned out that this was a new boyfriend and, at long last, it sounded as though Lucy might finally have decided to abandon her wild ways after finding Mr Right. Needless to say, in return for this revelation, Amy had to sit through an interrogation of her own that finished with Lucy wagging her finger at her.

'Your man is obviously off his head. From what you've told me, and from the way you speak about him, it's clear to me that the two of you are made for each other. Now, if you'd just listened to Auntie Lucy and jumped on him, you wouldn't be in this position now.'

'What position?'

'Sitting here with a face like a wet weekend. You should be bubbling over with joy. You've found out who your dad was and that he was a famous writer; you've discovered you've got a brother you knew nothing about; you're the owner of a medieval palace, and you've got more money in the bank than I could even dream of having. Instead, look at you: you look as miserable as sin.' She produced a mischievous grin. 'Although in my experience sin can be a lot of fun.'

'No, I'm not really miserable.' Amy held up her hand to prevent Lucy from interrupting. 'I'm just confused, that's all. I'm looking forward to going back to work on Monday but at the same time there's a part of me that questions whether I'm doing the right thing. Maybe my future lies in Tuscany. Just give me a few weeks to sort my head out.'

After ordering their meal, Lucy returned to the subject of Adam. 'Do you think he's got another woman? Is that it?'

Amy had been doing a lot of thinking about this. 'When I told him I'd broken up with Gavin he made a comment along the lines of, "That's tough, I know what it feels like," or some such. I wonder whether he was in a relationship that ended badly and it's a question of once bitten, twice shy.'

'You could be right, but if that's the case you just need to work on him. Get him talking about it and let him get to know you properly.' Lucy waited until the waiter had brought them two bottles of beer. 'The only thing is that in order to do that, you need to be there, not here.'

Sunday was overcast but Amy did her best not to let the weather affect her mood, which was subdued enough as it was. She spent the day cleaning the flat, doing the laundry and she only went out briefly for a food shop to refill the fridge. She only had one iffy moment when she saw a blind lady with a black Labrador guiding her along the pavement. Amy had to struggle for a moment not to drop her bags of shopping, fall to her knees, and embrace the dog, who just wandered stolidly past her. Yes, it wasn't just humans over in Italy that she was missing.

–

On Monday morning Amy went back to the office. It came as no surprise to find slimy Christian with his feet still quite literally under her desk. He had the cheek to look surprised when he saw her.

'Hi, Amy, you've come back. I didn't think you were going to.'

She felt her hackles rise. 'What did you think I was going to do? Stay on holiday forever?'

'Something like that. After all, you're not well, are you?'

She took a deep breath and somehow managed to paste a smile on her face. 'I'm fine now. I was just a bit rundown, that was all. I'm looking forward to getting back to work…' She let the smile slip slightly. 'In my own office. So while you collect your stuff and move out, I'll go and tell Scott I'm back.'

The interview with her boss was far less confrontational, and he looked genuinely pleased to see her back. She came straight to the point. 'How have things been while I've been away, Scott? I hope Christian didn't disgrace himself.'

'Christian did okay. He's not like you; he needs a lot more watching, but he coped. Now, are you sure you're fit and well again? You had us all worried you know.'

'That's kind, Scott, but I'm fine again now. I've just had five weeks' holiday in Italy and I feel revitalised.'

'I'm delighted to hear it, but just make sure you don't overdo it. You're an important part of the company, and we wouldn't want anything to happen to you.'

This sounded pretty good and she returned to her now empty office with a smile on her face. Unfortunately, as the day continued, the smile gradually wore off and when Scott shooed her out of the office at half past six, she was once again feeling dispirited. Unusually for her, throughout the day her concentration had repeatedly been interrupted by thoughts of that little town in Tuscany and its inhabitants. As a result, things hadn't gone as smoothly as she would have hoped, and she went home feeling even more confused and uncertain about the direction of her life.

It took her until Wednesday to come to a decision. That evening she made up her mind that the time for a change had come. What this change would be, remained to be seen. She found herself thinking more and more about Sant'Antonio, her father, the house and, inevitably, Adam. He hadn't been far from her thoughts all week, and a couple of times she had come close to calling him or texting him to check that he was all right in Somalia. Only the memory of his reticence to let their relationship develop into anything more intimate stopped her from contacting him, for fear of just making herself look foolish. Interestingly, she also found herself thinking more and more about Max the Labrador. She really missed him and she realised just how much he meant to her after such a short time. She took heart from this. At least she could honestly say that she wasn't just considering abandoning her career because of some forlorn longing for a man who patently wasn't interested. *He* might not love her, but she felt sure that Max the Labrador did.

On Thursday morning when she got to work, she went straight in to see Scott. She had been preparing her speech all night long and had slept only intermittently as a result. He must have seen something on her face when she went into his office and he looked up with concern.

'Hi, Amy, what's up? Is something wrong? Are you all right?'

She cleared her throat nervously before embarking on her speech. 'Hi, Scott. We need to talk. It's like this: something's changed in me. I'm not concentrating like I used to and I keep thinking about everything that happened in Italy and everything I've left behind over there.'

In response to his quizzical expression she gave him a quick outline of the amazing discovery of her long-lost father, the inheritance, and the way the little town had got under her skin – although she omitted to mention the big black dog and the man who had also got under her skin. By the time she finished, she was feeling quite emotional but she managed to keep a lid on it while she added her last words. 'I think I've got to accept that I'm no longer pulling my weight here. My head's too confused and something deep down inside is calling me back to Italy. I'm very sorry, Scott, but I've come to tell you that I've decided that I'm handing in my notice. I'd like to thank you and everybody here for giving me some very happy years, but I need to move on. Of course I'll work out my notice and I'll give Christian as much help as I can before I go. I'm sure he'll be able to take my place. The last thing I want is to leave you in the lurch, but please accept my resignation.'

'No.'

She looked up from her feet, puzzled at his response. 'No? No what?'

'No, I don't want to accept your resignation. We *need* you, Amy.' Scott stood up and waved her into one of the comfortable chairs by the window and then he came and sat down opposite her. Her eyes were on the dark waters of the Thames far below, but without it registering, as she listened intently to what her boss had to say. 'Karl and I've been talking. We were wondering how you were going to react when you came back from that collapse. That must have given you a hell of a scare. I was going to talk to you tomorrow but seeing as you've brought up the subject, we have a proposition for you.'

Amy leant forward, surprised and intrigued.

'The fact is that we don't want to lose you. The solution we've come up with is to promote you and, at the same time, to reduce your workload.' Before she could query what he meant by that, he explained. 'Like I told you on Monday, Christian did a pretty good job while you were away, but he and the rest of the department need somebody to keep an eye on them. As the company expands I'm getting busier and busier, and that's why we've come up with a proposal for you. How would you feel about overseeing this whole department, but there's no reason why that can't be from a distance? Do you have a good Internet connection over in Italy?'

She nodded and he continued.

'This would be a supervisory role, so we wouldn't expect you to work all day every day, so there should be no risk of you having another collapse. All our dealers here would be instructed to run all major transactions over a certain limit past you for authorisation, and you'd have the authority to advise and step in where necessary. We reckon you could easily work from anywhere in the world and just stick your nose back into the office every month or two just so you remember what we all look like. How does that sound?'

It sounded almost too good to be true.

By the time she emerged from Scott's office, her head was swirling. To her amazement, everything had happened so fast. She had told him she was delighted to accept his proposal and it was agreed that her new job would commence with immediate effect. This meant that if she wanted to head back to Italy even as soon as this weekend, that would be fine. Needless to say, the first thing she did when she got home was to call Lucy and ask her to come round for a drink. She had no qualms about buying a bottle of good champagne and a couple of slices of a totally decadent sticky chocolate cake from the delicatessen on the corner to celebrate. Lucy listened eagerly as Amy recounted what had been agreed between her and Scott and gave her a warm hug at the end of the exposition.

'That's perfect, isn't it, Amy? You get the best of both worlds: you keep the job you love but you also get to go and live in the place you love.' She reached for her glass of champagne and clinked it against Amy's. 'Cheers, sweetie, and talking of things that you love, or more precisely somebody you love, what happens now?'

Amy had been expecting the question and had been rehearsing her answer. 'The first thing I'm going to do when I get back to Sant'Antonio is to take him for a long walk so he can pee on all the trees to mark his territory.'

Lucy spluttered into her champagne. 'I'm assuming you're talking about your friend the Labrador, but I knew a man like that once.' She caught Amy's eye. 'So what about your man, then? What happens next?'

'I don't know and I don't care.' Amy nodded a couple of times to reinforce her words. 'I mean that, Luce. I'm going back to Sant'Antonio for all sorts of reasons and Adam is only one of them. Who knows how things might turn out between us over time but, for now, all that counts is that I have a clear idea of what I want to do with my life.'

Chapter 29

Amy arrived back in Sant'Antonio late on Saturday afternoon. She had spent most of Thursday and Friday evening and most of that morning severing her ties with London, informing her landlord of her decision to leave, cancelling utilities, and making arrangements with an international removal firm to pack up her things and bring them across to Italy. She emailed all her friends with her new address and sent Scott and Karl, the CEO, a handwritten letter, thanking them for their consideration and promising to continue to do her best for the company. When she arrived at Pisa airport, she rented a car just for one week. Now that she was definitely coming here to stay, she would go out and buy a car. Thanks to her newfound father, she had ample money to do that.

The first thing she did when she got back to l'Ospedaletto was to dump her bags, change into shorts and a T-shirt and head across the road to see Signora Grande and Max. Both of them greeted her effusively. The dog, in particular, looked positively ecstatic to see her and when he came out of the door into the street he started jumping up and down and running around in circles like a wild thing, growling and yelping happily. His joy did not go unobserved by the old lady.

'Just look at Max! He's so happy you've come back.'

'And I'm delighted to see both of you.'

'Does this mean you've made up your mind to stay and live in Sant'Antonio full time?'

Amy nodded. 'Yes, and I wanted to tell you that I'm very happy to look after Max whenever you like, or even to take him off your hands completely, if that's what you prefer.'

To her relief, the old lady beamed at her. 'That would be absolutely wonderful, Amy. If you're sure, then I'd be delighted if you felt like taking him on. I'm just too old now to give him the sort of exercise he needs and I'm sure not having him around will be a relief for Felix.' She pointed back into her garage where the cat was sitting on top of a cupboard, staring blankly at the dog's excited antics out in the street. 'He's getting on a bit, just like me.'

After being cooped up at the airport and in the aircraft most of the day, Amy was only too happy to take Max and set off up through the vineyard for a long walk in the warm summer air. Being back here felt so very good and she knew she had made the right decision. The temperature was high but there was a pleasant little breeze blowing in from the sea and she relished the warmth in the air along with the blissful silence after a week in the big city. Needless to say, her thoughts very soon turned, yet again, to Adam, and she wondered how he was getting on in Somalia. He had told her he was going for ten days, so hopefully he would be back by the middle of next week.

She received confirmation of this later that day when she went for dinner at the Corona Grossa. It was early July now and she realised as she got to the restaurant that she should have booked in advance. From the look of it, most of the diners were visitors, and the tourist season was well under way. Almost all the tables out on the terrace were taken and she was just standing there with Giuliano, who was trying to work out how he could fit her in, when she heard her name being called and looked up to see Danny and Pierpaolo coming across the square towards her. They were delighted to see her and insisted that she join them at the table they had had the foresight to book. They made a fuss of Max and both were far more affectionate towards her than Danny's big brother had been.

She insisted on getting a bottle of the local spumante and telling them all about the solution her employers had come up with and both men approved. Danny, in particular, looked delighted for her.

'You're obviously good at your job and it's clear they don't want to lose you. Sounds like a perfect solution.' He raised his glass and clinked it against hers. 'I know you're doing the right thing. We're so pleased you're here to stay, and when Adam gets back on Thursday, I know he'll be over the moon.'

She couldn't help shooting him a sceptical glance. 'You think?'

He grinned back at her. 'I definitely think.'

Pierpaolo added a bit of clarification. 'He's crazy about you, didn't you know? Anybody can see it.'

Amy blinked and took refuge in her glass of wine, taking a big mouthful without thinking. The bubbles went up her nose and she found herself spluttering. Pierpaolo leant over and helpfully slapped her on the back while Max looked up from her feet in concern. Finally recovering her voice, she queried what she had just heard.

'Either you two are talking about the wrong guy, or you know something I don't. The impression I get from Adam is that we're friends, hopefully good friends, but it doesn't go any further than that.'

Pierpaolo held out his open hands towards her in exaggerated amazement. 'What's wrong with you, woman? Like I say, it's so obvious.'

Danny started to explain but at that moment Giuliano arrived to take their orders. The two men both chose the same thing, mixed antipasti followed by *fritto misto*, and Amy followed suit blindly, much more interested in what Danny might have to say.

'The thing you have to realise, Amy, is that Adam's been badly burnt.' Seeing the expression of shock on her face, he clarified. 'That's emotionally burnt, I mean. Hasn't he told you about Jennifer?'

'Jennifer...? Who's she?'

'She was his fiancée until it all went belly up four or five years ago. That's why he left LA and came over here.'

Pierpaolo joined in. 'I never met the woman, but from what Adam's said, it's quite clear he was madly in love with her.'

Amy was gradually beginning to make sense of what she was hearing. 'So what happened?'

Danny picked up the story again. 'You know the work he does. He's away a lot and he goes to some pretty scary places, and she couldn't handle it any longer.'

'So she dumped him?'

Pierpaolo gave a little snort. 'She broke his heart, poor man. Callous bitch.'

Danny once again stepped in to clarify. 'That's not the way it was, Pierpaolo. You don't know the full story.' He returned his attention to Amy. 'She gave Adam an ultimatum: either the job or her. When he chose the job, she called off the engagement. It was tough for Adam, but it must have been just as tough, maybe more so, for her. I met her a few times and I liked her. I'm quite sure she was just as deeply in love with Adam as he was with her.' He took a mouthful of wine before continuing. 'It can't have been easy for either of them.'

The sinking feeling in the pit of Amy's stomach ever since Danny had started speaking was becoming worse and worse. The truth was now emerging. Presumably Adam, if he really did like her a lot, knew that there could be no future in a relationship with her, and he didn't want either of them to get hurt. On the one hand, this demonstrated a lot of consideration and wisdom on his part, but it didn't bode at all well as far as anything more developing between her and him was concerned. Even the arrival of the bruschetta, some topped with chopped tomato, others with chicken liver and some with roast aubergine and goat cheese, did little to cheer her up. Lucy had been right. There had been another woman in Adam's life, but that wasn't the reason he was keeping his distance. He had already once had to make a big decision, and he had chosen his job. From the way he was behaving towards her it was clear that he still felt the same way.

The *fritto misto* was as good as ever and in the company of the two men Amy gradually cheered up again – to a certain extent. By the end of the meal she felt able to put into words the way she was feeling.

'There's something about Sant'Antonio. Sitting here now with you guys I know I've made the right decision. It's so good to be back. I'm looking forward to seeing Adam again and I know he's going to continue to be a really good friend, but I can be happy with that. I've got my wonderful house, my new brother, my new job, you guys and, of course, my four-legged friend.' She shot an affectionate glance down at the big dog sprawled at her feet. 'What more could I ask for?'

Pierpaolo gave her a cheery smile. 'That's the spirit, Amy.' He then changed the subject. 'Now, I seem to remember you promising to throw a party, but then you scampered off to London. Now you're back I think it's only fair that you keep your word.'

She grinned back at him. 'You're quite right. There's a whole heap of people I want to invite. I just need to get settled back in first.'

Danny came up with an idea. 'Adam said he should be back some time on Thursday. Why don't you plan your party for that night, make it a surprise welcome home party?'

Pierpaolo clapped his hands together excitedly. 'Great idea. That way, Amy, you can get him drunk and have your way with him.'

Amy shook her head and smiled. 'Haven't you been listening to what I've been saying, Pierpaolo? You sound just like my friend Lucy. Adam and I are just going to be good friends and that's fine by me.' Hopefully the more often she said it, the more she would come to believe it. She held up a hand to stop him protesting. 'You two will both come on Thursday evening, won't you?'

'Of course, and we'll make sure your party's memorable. You're going to need food, drink and music.' Danny was also smiling. 'You look after the first two, and Pierpaolo and I'll look after the music. Okay?'

'That sounds great, but what sort of music were you thinking of? There'll be quite a few older people like Signora Grande coming, and we don't want to deafen them.'

Pierpaolo tapped the side of his nose and gave her a reassuring smile. 'You leave that to us.'

Chapter 30

The next few days flew by. Amy set up her office in her father's study and after a lot of soul-searching she finally gave in to Max's persistent demands to be allowed to be up there with her. On Monday she went shopping and bought two dog beds – one for downstairs and one for upstairs in the study – but it came as no surprise to find him stretched out on the wooden floor beside her bed every morning all the same. She didn't tell him off. It was good to have his company and as long as he didn't try and climb into the bed with her again, she was quite happy.

She spent several hours phoning around or calling in on friends – not forgetting all the wonderful tradesmen – to invite them to Thursday's party and she was delighted to find that almost everybody was prepared to come. When she was visiting Rosa and Vincenzo's home, she received an excellent suggestion from her.

'Why don't you have a word with Giuliano at the restaurant and see if he can lay on the food for Thursday night? He's done it for us in the past. His charges are very reasonable and it'll save you an awful lot of bother.'

Amy did just that and came away from the restaurant later on feeling relieved. As far as she could count, there were going to be well over twenty people coming and she had been dreading all the preparation and cooking that would have been involved. This way she could carry on with her work, which looked as if it was only going to occupy a few hours of each day, and she would have plenty of time to go shopping for essentials ranging from plates and napkins, bottles of spirits, beer, mixers, to a selection of nibbles and nuts.

On Tuesday evening, she had just finished mopping all of the floor downstairs and she was sprawled on the sofa resting and recuperating, trying to summon up the energy to get up and make herself a snack, when the doorbell rang. Max, who had not been involved in any of the cleaning just glanced up from his recumbent position on the mat, yawned, and left it to her to heave herself to her feet and go and see who it was. She opened the door and her heart leapt.

'*Ciao, bella*. I'm back!'

She gawped at him in disbelief. 'Adam? I thought you weren't coming back till Thursday.' Before he could answer, she stepped forward and gave him a hug and a kiss on the cheek, doing her best to ignore the little electric charge that went through her as she touched him. 'Come in, come in.'

He followed her inside and closed the door behind him. Max, realising who it was, jumped to his feet and came across to give him a warm welcome. Adam bent down to make a fuss of him and spoke to Amy over his shoulder. 'To be honest, we were supposed to be there for another couple of days, but I cut the trip short.'

'Why was that? Did you get caught up in the fighting?'

Before he could answer, her phone started ringing and she gave him an apologetic look before answering it. It was Lucy with some good news. Amy had sent her an invitation to Thursday night's party without any great expectation of her being able to come all the way to

Tuscany, but it now appeared that this wasn't going to be a problem after all.

'I'll see you on Thursday. Jack's flying me over. By the way, is it all right if I bring him?'

'Of course it is, I'm dying to meet him, and there's bags of room here. What's he doing? Chartering his own aircraft?'

'No, he's just swapped with another pilot on the Pisa run that day and I'll fly over with him that afternoon and back again first thing next morning.'

'I'll come and pick you up from the airport.'

'Don't worry, Jack says he gets a special deal from a rental agency so we'll make our own way there and back. Be with you about six.' Lucy then unwittingly put Amy on the spot. 'How are things with you and your man? Have you done the deal yet?'

Amy chose her words carefully. 'Adam's here with me at the moment. Hopefully he'll be at the party and you can meet him.'

'Do I deduce from your cautious tone that you still haven't followed my advice? Either you've got far more self-control than I have, or you're getting old.'

'I'm six months younger than you and you'd better remember that. Anyway, must rush, I'm really pleased you're coming on Thursday and with your very own pilot as well. Swanky.' And she hastily rang off before Lucy could ask any more embarrassing questions. Returning her attention to Adam, who was now squatting on the rug alongside the dog, fighting over possession of one of the logs by the fireplace, she pointed towards the kitchen.

'I've got a fridge full of fizz. Feel like a glass?'

He looked up and smiled. 'As long as I'm not disturbing you.' In spite of the smile, he was looking a bit less confident, a bit more insecure than usual, and she wondered what this might presage.

'Definitely not.' She went through to the kitchen and, as always, the slight squeak when she opened the fridge door reached the whole length of the house to Max's acutely tuned food-oriented Labrador hearing and he abandoned the log and came trotting through just in case there might be food on offer. Adam followed behind a bit more slowly.

'Here, I'll do that.' He took the bottle from her and whistled as he saw the label. 'Wow, real French champagne. Are you celebrating something?'

'I don't know if you've spoken to your brother yet, but I'm having a party on Thursday night and you're invited. I'm celebrating the fact that I finally made up my mind to leave London and settle here in Sant'Antonio.'

'No, I haven't seen Danny yet and, yes, I'll be delighted to come to your party. Let me know if I can bring anything or do anything to help.' He opened the bottle and filled the two glasses she had set on the table. Picking up his glass, he held it out towards her. 'Cheers, I can't tell you how pleased I am that you're going to settle here. Have you managed to figure out how you're going to spend your time?'

She explained to him about her new role in the company and his enthusiastic reaction was the same as his brother's. 'It sounds as though you've got your life mapped out. I'm so glad for you.'

She was desperately curious to ask him about his former fiancée, but she knew it wouldn't be appropriate – at least not yet. Instead, she just clinked her glass against his and took a sip before changing the subject. 'So how come you decided to cut short the Somalia trip? Did you run into trouble?'

He looked uncomfortable. 'No, it all went well and we got some excellent footage but…' She saw him take another mouthful of wine. '…to be completely honest, the reason I came home early was you.'

'Me?' Her ears pricked up.

He nodded. 'I got a text from Danny telling me about your decision to settle down here and I knew I had to come back and see you, to speak to you.' He was still looking very insecure and she took pity on him.

'It's a beautiful evening. Why don't we take our wine outside into the garden and you can say what you want to say.' She led him out through the French windows to the bench under the palm tree and they sat down side by side. Max trotted out behind them and slumped down at their feet. The sun was starting to drop towards the horizon and there was a sweet scent of pollen in the air – accompanied by a continuous background buzz of bees. Apart from that, there was near perfect silence. Even without Adam and any possible revelations he might have, it would have been lovely out here, and she could feel a smile forming on her face. She settled back and glanced sideways at him. 'Feel like telling me what's on your mind?'

He answered immediately. 'You. You're what's on my mind and you've been on my mind ever since I first saw you sitting outside the Corona Grossa that time.'

He hesitated, but Amy didn't interrupt his train of thought, not least because she had a feeling she might find it hard to speak. Her mouth had suddenly dried as she began to register what might be happening. It sounded as if he was in a similar state as she heard him clear his throat before speaking.

'All the time I was over there in Somalia, I couldn't stop thinking about you. The idea that you had effectively disappeared from my life was unbearable. How could I have been so stupid as to let you go off without saying anything? I couldn't concentrate on my work; I was a mess.' He had been looking down at the dog but now he raised his head and caught her eye. 'I like you a lot, Amy.'

She took a sip of wine and struggled to reply in even tones. Her mind and her heart were racing and she felt as though she was going to be swept away by a tsunami of emotion. 'Well, I like you too, but I wasn't so sure about how you felt towards me. You've kept any feelings pretty well hidden.'

'I had to; it wouldn't have been fair on either of us.'

After what she had heard about Jennifer, Amy felt sure she knew what he was talking about but she let him tell it his way.

'For the last nine years, ever since I set up the company, I've been focusing on building it up and making it a success.' He paused for a moment and she saw his fingers twisting and turning nervously. 'A few years ago, back in LA, I met a girl. We got engaged but we ended up splitting up because of my job. The only thing that mattered to me back then, more than anything else, was my work. I felt that way right up until a few weeks ago when I first set eyes on you. Don't laugh, but in the darkest moments over in Amazonia, with snakes all around and the constant assault of vicious bugs, it was the thought of you that kept my spirits up. All the time over this past week in Somalia, when I thought I'd lost you forever, I've been unable to concentrate on the job in hand. When I got the message from Danny saying that you'd come back again to stay, it felt as if something had exploded inside me. I knew what I had to do.'

'And what was that?'

'I had to tell you how I felt.'

'And how do you feel?'

He reached over and caught hold of one of her hands and squeezed it gently. 'I want you in my life, Amy, if you'll have me.'

A wave of joy swept through her, but she had to be sure. 'You *are* in my life. Maybe not as fully as I would want, but we're good friends and that's not going to change. Are you saying you'd like to be more than friends?'

He didn't say a word; he just gave her hand another little squeeze and nodded his head. Delighted as she was at this admission, Amy needed to be sure.

'Last week, after three days back at work, I went to my boss to hand in my notice. Do you know why? Because, just like you've been describing, I found I couldn't concentrate fully on the job. I kept thinking about this place, my father, and the friends I've made here.' She placed her free hand on top of his and gave him a little smile. 'That means you, in case you didn't know it. The thing is, the way I resolved my dilemma was to change the nature of my job. From what you've told me and from what your brother has told me, that's not something you're prepared to do.'

'You don't understand...'

'I like you an awful lot, Adam, but you need to know something. My mother screwed up her life for all sorts of reasons, and one of them was that she married a man who was doing a dangerous job, and the job killed him. The idea of allowing myself to get close to somebody like you who's forever zooming off to one warzone or another is just too frightening for words. I can't bear the idea of ending up like my mum or...' She paused, wondering if she should give away what Danny and Pierpaolo had told her before taking the plunge. 'Or Jennifer.' She saw his eyes open wide and rushed to explain. 'The boys told me what happened. It would break my heart. I get that you love your job and that you want the company to thrive and prosper, but I'd prefer to lose you now than to go through what my mum went through – or Jennifer, for that matter.'

She would have said more, but he stopped her. 'That's what I came back to tell you, Amy. When I was over there in Somalia I made a decision and I promise I'm going to stick to it. First thing tomorrow morning I'm going to start advertising for a presenter, a roving reporter if you like, somebody who's prepared to spend a few nomadic years travelling around the globe for the company, dodging the bullets like I've been doing. That way I can concentrate on the creative and administrative side of the business – and on you, if you'll have me.'

Amy's immediate instinct would have been to throw her arms around him and kiss him madly, pledging her life to him, but something still held her back. She threw out a quick question to see what kind of answer it provoked.

'You're saying you're prepared to change your whole way of life just for me?'

'That's pretty much what I'm saying... if you'll have me.' He was repeating himself but she barely noticed.

Her head was swimming with the ramifications of what he had just told her. There was a movement by her feet and the next thing she knew there was a heavy Labrador head resting on her lap and a pair of big brown eyes staring up at her in solidarity. She removed one of her hands from

Adam's and gently stroked Max's ears before looking back at Adam.

'Have you ever seen *Casablanca*, the film with Humphrey Bogart and Ingrid Bergman?'

He looked surprised at the question. 'Only about two dozen times. It's one of the greatest movies ever made. Why do you ask?'

She left her other hand in his as she did her best to explain what was worrying her. 'Right at the end of the movie, when Bergman tells Bogart she'll leave her husband and stay behind to be with him, Bogey tells her something like, "if you don't leave now, sooner or later you're going to regret it." Does that ring a bell with you?'

He nodded slowly. 'I remember it well. The screenplay was a masterpiece by a guy called Julius J. Epstein.' A shadow crossed his face. 'Are you saying you think this might apply to me? Do you think I'll regret giving up my current lifestyle for your sake?'

'That's exactly what I'm saying. I can't ask you to give up such a major part of your life. Aren't you afraid that sooner or later it might start to gnaw at you and rankle with you? It might even make you come to resent me.' He started to protest but she held up a hand to stop him. 'Over the past few weeks that I've known you, I've grown to like you enormously, in fact I suppose the truth is that I think I've fallen in love with you, in spite of knowing you for such a short time. My father wrote in his letter to me that when he first set eyes on my mother it was love at first sight for him and I now know exactly what he meant. What I'm afraid of is: what if we get together only for your job to tear us apart? It would break my heart. It might break *me*.'

She felt his hand squeeze hers reassuringly. 'I promise you that isn't going to happen. Just like you've been able to modify the job you love so you can come and live here in Sant'Antonio, so I'm going to do exactly the same thing. If it works for you, it can work for me.' He gave her hand a gentle tug and pulled her towards him. 'You and your father aren't the only ones for whom love at first sight was a real thing. I think I love you too, Amy, and I want to spend my life with you.' Her eyes were already closing in anticipation of the kiss when she heard his voice again. 'Unless there's already somebody else in your life.'

A happy smile formed on her face as she pointed down at the Labrador.

'Love me, love my dog.'

Epilogue

The arrival of Lucy and her new man on Thursday afternoon brightened Amy's already joyous week. The moment she saw the two of them together and saw the way that Lucy looked at him, she knew that this had to be The One. She was delighted for her friend and the more she got to know Jack in the course of the evening, the more she approved of Lucy's choice. Here, she felt sure, was a relationship that looked as if it should go the distance – just like hers with Adam.

Later that afternoon Danny and Pierpaolo called in to help her get ready for the evening's party. Together they shifted furniture, washed dishes and prepared cutlery and napkins for the guests. At just after six there was a knock at the door and the boys introduced her to the musician they had arranged. To Amy's delight this was a young Spaniard called Miguel who played classical guitar. Wonderfully.

Amy had told people to come any time after seven so she hurried upstairs at six to shower and change. Tonight she was determined to look her best and she dug out a gorgeous Dior dress she had bought in the Harvey Nicks sale for half price – although that had still been an awful lot of money.

As she was drying her hair, the strangest thing happened.

She was standing in the bathroom, humming along to the strains of the *Concierto de Aranjuez* drifting up from downstairs, when she had a feeling. When she recounted it to Adam later she found herself struggling for words to describe what had happened. There was no question of an apparition or a haunting or anything scary, but she just suddenly started to feel a warm, cosy glow spread throughout her whole body. It was as if a loving, supportive arm had encircled her shoulders and hugged her. It only lasted for a few seconds but its effect on her was immediate and overwhelming. She walked through to her room and sat down heavily on the end of the bed, looking across at the closeup photo of her father she had hung on the wall. She could feel her eyes stinging with emotion but, as she told Adam later, she didn't feel sad or sorry, she just felt a wave of contentment that she had never felt before flood throughout her whole body.

Half an hour later, she greeted the guests as they started arriving with a broad smile on her face that never shifted all night. The first to comment was the first guest to arrive: Adam.

'*Ciao, bella.* You're looking gorgeous but, above all, I've never seen you so happy. You should have parties more often.'

She threw her arms around his neck and kissed him until the repeated prodding of a cold wet nose against her bare leg forced her to step back and reassure the Labrador, who was looking concerned. She crouched down and gave him a hug before straightening up and catching Adam by the hand and leading him across to the drinks table. As she did so, she responded to his comment.

'You're right about the happiness. I've never felt this happy before and much of it's because of you.' Before he could ask, she added, 'But a lot of it's down to Martin Thomas Slater, my father and your friend.' She waved a hand around the massive room, from the vaulted ceiling to the ancient terracotta floor tiles. 'You can't imagine how it feels for me to know where I come from – the real story – and to know that my father was such a brilliant man. Everywhere I look in here I see him, and it feels wonderful.'

The party was a great success. Rosa and Vincenzo arrived with Coco, and the two dogs spent most of the evening wandering from guest to guest, doing their best to look as if they were on the brink of starvation. Signora Grande surprised Amy by suddenly launching into a very convincing flamenco that drew applause from all the onlookers and then she grabbed her nephew and whirled him around the room in a Viennese waltz. By the time Pierpaolo returned to the drinks table for a well-earned glass of spumante, he was looking flushed while his aunt continued to whirl. He took a big mouthful of wine and explained to Amy.

'Zia Valentina's famous around here as a dancer. She and my uncle used to win competitions. Not bad for eighty-two, is she?'

Amy shared his admiration and she also admired the way Lucy barely glanced at Lorenzo Pozzovivo, who arrived looking as hunky and appealing as ever. No, it looked as though Lucy only had eyes for her Jack, and Amy was delighted for both of them. Angelo and Emilio Rossi arrived with their wives and Amy was able to break the news to them that she had now discovered the truth about her paternity. They looked genuinely happy for her and greeted the news that she was settling down here in Sant'Antonio with enthusiasm. Domenica and Rolando arrived with smiles on their faces and Amy even took her little brother for a dance at one point. All trace of his former hostility had disappeared and she felt genuinely comfortable in his presence.

It was a warm evening and the French windows were wide open to the garden. Towards the end, after excellent food produced by Giuliano from the restaurant, Amy wandered outside, accompanied by Max, and stood there, looking down the hill and across the roofs of the town. The orange glow of the street lights illuminated the aerobatic antics of families of bats as they swooped between the houses in search of insects for their evening meal. It was a delightful view and she never tired of it. She heard a movement behind her and felt a pair of strong arms catch her around the waist and a familiar voice at her ear.

'What a magical night. I can't imagine anywhere else I'd like to be and I definitely can't think of anybody I'd rather to be with.' She felt his lips press against her ear lobe and she turned towards him, looking up into his smiling face.

'*Ciao, bello*, and there's nobody else I'd rather be with either.' A cold wet nose nudged her knee and she glanced down. 'It's all right, Max, I haven't forgotten you. I love you, too.'

Adam gently turned her towards him and leant forward, brushing her forehead with his lips.

'You're the best thing that's ever happened to me, Amy.'

She smiled back at him. 'I thought the best thing to happen to me was finding out about my father, but it looks as though Sant'Antonio had another trick up its sleeve.' She kissed him softly on the lips. 'I love you, Adam. I've never been so happy in all my life and I never want it to end.'

He kissed her in return. 'Amen to that.'

A big hairy head nudged her leg again. Max agreed.

Acknowledgements

Warmest thanks to Emily Bedford, my lovely editor, and to everybody at Canelo publishing, who do such a great job.